GODS
OF
CHAOS

JEN McCONNEL

Month9Books

Month9Books

To Laura, who loved Darlena from the first.

GODS
OF
CHAOS

JEN McCONNEL

1

"Darlena, sweetie, it's time to light the fire." Mom's voice was muffled by the clothes in my closet, but I couldn't pretend I hadn't heard her. I'd promised to celebrate Solstice with her and Dad, even though all I wanted to do was hide in my room, and my mother wouldn't take kindly to a broken promise. That was one of the downsides to having a Witch for a mom; in our world, words had power, and promises couldn't be made lightly. With a sigh, I crawled into my room, feeling the familiar tingling as I passed through the protective ward. My closet was the one place nothing magical could reach me. I looked into the sanctuary with regret, but I had hidden long enough.

I made a halfhearted attempt at untangling my long red hair, but after a moment, I gave up. My parents already knew the worst thing about me; it was too late to start worrying about their opinion of my knotted hair. I wasn't sure what they thought about everything that had happened last fall, but they didn't seem to hold Rochelle's death against me.

That didn't mean I wasn't guilty.

Weary, I rubbed my eyes and glanced in the mirror mounted on the front of my closet door. I looked like a ghost; Rochelle would have laughed at my pathetic expression and deeply sunken eyes, but Rochelle wasn't here anymore.

She was gone because of me.

My parents knew I was a murderer, but they hadn't said anything after I killed Rochelle. They let me retreat into the darkness of my room, and it wasn't until last week that Mom had started trying to talk to me through the door. She told me she loved me, and she offered to do anything to help me with my path. Her words pierced my gloom, and, like an idiot, I promised to come down for Solstice. I would have had to leave my room tomorrow anyway, since I was picking up the threads from the fall and starting my quest to find another Red Witch, but in reality, I would have rather not faced my parents before I left for Scotland. Still, a promise is a promise, so I headed downstairs.

Candles glowed on every surface, casting the living room and kitchen in a strange, buttery light. I blinked; after months shrouded in the darkness of my room, even the candlelight felt bright. Xerxes stalked by me, his tail lifted imperiously. I hadn't realized how much I'd missed the old cat until that moment. I knelt down to scratch his ears, and the candles flickered as my vision clouded. For a moment, it looked like I was in a cavern, surrounded by flames. Sharp rock walls pressed in on me, and everywhere I looked, I saw the orange-red glow of fire. The heat singed my skin, but I wasn't afraid. It was as if I *were* the fire.

I'd had this vision repeatedly ever since Rochelle's death, but that didn't mean I had any idea what it meant.

The cat hissed, shooting up the stairs as if he'd been scorched, and I blinked rapidly, trying to clear my mind. I could still hear the sound that always accompanied the vision of the cave: a wailing, inhuman voice. It sounded like it was screaming my name.

"Lena?" My dad stood in the kitchen, watching me warily.

I glanced down, and noticed my hands were covered in red sparks. Sticking them behind my back, I shook my head, dispelling the lingering vision. "Sorry. Just a dizzy spell."

He nodded, looking relieved. Dad didn't pry about Red magic. Sometimes, it seemed like he pretended I'd declared to the Green path like him and Mom. Once, I had minded his aloof, distant attitude, but ever since fighting Rochelle, I wished my parents didn't know I was a Red. If he wanted to pretend it had all never happened, I wouldn't begrudge him that.

Dad forced a smile. "Help me with the cider, will you?"

He handed me two cups of steaming cider, and ladled a third from the silver Crockpot on the counter. With his free hand, he opened the sliding door, and I followed him outside.

The cold air bit into my face, and I looked at the yard in shock. Frost hung on the branches, and even the evergreens looked brown. Winter had come on with a vengeance while I hid in my closet; the last time I'd been outside, the air was still crisp and apple-scented. Now, it was like everything green was dead, and I had the terrible, irrational fear that the earth wouldn't wake up from this bitter season.

"It hasn't been a mild winter," Mom said, glancing up from the fire pit and noticing my stunned expression. She'd built a nest of leaves and newspaper for the Yule log to rest on, but she hadn't lit it yet.

"Strange for North Carolina," Dad added, settling into his lawn chair. He scooted closer to the fire pit, holding his cider in one hand. Steam curled lazily into the air. I watched it drift into the clear sky, and I shivered.

I started to hand Mom her cup, but she shook her head and stood. "The fire's ready."

I closed my eyes and began the familiar incantation without setting down the mugs. "Let this fire burn away the dark."

My dad joined in. "Let our lives make their mark."

My mother spoke the next line in her calm voice. "We celebrate the longest night, and look for the coming of the light." The smell of sulfur filled the air as she struck a match.

Power suddenly surged in me, and I fought down the impulse to light the fire with Red magic. My hands felt like I had dipped them in flames, and my eyes flew open. The cups of cider had exploded in my grasp, and hot liquid scalded my palms. Red sparks danced up and down my arms for the second time that night, searing my flesh.

I must have whimpered, because Mom looked up from the now-lit fire. "Oh, sweetie," she said softly. "I'll get some more. Do you want a dish of cool water for your hands?"

I shook my head, wiping my sticky hands on the frosty ground. The pain dimmed, but my palms still pulsed faintly. The red sparks had subsided, but I knew what they meant. I had used Red magic without meaning to.

Dad opened his eyes and shot me a curious look. I was glad he hadn't seen the explosion.

"I'm fine," I lied, sliding into my seat beside the fire. I stared at the flames, stewing. I had never hurt myself with magic; it was like it had acted of its own accord for a minute. I shook my head, denying the frightening thought. The orange flames licked at the wood and I stared at them, trying to feed my worries into the fire. Whatever had just happened with the fire and the cider couldn't happen again; I couldn't risk losing control of my magic. What if I hurt Mom or Dad?

A gentle hand touched my shoulder, and Mom wrapped my fingers around another mug. She smiled at me, but her eyes were full of worry. She didn't say anything, though, and I was grateful. If she'd asked what happened, I don't think I would have had an answer.

It was hard to be outside with my parents. What did they *really* think of me now? Were they relieved that I was leaving tomorrow? How the hell was I supposed to know? Mom had offered her support to coax me out of the closet, but she seemed just as awkward as Dad now that I was with them again.

Nervously, I tried to talk to them, but mostly, I just listened. They spent the evening talking of small things, avoiding any serious topics. Dad hardly looked at me, but every now and again I caught Mom's worried glance across the fire. I sank deeper into my seat, wishing I had learned how to turn myself invisible. At midnight, my dad raised his glass of spiced cider in a toast and smiled awkwardly at me. "Here's to our little Red Witch. May your fires always bring warmth without burning." He thought he was just teasing, but his words stung. Of course he wouldn't understand; he was a Green, and he'd never used magic to bring harm. He probably never would, and yet harm seemed to be the one thing I was capable of causing ever since I swore to follow the Red path.

Just before dawn, when the fire had all but died down to embers, my mom stood up. Spreading her arms wide, she looked into the last of the flickering flames.

"The coming year will bring challenges, but I am ready to face them." Her voice was strong and clear.

My father stood, adding the next words of our annual ritual. "The coming year will bring sadness, but I am ready to weep."

I rose and lifted my arms, mirroring them. "The coming year will bring surprises, but I am ready to learn." The words were bitter in my mouth; what more could I possibly learn, except that I was dangerous?

Dad reached out and clasped my hand, and I leaned forward to grab my mother's hand, too. Standing there linked around the fire, I felt the strength and support of my parents holding me up. Energy surged through me, and I felt strong and confident for the first time in months. In that moment, I was sure that I could face anything that Hecate might throw at me, and despite everything that had happened that fall, I almost started to look forward to my upcoming trip.

Because of a dream I'd had right after defeating Rochelle, I had a pretty good idea that I'd find another Red Witch in Scotland. Even though it would have been easier to just leave it alone and let chaos take over, I still wanted to resist the darker nature of Red magic. Hecate had been thrilled I'd been so dangerous up 'til now, but I thought I could change that if I found another Red. If I wasn't strong enough to stand against Hecate on my own, maybe two Reds together would tip the balance.

I had almost given up on opposing Hecate after Rochelle died, but Justin, my sort-of ex, had snapped me out of it. Every day, I woke up to another series of texts from him on my phone, and finally, last week, I read what he'd sent. It was chilling; while I'd been hiding in my room, chaos had been bubbling up all over my territory. I had thought by stepping back and stopping magic altogether, I might abate chaos, but that didn't seem to be true; fires, small explosions, shootings, and other disasters had been plaguing the Americas, and they seemed to be getting worse the longer I stayed incommunicado.

I don't know why Justin didn't give up on me; I still hadn't called or messaged him back, but his constant, frightening updates had snapped me out of my depressed stupor. Determined to find a way once and for all to stop causing destruction, I booked a flight to Edinburgh and started to pack. I didn't think to ask my parents' permission; ever since I became a Red Witch, it felt silly to act like everything was normal, but they saw the credit card bill. Mom didn't ask any questions, just bribed me into agreeing to celebrate Solstice with them, and Dad hadn't mentioned the trip at all.

Being a Red Witch was proving to be even lonelier than I had anticipated, but at least they didn't try to stop me.

2

The plane jerked, and I fought back a wave of nausea. The woman in the seat next to me had her eyes shut, and her mouth was moving silently. Looking out the window, I pictured Persephone somewhere beneath me, and I whispered my own prayer. We hadn't spoken since her return to the Underworld after Rochelle's death, but I had a feeling I wasn't done with the goddess's influence in my life.

Because of Hecate, I had learned the destructive powers of Red magic, but Persephone had sought me out and given me a chance to change the chaos. In her marriage, she strove for balance of the world of her husband and the world of light above, and the time I'd spent with her convinced me that I wanted to help find balance, too, but to do that, I would need a better understanding of the forces that controlled my magic. Maybe another Red could be my teacher as well as my ally. It was worth a shot.

Sighing, I pressed my head against the small, cold window. The plane jerked again, and I bit my tongue. The sharp taste of blood filled my senses, and my head swam. I never used to have any reaction to the sight or smell of blood, but the more I worked with Red magic, the more blood seemed to affect me.

It made having my period even worse than before.

"I hate flying." I turned, surprised at the voice. My seatmate hadn't spoken to me once during the six hours we'd been in the air, and I hadn't expected her to stop praying any time soon; the plane was still jerking around like a panicked bat, and even I was starting to get nervous.

Sweat glistened on her forehead, and she fingered a small gold cross around her neck. She was dressed in a rumpled blue business suit, and something about her gray hair and eye makeup reminded me of my grandmother. I felt kind of bad for the Non.

"It'll get better." Despite my efforts, I failed to sound chipper.

She shook her head. "I'm being punished."

"What do you mean?" *Great, I ended up next to a nut.*

"God is testing my faith."

I sighed. "Well, I think we'll be on the ground in a couple more hours, and then you can tell God that you still believe."

She shook her head. "I will never be forgiven."

I forced a yawn. "I'm sorry, I really need to try and sleep." I leaned against the window, hoping that would shut her up, but she kept talking to herself.

"I have dabbled in sorcery and will not be forgiven."

My ears pricked up at her words.

"I made a bargain with the dark lady, and the Lord knows."

A chill ran down my spine. I turned around. "What dark lady?"

She stared at me emptily. "The one who is seeking you."

Shit.

Before I could ask her anything else, the plane lurched sickeningly and the lights flickered. There was a pause, and then the entire cabin was plunged into darkness. For a moment, I felt the urge to use magic to bring the plane crashing down. My hands started to tingle, and with a shock, I saw red sparks dancing on my skin. My seatmate gasped, but I ignored her and dug my nails into my palms. Where did that come from? It was the third time in two days I'd almost lost control of my magic, and I was starting to freak out.

A woman in the back of the plane shrieked, but otherwise, everything was deathly still. The intercom sprang to life, and the pilot's voice came on.

"Don't worry, folks," she said, "just a slight power malfunction. Stay in your seats and remain calm."

Sobs echoed through the dark, and I realized the woman beside me had started crying. "Lord, save me!" she moaned.

I leaned over. "What did you tell the dark lady?" I hissed, my voice sounding loud and hollow in the dim cabin. I hated the way she recoiled from me, but I had to know.

"I said I'd help her catch you," she whimpered.

"How?"

Hesitantly, she pulled a knife out of the seat pocket in front of her. It was serrated, like a jumbo steak knife, and I leaned back involuntarily. She must have had it glamoured to get through security, and I looked around, nervous. Had anyone noticed? The panicked passengers seemed too worried about the jerking plane to notice that a little old lady had a blade pointed at me.

"I told her I'd keep you on the plane. I told her when we landed, I wouldn't move. You'd be trapped here in your seat until she came." Her words came so fast, she almost sounded drunk, and I stared at her for a minute, trying to process what she'd said.

The panic in the woman's eyes was obvious, and I could tell she didn't want to use the knife. "What did she offer you?"

The woman's hand shook. "She said that I would die with you if I didn't help her."

As far as I knew, the gods couldn't directly interfere with humans, so it was unlikely that Hecate would kill us. However, if she had another Witch messing with the weather, I'd be just as dead as the next person if the plane went down. I glanced out the window just as a bolt of lightning jumped between clouds. The intercom snapped to life again.

"Folks, please stay calm. We're going to have to take a slight detour, but we'll get you to Edinburgh in no time. Flight attendants, prepare for emergency landing."

I thought the woman next to me was going to pass out. "We're going to drown!" She waved the knife frantically, and I ducked.

"No we're not." I touched the screen on the seat in front of me, forcing myself to stay calm. "Look."

The red line that showed the plane's trajectory had shifted on the map, and we weren't hovering over the Atlantic Ocean anymore. We were headed for a small island.

"Is that Greenland?" she panted.

I squinted at the map. "No. Iceland."

For an emergency landing, things seemed to go remarkably well. I was tense until the wheels ground down on the runway, but luckily, the landing distracted the woman beside me. She was still holding the knife, but it was no longer pointed at me.

Hecate had almost seen me dead twice. I worried the third time might do it.

"I'm so sorry," the woman next to me whispered when we landed. She gripped the blade and stared at it.

I glanced at the aisle. Frightened passengers streamed off the plane. "We aren't in Scotland. Isn't that where you told her you would hold me?"

She nodded uncertainly, and I threw as much glamour as I could into my words.

"Well, we aren't in Scotland yet. You don't have to do anything."

She hesitated, looking confused.

I kept pouring magic into my voice. "She'll never blame you. The plane had to land in Iceland. You lost sight of me at the airport. Maybe they'll even route me on a different flight. No one would blame you," I repeated firmly.

She sighed, dropping the knife. I leaned over and grabbed it before she could notice. "No one would blame me," she whispered, squeezing her eyes shut.

When she opened her eyes, they were clear. "Good luck getting to Scotland. I think I need to find a bar and rebook my flight." She stood up with a little wave and joined the crowd filling the aisle.

I pocketed the knife and smiled weakly at her, not surprised by her abrupt shift. Glamour magic worked on more than just appearances, and it seemed that whatever spell Hecate had cast on the woman hadn't been designed to hold up under pressure. How had Hecate even known which flight I'd be on? She hadn't tried anything since I defeated Rochelle, and I'd started to believe I might finally be safe from her. So much for that fantasy.

I waited until a dozen passengers were between the woman and me before standing to grab my backpack. Once I stepped into the airport, I dropped the knife in the closest trash can and then headed straight for a harried-looking airline employee. His nametag spelled out "*CARL*" in blue letters, and white-blond hair framed his young face. I took a deep breath and summoned my magic.

"Look," I began, "I need to get to Scotland." The glamour I was using made my voice musical, and Carl grinned sappily at me. "I'd be happy to fly out tomorrow if the airline would find me a hotel."

Carl sighed in relief. "No one has agreed to fly out later—everyone wants to get where they're going now! I'm sure we can arrange a voucher for you. Does it matter when you fly tomorrow?" He headed to a computer kiosk, beckoning me to follow him.

I thought for a moment. I didn't want to delay my search for too long, but I figured I could spare a day. "I'd like to get there before tomorrow evening, but anytime in the day should be fine."

He sighed. "I love travelers with flexible plans. You have no idea how rare you are, miss."

"*You* have no idea," I muttered. With a few quick strokes of the keyboard, Carl was printing me a new ticket for the following day. I eyed it gratefully, while Carl kept typing.

"Flying out on Christmas Eve. I guess you don't have family waiting on you in Scotland."

I shook my head. "I'm just traveling for fun."

"Don't your parents mind you not being around for Christmas?"

Wordlessly, I shook my head. If they minded the trip at all, they hadn't let on. Not that that would have stopped me; I was determined that the next time I faced Hecate, I wouldn't do it alone.

3

I headed to the curb outside the airport, following the directions Carl had given me to find the hotel shuttle. He'd been nicer than I expected, but then again, magic tended to make people larger versions of themselves. I guess Carl was already a pretty nice guy, because under my spell he'd printed me fifty dollars in food vouchers, a hotel voucher for a luxury resort for the night, plus a free one-way ticket to anywhere. I hadn't expected the free ticket; my spell had taken on a life of its own.

A small white van with the hotel logo on the side pulled up to the curb, and I opened the door.

The big, smiling driver looked like a Viking right out of an old Hollywood movie, complete with messy long hair and bulging muscles, and I almost cracked up when he stuck out his hand and said, "My name is Odin. Welcome to Iceland!"

The ride from the airport to the hotel was over pretty fast. Grateful, I handed Odin a tip when he opened the door for me.

He shook his head. "No tip. Just have a nice trip!"

He trundled off toward the van with a wave, and I pocketed the money as I waved back. Maybe I should have asked Carl to give me a couple of days to explore Iceland, I thought, as I carried my backpack inside the hotel. I'd never had an interest to travel there, but the people had been really nice so far. I sighed. This wasn't a vacation, I reminded myself. I was on a mission, and based on my encounter with the woman on the plane, time was running out.

I'd been counting on meeting with the other Red in secret and joining forces with her, but it looked like the Queen of Witches was a step ahead of me. It was sick how she was willing to use anyone; that poor woman on the plane had freaked me out, but Hecate hadn't thought twice about getting an innocent Non involved in our fight. I realized I was shaking, and it took me three tries to swipe the key card and get into the safety of my hotel room.

Carl had done a really good job with my voucher: the room was a suite with a kitchenette, a king-sized bed, and a balcony. Poking my head into the bathroom, I grinned in delight when I saw the massive claw-footed tub. Even if I hadn't narrowly escaped death on the plane, a hot bath would have still sounded amazing.

Dropping my backpack, I began rooting around in it. Finally, I found the pill case I had filled with herbs. I'd wanted to keep them separate, so I'd used one of those "pill a day" cases that I'd picked up at the dollar store. I fished out a pinch of rosemary from the Wednesday slot, some peppermint from Tuesday, and a dried clove from Sunday.

I ran the water extra hot, and soon the suite was filled with the scent of my magical bath. I had begun dabbling in Herb magic over the past year, before I went Red, and Mom had insisted I take the herbs with me to Scotland.

"Herbs can help you," she'd said when she helped me pack early this morning. "Clove will protect you, and if you charge it right, it'll help you to divine the truth." The peppermint was for calming, and the rosemary for protection when traveling. Most of the other herbs she sent me with served similar purposes. Having the herbs with me made me feel like I wasn't traveling alone; it was almost like having Mom there with me, and that thought was comforting.

As I eased myself into the steaming water, I made a mental note to thank her when I called home later that night. I'd sent a text as soon as the plane landed to let them know about the change in plans, but they hadn't been surprised. Mom had texted back to say Dad had been watching my flight on the computer. He probably knew about our change of course before I did. At least they weren't worried about me … yet.

Leaning my head against the cold porcelain lip of the tub, I closed my eyes and concentrated on breathing deeply. I hadn't just wanted to take a bath to relax: I was hoping that the combination of herbs would stir up some visions to help me strategize. I didn't have any delusions about Hecate, despite the fact that she hadn't moved against me again until tonight. I was sure that if she could arrange it, I wouldn't live very long.

Suddenly nervous, I sat up, sloshing water onto the floor. I realized that I hadn't cast any kind of ward on the hotel room. I'd been in such a rush to soak in the tub that I'd ignored my safety. *Stupid move, Lena.* Grabbing a white towel off the floor, I hurried to stand up. Water cascaded down my legs as I climbed out of the tub. Quickly, I muttered the words of protection that would create a temporary ward around the room. Holding out my left hand, I started to walk around the suite, moving clockwise.

I was almost to the door when the knob began to rattle. I froze for a moment, and then hurried to seal the circle. The handle of the door went still. A second latter, a loud knock sounded and I jumped, clutching my towel with both hands.

"Room service," a muffled voice called from the hall.

Cautiously, I crossed to the door and tried to look out the peephole, but the distorted image in front of me was just the top of someone's dark head. I couldn't see anything else.

"I didn't order anything," I called, trying to sound confident.

"Complimentary for our special guest." The woman looked up then and I saw the flash of her red eyes.

I swallowed. Why wasn't she just blasting the door down? Pele had popped into my bedroom uninvited before, and I was sure she could do it again. My skin crawled as I looked at her.

"Swear a truce." The words left my mouth before I had time to question them. I saw her sneer through the door.

"Why would I do that?"

"You could have just come in here. But you wanted me to know who you were. Well, lady, I'm not opening the door until you swear you won't harm me."

She laughed roughly. "Surely you know your time grows shorter with each breath."

"Swear it."

Her eyes seemed to bore into mine through the door. "Very well. I swear by my great mountain that I will not harm you tonight."

I paused, trying to see if there was any loophole in her words. Finally, I shrugged. "Okay."

I opened the door and the Mistress of Volcanoes swept into the room.

I faced her, holding my towel tight. "Well? What are you doing here?"

She laughed, her fiery eyes sparking. "You are the one who entered my realm."

"What are you talking about? You're a Polynesian goddess."

"Any land that has one of my fire mountains belongs to me."

For a minute, her words didn't make any sense, but then I remembered the recent volcanic eruptions in Iceland. That had been one of the news items Justin forwarded to me while I was comatose.

Pele smiled as she saw the realization dawn on me. "Yes. You are in my domain now, Darlena."

I gulped when she said my name. She sounded … hungry. "What do you want?"

She bared her teeth. "A bargain."

"What?"

"You are without a goddess again, are you not?"

I nodded, wondering how she knew.

"It has been long since I had a Red to represent me. If you would swear to me—"

"Why in the world would I do that?" I exploded. "You told me yourself you demand sacrifices, and that's not what I want to do with my power."

Pele glared at me. "Foolish girl. Do not cross me. With me as your patron, you would grow more powerful. And none could harm you."

"I'll take my chances." I clutched my towel tighter, and the goddess smiled.

"I will not make this offer again."

"That's fine. I won't swear to you."

Her eyes blazed. "Fine. But remember this. You are in my land now. Watch where you walk."

She turned on her heel and left, slamming the hotel door behind her. I let out my breath in a rush and locked the deadbolt.

I glanced into the bathroom, but lounging in a tub seemed like the last thing I wanted now. I drained the water and looked around. Catching a glimpse of my reflection in the huge wall mirror, I shuddered. I looked far worse than jetlagged: I looked like I was on death's door.

Hurriedly, I pulled on my sweats and an old T-shirt I'd stolen from Justin. He was tall, but he wasn't a bulky guy. When I glanced back in the mirror, I realized with a shock that his shirt hung on me like a circus tent. *When did I lose all that weight?* My sweats were slung low on my hips, and I cinched the drawstring as tight as I could. Stepping closer to the mirror, I shook my head.

I studied my face, and it was like staring at a stranger. My eyes were sunken into my skull, and I could see the bones of my jaw like ragged edges underneath my skin. I pressed my fingertips to my cheeks. I'd never had a problem with my weight, but I'd always been closer to curvy than skinny. Justin said he liked me that way, and the memory of his hands caressing my skin made my face flush. Instead of a normal blush, however, my cheeks turned blotchy, like I'd been experimenting with makeup. I looked awful.

What had happened to me? I crossed the room to the bed and snuggled down under the thick, white comforter. I hadn't been eating very much lately, true, but I hadn't felt like eating ever since Rochelle died. I didn't realize how much my body had changed since Halloween.

Burrowing under the blankets, I wondered what else about me had changed.

4

Before I succumbed to sleep, I heard my cell phone buzzing in my bag. I crawled out of bed, shivering, and pulled it out.

"Hello?"

"Hey, sweetie. Did I wake you?" Mom sounded so normal, her voice almost made me cry.

"Um, no. I was in bed, but not asleep. I'm sort of wound up."

"I bet the detour shook you up a bit."

You have no idea. "Yeah. But I fly to Edinburgh tomorrow."

"That's good." She paused, and even thousands of miles away, I could tell she was choosing her words carefully. "The sooner you get there, the sooner this will all be done."

I crawled back into bed, taking the phone with me. "I hope so. But Mom, what if I don't find the other Red?"

"You said your dreams point to Scotland. Trust your dreams, Lena."

"Right. It's just … things aren't what I expected."

Mom paused. "Is everything okay?"

I sighed, remembering Pele's flashing eyes. "Yeah, sure. I have a feeling this will be harder than I thought is all."

Mom didn't say anything for a minute, and I yawned loudly.

"Look, Mom, I should—"

"Your father wants to say good night."

I stared at the phone, surprised. "What?"

There was silence on the line, and then Dad chirped a greeting. "How's Iceland?"

I rolled my eyes. "Fine. I'm not here to sightsee, you know."

"I know that, but you're there, so you might as well make the most of it."

"I'm leaving tomorrow. But Dad, it's late here. I really ought to try and get some sleep."

"Oh, sure. Of course." He sounded hurt, but that was silly. "Just be careful, sweetheart."

"I'll be fine."

I wasn't so sure I'd be fine, but I wasn't about to tell him that. I didn't want to risk a lecture, or worse, a fight about me giving up and coming home. Mom and Dad had been surprisingly chill about this trip, but I had a feeling that they would try to order me home at the first sign of danger. There was no point mentioning the woman on the plane or Pele's visitation; it wasn't like they could do anything to help. I was on my own.

"Night, Dad."

"Good night, Lena."

When I hung up the phone, I felt a strange lump in my throat. Staring around the vast hotel room, I pulled the covers up to my chin and snapped my fingers. The overhead light shut off, and the bathroom light dimmed until it cast a warm yellow glow into the room, like a nightlight. My thoughts were racing, but I knew I'd be worthless tomorrow if I didn't get some sleep, so I began counting backward from one hundred. I was out by the time I hit twenty, and I was immediately plunged into a bizarre dream. It started out like my regular recurring dream of the flaming cavern, but then it shifted.

A man was lying on his back on the tip of a twisted stalagmite. His hair looked like fire. There was something familiar about him, but I couldn't place it. In the dream, a woman was standing beside him, holding a bowl over his face. Something kept dripping into the bowl. The slow dripping sound filled the cavern, and I stared at the strange man.

"Is that the Red Witch?" His voice was harsh from disuse, and I felt the hair on the back of my neck stand up. He called out again, and I stepped toward him.

"I am a Red Witch," I answered. His smile twisted his face as if he were in pain, and he crooked his finger in my direction.

"I have an offer for you, little one."

Wary, I shook my head. "I've had enough offers."

He barked a laugh. "Offers from goddesses, yes, but have you had any offers from a god?"

I moved closer to him. "Who are you?" I asked in my dream.

"I am the Twisted One. I am the Red One. I am Loki, Lord of Chaos."

I took a quick step back. "I've had enough of chaos."

"It is your vow: you cannot escape chaos, and where there is chaos, there am I."

The woman spoke softly to Loki. "The bowl is filling, husband."

He gripped her arm. "Stay just a minute, sweet. Let me speak my piece first."

"It will fill soon." She glared at me, but she stayed where she was. Even in the dream, I didn't have a clue what was going on.

"I will speak plain, then," Loki sighed, "and dispense with my riddles. You and I could help each other."

"How?" I was skeptical, but something inside me was listening to this god.

"I am stronger than the other Red gods. I can even bring Hecate down. I can make sure she doesn't harm you."

"But what's in it for you? Do you expect me to take you as my patron?"

He cackled. "Silly girl. Bargains do not have to be that binding."

"Then what do you want?"

"I can protect you, but only if I am free. You must set me free."

"I still don't understand."

"Husband," the woman said urgently, "I must empty it."

"Wait." He gritted his teeth but she shook her head sadly.

With one swift movement, she whisked the bowl away from his face and hurried into the shadows. Loki screamed out in pain.

"It burns! After thousands of years, it still burns! Haven't I suffered enough?" He cursed and wept, thrashing about from side to side, and I saw that not only was he balanced on the rock, he was bound to it. This god of chaos was a prisoner.

I felt myself sliding out of the dream, and Loki called out, "Just make it seem as if the world is ending! Then I will be free, and I promise, I will come to your aid."

I woke up drenched in sweat, a feather pillow clutched tight across my face. What in the world had that been about? I had always listened to my dreams, but since my declaration of Red magic, it seemed that I dreamed more vivid and disturbing things than I ever had before.

I glanced over at the glowing green numbers on the nightstand. The clock said it was close to four a.m. Too jostled to sleep, I got up and padded over to the hotel desk. My tiny laptop was where I had left it last night, and I turned it on. As it booted up, I thought back over the details of my dream, but they were beginning to fade. Hastily, I grabbed a pad of hotel paper and a pen and began to scribble down everything I could remember.

I shuddered as I recalled Loki's screams when the woman had removed the bowl from his eyes. What was all that about? And could he really help me? I shivered at the idea. He didn't seem like the kind of god I wanted to work with, but then again, I didn't have a lot of options.

Quickly, I connected to the hotel's wireless and opened a search engine. A few clicks later, I was reading about Loki. What I found horrified me.

According to one site, Loki always liked to prank the other gods, but he went too far one day and caused the murder of the god Baldur. The gods punished him by binding him and sending a serpent to drip poison into his eyes. The woman I had seen in the dream could only be his wife, who stayed by his side in his torture and caught as much of the venom as she could to spare him the pain.

But, just like in my dream, sometimes the bowl would fill. When it was being emptied, the website said, Loki would thrash in pain and fury. His movements were thought to cause earthquakes and volcanic eruptions. I swallowed even though my mouth was dry.

Loki had been right about one thing: nothing short of the end of the world would release him from his prison. And I didn't like Ragnarok, the Norse version of the end of days: mass chaos, unmanageable natural disasters, and the deaths of many gods.

I had reason to believe that mythology was a lot closer to reality than most people knew, and I didn't want to be around when the world flooded and Loki escaped from his cave. And yet that seemed to be exactly what he wanted: he'd asked me to free him.

I drummed my fingers against the desk, frowning. Why would I free such a dangerous god? The Internet referred to him as "the power of fire bound," and that wasn't something the world needed. I had good cause to know and fear the power of unbound fire; she'd been in my room a few hours ago. Did I really want to be responsible for turning another crazy god loose on the world?

On the other hand, Loki had offered to help me. And from my brief Internet research, it seemed like he might be powerful enough to do what he had offered. At least, he might be that powerful if he were free. I just had to make it seem like the world was ending.

I buried my head in my hands. I'd been a Witch all my life, but I hadn't realized just how complicated magic could get until this year. All the gods and goddesses of chaos were starting to get on my nerves; first, they had courted me, trying to get me to choose one of them to be my patron, but now they were just out to get me.

I'd tried the whole patron thing with Aphrodite; it hadn't exactly worked out.

I'd unbound myself without meaning to, but since I'd been given the chance to turn back that decision, I was hesitant to vow myself to any other gods. I knew Mom had a patron; she made no secret of her relationship with Demeter. Dad never talked about having one, and most of the other people I knew seemed to think taking a patron was old-fashioned. I'd pledged myself in desperation, but now that I was free again, I wasn't too keen on working with another Red god, particularly one like Loki.

I sighed, thinking about Aphrodite. She had saved me from Hecate, not to mention a trucker who wanted to get in my pants, and I hadn't even talked to her since I broke my vow. I had tried to explain, but I still didn't understand how I broke that vow. She hadn't killed me yet in some freak perfume accident, so I didn't think she was mad, but I had no way to really know.

Suddenly lonely, I crossed to my bag and dug out the little copper mirror that Aphrodite had given to me when I first dedicated to serve her. I'd tried to give it back when our bond was broken, but she had implied I might need it. I didn't know what good the mirror would do, but it occurred to me that it might be a way to contact my former patron. If she wasn't mad at me, maybe she could help.

Concentrating hard, I stared into the shiny glass. My eyes began to cross and it was like I was seeing through the mirror. At that moment, I whispered a prayer to Aphrodite to reveal herself to me. I closed my eyes for an instant, and I heard the rustle of fabric behind me. Cautiously, I turned and opened my eyes.

Instead of the beautiful blond goddess I'd been expecting, I was facing a tall woman who looked like a warrior queen. Her brilliant red hair cascaded over her shoulders, and her torso was swathed in a shining breastplate of gold. Her green eyes reminded me of my cat, Xerxes. I gulped at their fierceness and clutched the mirror to my chest.

"Who are you?" I took a cautious step back, trying to put some distance between me and this new goddess.

"You summoned the goddess of love, did you not?"

I started to shake my head, then stopped, confused. "I was looking for Aphrodite."

The goddess waved her hand dismissively. "What makes you think you can call to one of the Greeks? You are across the world from their land."

I looked at her in puzzlement. "But I've never had trouble before."

"Before in America, you mean?"

I couldn't answer, and she laughed.

"I know who you are. You cannot think to travel in anonymity, not when you have made enemies of the most powerful goddess."

"Hecate." I whispered her name, truly frightened. If this strange goddess wanted to, she could hand me over to Hecate. I was sure I couldn't beat the redhead in a fight; power radiated off her in waves.

She nodded. "The Queen is not pleased with you." Eyeing my messy hair and sweats she added, "Although I do not see why."

I shook my head. "I'm still confused. Why didn't Aphrodite come?"

"Silly girl. The gods are bound to the lands that know them. In Iceland and all Norse lands, I am the Goddess of Love. I am also the Goddess of War."

A name stirred in my memory. "Freya."

She nodded her approval. "Much like my Greek sister, and then again, much like myself."

"But why could Aphrodite come to me when I was at home?"

Freya laughed. "Even I could come to you there. There is not a god that cannot enter America; your people are such a mottled mass of immigrant blood that all gods feel at home there."

I paused, thinking about what she said. I'd never heard anything like this before, but Freya's words made a lot of sense. "So Hecate can't find me here?"

She tsked in exasperation. "Some gods transcend boundaries. Hecate has been worshiped in many places. Do not believe you will escape her if she truly hunts you." She snapped her fingers, and a huge cat crept out of the shadows.

I backed away, staring at the thing. It looked more like a mountain lion than a house cat, and it snarled at me, showing its sharp teeth.

"I do not think this Witch smells like prey, Bygul. At least, not yet."

I felt myself growing angry. "Why are you here?"

She feigned innocence. "You summoned a goddess of love, and I heard your call."

I shook my head. "There's more to it than that. I may be mortal, but I'm not stupid."

"That remains to be seen." Her tone was hard, and the cat growled and stared at me.

"What do you want?"

"A promise."

Startled, I paused. Bygul growled again. "What kind of promise?"

"That you will avoid dealings with the Red One."

I rolled my eyes. "A name like that doesn't really narrow it down, you know."

Freya didn't laugh.

I tried again. "Could you be more specific, please?"

"Loki." She spat his name as if it was poison, and Bygul hissed.

I stared at her, amazed. "How did you know about my dream?"

She showed her teeth. "I didn't until you spoke, you fool."

Bygul took a step toward me, and I stepped back cautiously.

"Why would I promise you not to help Loki?"

Freya's eyes blazed with hatred. "A thousand lifetimes will never be enough for him to pay back his crime. He cannot go free."

I paused, weighing my options. It occurred to me that I should try to bargain with Freya, but I rejected that idea almost immediately. She didn't seem like the type to make a deal. Still, I didn't want to promise any god anything until I found the second Red Witch and formed an alliance with her.

Drawing a deep breath, I kept my face calm. "Loki won't be released until the end of the world. I don't think I have any say when that will be."

Her eyes bored into me, but I didn't flinch. Bygul growled again, this time low and throaty.

"Very well. I see that mortals have not gained much intelligence over the centuries. You would do wise not to cross me, Witch Darlena."

"I'm not trying to cross you. I'm trying to stay out of this."

"When do you leave my land?"

I looked at the clock over her shoulder. "Later today."

She pursed her lips. "And when do you return?"

"Never, if I have anything to say about it."

She smiled. "Mortals rarely have a say, Darlena."

5

Despite my disturbing encounters with the local gods, I made it to the airport later that morning in one piece. When I was going through security, I caught a glimpse of an ice-covered volcano spewing lava on the local news station, and I shuddered, remembering Pele's warning.

I had arrived way too early for my flight and was quickly bored. Sitting there on the hard vinyl chair, my backpack under my feet, I pulled out my cell phone. Before I could think too much, I sent a text to Justin. I hadn't told him I was leaving, and I wondered if he knew how much his texts had helped pull me out of the dark hole I'd dug for myself in the past few months. I hated the idea of being dependent on him, but that seemed to be something I couldn't escape.

We'd dated and split up long before I became a Red Witch, but that hadn't been the end of us. My emotions always went into overdrive when he was around, and even though I'd told him I loved him last fall, I didn't think we had any future together. Hecate would have no problem using him to hurt me, and I couldn't bear the thought of putting Justin in danger, so I had kept him at arm's length ever since I killed Rochelle.

Still, I felt an odd sense of comfort when my phone buzzed an instant later. "Miss u" was all his text said, but I grinned at the phone like an idiot. I was texting him back when I heard a disgusted snort behind me.

I glanced around and was startled when I locked eyes with Freya.

"Haven't you mortals learned a better way to speak to your lovers?"

I flushed. "He's not my lover."

"But you wish he were, do you not?"

I refused to answer, but I felt my face growing hot. The first time we'd broken up, it had been because I wanted to take our relationship all the way, but for some reason, Justin refused. Freya smiled slowly at something in my eyes.

"I could help you win his heart. It is one of the things I do."

"No, thanks. No more love spells for me." I shuddered at the memory of Justin's face when he realized I'd used a spell to bend his will.

Freya looked surprised. "But they are so fun, so simple!"

I shook my head. "Look, why are you here? I'm leaving, just like I told you."

She nodded. "I came to see for myself that you *will* get on that plane."

I studied her, confused. "Why don't you trust me? You don't even know me."

Her expression darkened. "I learned long ago to never trust Red Witches."

Eagerly, I leaned forward. "What other Reds have you met?"

"Enough to know that you are all lying, dangerous creatures."

I ignored her insult. "But aren't you a Red goddess? I mean, I bet you don't think Red magic is awful."

"Red magic and the mortals who wield it are two very different things."

"What do you mean?"

Freya glared at me. "You are a tricky Red, trying to coax wisdom from me. But I know enough of your kind. You will never learn the secrets of Red magic, Darlena. It is foolish to try."

I crossed my arms over my chest. "I have to try, because otherwise I'll never defeat Hecate."

The silence was tense. Freya's hand went to her waist as if she was reaching for a weapon, but nothing appeared. Finally, Freya said, "Why would a mortal dare to take on the Queen of Witches?"

"She tried to kill me!" I snapped. An airline employee looked over at me in concern, and the mother sitting across from me grabbed her toddler by the hand and stood up. I lowered my voice. "She wants to control me, and when she found out that she couldn't, she tried to have me killed."

"Death is a part of life. Besides, Reds never live very long."

I felt cold at her words, but I persisted. "But I want to use my magic to create balance! If Hecate kills me, the next Red Witch isn't likely to care about balance."

Freya eyed me with interest. "Why is this so important to you, this balance within chaos?"

I struggled to put my thoughts into words. I still wasn't sure why I was driven to find balance, but anything was better than becoming a monster. "Chaos is powerful and destructive, but I've learned that chaos isn't the same thing as destruction. I used Red magic to change things, and … " I trailed off feebly, realizing how naïve I sounded.

But Freya's eyes lingered on me. They were still wary, but there was a spark of something that might have been respect buried in their depths. "Many gods do not learn the lessons you have learned in your short life." She sighed and looked down at her long, elegant hands. "It is true, I am a goddess of Red magic. But unlike some, I do not thirst for blood. I seek justice, which sometimes brings chaos, but I also bless the marriage beds of the young ones. I have spent eternity striving for balance, and never have I met a mortal who could speak the words I keep close in my heart."

Stunned, I gaped at her. That was almost exactly what Persephone had told me when we first talked, and she'd proved to be a valuable ally. "So you'll help me?"

She laughed. "I never said that. No, mortal, I won't interfere. But your words make me question what I have always believed about your kind."

"We're not all bloodthirsty."

"*You* are not, I'll grant you that. But how can you know what the other two Reds are like?"

I took a deep breath. "I can't. That's why I'm going to Scotland: to find another Red Witch."

Freya stared at me for a long minute. "Why Scotland?"

I hesitated, not sure I wanted to tell her about my dream. Finally, I said, "It's a gut feeling."

"Did that gut feeling happen to come from a vision while you slept?"

I glanced at her, surprised, and nodded.

"Be wary of dreams, Darlena. They are not always as they seem."

Trying not to shiver, I looked her square in the eye. "So far, mine have been pretty accurate."

She shrugged. "Then I wish you well. But remember that this quest of yours may not follow the path you intend." She brushed her fingers across my forehead in a gesture of blessing before sweeping off into the crowd. When I blinked, she was gone.

"Now boarding flight 1183 with service to Edinburgh. All passengers, all rows."

I grabbed my backpack and joined the line queued up at the gate. When the ticket attendant scanned my boarding pass, the computer beeped insistently at her.

"Look at that! You've just been upgraded to first class. How lucky."

I thanked her, grinning. Luck had nothing to do with it; Carl had certainly fallen under my spell.

As I stretched out in the luxurious seat, I thought about Freya. I wasn't used to seeing goddesses that frequently, but I'd seen her twice this morning. What was it she had said about gods and their homelands? I glanced out the window as the plane took off, watching as the white landscape receded beneath me. I saw a brief flash of orange against the ice, and my muscles tensed at the thought of the volcano erupting on the ground. I pressed my face to the glass, watching plumes of black smoke and molten fire bubble beneath me. Scanning the hillside, I sighed in relief. It didn't look like the volcano was close enough to any homes to do damage, but I was still on edge. Seeing it reminded me that Pele could cross some boundaries, but even she was governed by her element. I didn't think there were any volcanoes in Scotland.

With a shock, it hit me that I wouldn't have the help of any of the goddesses I'd met so far: Aphrodite and Persephone weren't native to the land I was traveling to, and Freya seemed to indicate that in

Europe the gods were more tightly constrained by things like location. I leaned my head back against the seat, realizing that I was going to be completely without celestial support. I hadn't really planned on getting help while I was in Scotland, but now that I knew I'd be on my own, I felt an icy prick of fear between my shoulder blades.

6

I breezed through customs, but I wasn't prepared for the chaos of the Edinburgh airport. It was packed with travelers, and none of them seemed too happy.

"But I've got a meeting in Stockholm tomorrow morning!" I heard one exasperated man yelling at the harried clerk behind the counter.

"I'm sorry, sir, but due to the situation in Iceland, all flights have been grounded until further notice." She pointed to the large television screen on the wall, which was showing footage of black smoke. With a shiver, I realized that the volcano I'd spotted before I left was still going.

I passed by the crowded counter, clutching my backpack and thankful that my flight had landed; it wouldn't have been safe for me to spend another night in Iceland, not after Freya's warning and Pele's visit. I ducked into a restroom and splashed cold water on my neck, trying to revive my sluggish, jetlagged mind.

I hadn't booked a hotel ahead of time because I didn't want to run the risk of alerting Hecate to my plans, but now that seemed stupid. It was clear after last night that Hecate knew what I was up to. The only thing I didn't know was when she would strike next. In the meantime, I was surrounded by stranded travelers, and I didn't have a place to stay.

Taking a chance, I crossed to one of the airport pay phones and dialed the number for a youth hostel I'd marked in my travel guide. When the thick-accented receptionist answered, I crossed my fingers.

"I need a room for tonight."

"It's Christmas, lass. Don't you have family to stay with?"

I shook my head and then felt like an idiot. She couldn't see me. "No. I just landed. I guess I didn't plan my trip very well ... but I've always wanted to spend Christmas in Scotland!"

Her voice softened at my lie. "If you don't mind sharing one of the dormitories, I can find a bed for you. But I canna promise you a hot shower!" She chuckled softly.

"That's fine. What should I tell the taxi?"

She clicked her tongue. "No need to waste your money on a car, lass. We're two blocks up from the train station. Just take the tram from the airport. We're at the corner of Princes and Frederick. You'll see the sign."

I thanked her and hung up. It didn't take long to find the tram, and soon I was walking along the steep, cobblestoned streets.

Despite the short walk, my fingers were numb by the time I reached the hostel, and my breath hung frostily in the air. I hadn't packed any gloves for my trip, thinking foolishly that Scotland would have a temperate ocean climate. I had to grasp the door handle twice before I was able to turn it and step into the warmth of the crowded room.

The reception area was on the ground floor, and it was overflowing with people my age and a little bit older. Red and green decorations hung from every surface, and the clerk behind the desk was wearing a Santa hat that looked like it had been designed by Dr. Seuss. A big smile spread across my face as I walked up to the desk; the party spirit was infectious. The clerk spotted me and pounded on the old-fashioned bell that sat in front of him.

The chatter in the room quieted, and I felt everyone's eyes turn toward me. A wave of paranoia washed over me; what if Hecate had spies watching me?

"What can I do for ye?" the man asked with a smile, unaware of my tense mood.

"I called earlier from the airport. The lady said you still had room available?"

He grinned broadly. "Of course there's room at this inn!" He laughed, and a few people standing nearby chuckled at his Christmas joke. "Just need to see your passport, and your student card."

I pulled both items from the deep inner pocket of my backpack and handed them over. He turned to make a photocopy, and I looked around the room, trying to slow my racing heart.

The party looked like it was just getting underway, and I could hear snippets of conversations in heavily accented English from all corners of the room. No one was watching me, and I exhaled slowly and grinned. It should be easy to blend in to such a mixed group of travelers for a day or two while I figured out what to do next. However, as I glanced at the map of Scotland tacked up on the wall behind the counter, my heart sank. The country was much larger than I had thought, and I didn't have the slightest idea where to begin my search. It might take months before I found another Red ... unless I used magic to help me.

The clerk shoved my passport and student card back toward me and grabbed a key off the wall behind him. "I'll put you in dormitory five upstairs. Anything valuable in that sack?"

I shook my head, and he smiled.

"Just as well. If there were, I'm supposed to tell you to leave it locked up down here in the safe, but most folks don't want to do that. Most folks aren't traveling with anything of much value, either."

I followed him up the steep stairs, which turned sharply at three small landings before he announced, "Dormitory 5C. Home sweet home!" He unlocked the thick wooden door and gestured to an unmade bunk bed near the window. "No one's claimed that bed, so it's all yours. Pity it's not on the floor; are you scared of heights?"

I could tell he was joking, but I didn't feel like getting into a conversation right now. I shook my head silently and turned toward the bed.

"Lights out is at one a.m., so I canna make anyone be quiet before that. If you're wanting to sleep, I hope you brought earplugs!"

He shut the door and headed back down the stairs to join the raucous Christmas party in the lobby.

There were four sets of bunk beds lining the walls; I guessed that meant I had seven roommates. There wasn't much space on the ground in between the beds, but that didn't seem to hinder the other travelers: every bed but mine was strewn with clothes, bags, and other items. I tossed my backpack up on the blue and white striped mattress, and then climbed aboard. I set a loose ward on the door of the room which would alert me if anyone was about to enter. I didn't want to be interrupted, and I knew that I needed to get to work right away, no matter how tired I was.

Breathing deeply, I crossed my legs, perching precariously on top of the bunk bed. When I straightened my spine, my head hit the ceiling with a deafening *thwack*. I always preferred to meditate in a seated position, but that didn't seem possible tonight. Instead, I lay on my back on the bare mattress. One of the first things I'd learned at Trinity was the power of the mind to reveal necessary information. I didn't usually have the patience for meditation, but whenever I bothered to slow down enough, I got results. I'd used a fire meditation last fall to help me begin to figure out more about Red magic, and it had worked like a charm. Tonight, I decided I would meditate to figure out where the other Red Witch was.

Wary of drawing too much attention to myself, I didn't light one of the red candles buried in the bottom of my bag. Instead, I held Aphrodite's mirror in my left hand and my other prized possession, my mother's knife, in my right. There was one more magical item in the bag, tucked carefully in the bottom of a sock: the crystal sphere Hades had given me when I left the Underworld. These tools were bulky and it took a certain amount of magic to get them through airport security, but having them with me was worth the effort. I thought the tools might help ground me and remind me of the people and gods who were willing to help, and Witches always trust their instincts.

Mom had insisted I take her athame last year, even though I knew just how important her sacred knife was to her. I'd used it many times since she gave it to me, but I still thought of it as hers; a person's magical energy doesn't fade from an object just because it's no longer in their possession. Feeling my mother's presence through the knife made me breathe a sigh of relief. With a pang of guilt, I realized I hadn't called home to let them know I made it to Scotland. I almost got up to call them on the spot, but I didn't want to lose the opportunity of the empty dorm room. Doing this magic while the party was still going was my best chance to learn something.

Lying on my back with my hands at my sides, I stared at the ceiling. I let my focus go slack until it was as if I were looking through the ceiling rather than at it. The crack over my head doubled, and then tripled as my eyes started to glaze over. As my breathing slowed, I formed a question with my mind.

"Where is the Red Witch?"

At first, I only asked the question in my head, but as my trance deepened, I began to whisper the question like a chant. "Where is the Red Witch?" My voice grew slowly louder, until I was almost shouting. My vision blurred, and I could almost see the answer when the ward I had put on the door buzzed in my mind, yanking me back to consciousness.

Startled, I rolled over, concealing my tools with my body. Trying to look like I was asleep, I rested my head on my arm and shut my eyes, leaving them cracked just a sliver. The door opened and two girls stomped in. They looked like they might be a little bit older than me, but it was too dark to tell. I watched them through slitted eyes as they staggered to the bunk across from me.

"Come on, Joan. Where's my toothbrush?"

Joan giggled. "He still won't kiss you."

Her friend smacked her playfully. "He might! It's Christmas."

Joan spun around and flopped down on the floor. "Woopsie." She giggled again. I realized that she'd probably been drinking at the party; from the look of her, she'd never done that before, and I resisted the urge to laugh. She looked like an idiot.

Her friend rummaged around for a minute, then let out a triumphant shout. "Here it is! Come on, I have to hurry."

They didn't glance at me as they headed out into the hallway. Once the door was shut, I counted slowly to ten, and then breathed a sigh of relief. At least two of my roommates would be too hungover to pay much attention to me in the morning. For a minute, I thought about trying to restart the meditation, but weariness overcame me. Still clutching the knife and the mirror, I fell asleep. Almost immediately, I started to dream.

I was walking through a dark forest, approaching a woman who was standing in front of a bubbling cauldron.

Her back was to me, but she was draped in black and cobwebs, and panic filled me. I thought I knew exactly who she was; Hecate had found me! If she harmed me in the dream, would I ever wake up? I wanted to turn, to run, to stop walking, but my feet kept leading me toward her. I was trapped.

When she turned, I saw the brightest green eyes I'd ever seen. The woman's face was lined with age, but she was still frighteningly beautiful. I just had time to register that this strange woman wasn't Hecate before the dream shifted and the woman vanished.

Now I was standing next to a dirt mound as tall as my head. Stones circled the hill haphazardly, and two stones seemed to form an entrance. As I approached, I saw that there was an opening, leading into the dirt like a tunnel. I walked forward, curious, but just then the light in the dream shifted, illuminating the inside of the mound. Piles of human skulls and jumbled bones leered at me from the darkness, and I stumbled and fell over backward. As I fell, I thought I heard a deep voice.

"You shall not enter my domain alive. Go back; you are not of the dead. Yet." The voice rasped and echoed around me, and I sat up with a jolt, smashing my skull against the ceiling for the second time that night. I rubbed my head and bit back a curse, glancing around the dark room.

Still shaken by my dream, I lay there in the dark with my eyes open for a while. I had been so sure that Hecate had found me, but the woman at the cauldron was not the goddess I ran from. Whoever she was, she wasn't someone I wanted to get to know—the entire dream had been creepy. I shivered, remembering the mound of bones and the standing stones. I had no desire to go to such a place—the voice in my dream had issued an unnecessary warning.

As my fear faded, it was replaced by irritation. The dream and the meditation hadn't told me anything, and I was no closer to knowing where to look for the other Red Witch than I had been before. Sure, I was here in Scotland, but so far, that had been the only clue I'd had. How was I going to form an alliance with the other Red if I couldn't even find her? Annoyed, I drifted back to sleep.

7

The next morning, I stepped out of the shower to find the shared bathroom occupied by a tall, blond girl who was industriously plucking her eyebrows over the sink. After a moment, I recognized her as the girl who had interrupted my meditations to find a toothbrush. Our eyes met in the mirror, and she blushed.

"Sorry if we woke you last night. Everyone was enjoying the party a bit too much."

Her accent sounded Australian.

"It sounded like you were having fun. Did he kiss you?"

"You heard that?" Her long hair swayed as she laughed. "Nope. That bloke was gone by the time we got back downstairs. Pity," she sighed, turning back to the mirror with her tweezers. "I made up my mind to have a bit of a romance on this holiday, and I'm running short on time!"

I leaned against the sink. "Where are you from?"

"New Zealand. Thank God you asked; I hate when people assume I'm Australian."

I grinned at her. "Well, to tell the truth, I—"

"Don't say it!" She shook her head. "I think I like you, and I don't want a reason to hate you."

Her words were playful, but I felt a chill when I met her eyes. Had she meant something by that statement? Nervously, I clenched my hands. I needed to get over this paranoia; the whole world couldn't be working for Hecate.

She studied me for a moment. "You're new to the hostel."

I nodded. "Just got in last night."

"American?"

I nodded. "Right in one guess."

"You Yanks are easy to spot. How long are you here?"

I paused, considering my words. "I don't really have plans. I'm just winging it, I guess."

"Lucky! There's no way my folks would let me go on holiday forever." She pouted at her reflection and put her tweezers back in her bag. "I fly home on Sunday."

"You're not going to be here for New Year's Eve?"

"Nah. The winter term starts right up, and as much as I like a good party, I can't stand being jetlagged and hungover at school."

"Fair enough." I stood there nervously for a minute. "I'm Darlena, by the way."

She smiled, showing her perfect white teeth. "Sandra. Don't you dare call me Sandy."

I laughed. "Okay." I turned to leave the small bathroom, but her words stopped me.

"Want to explore with us a bit today? We're going to the vaults."

I glanced at her curiously. "What are the vaults?"

Her eyes lit up. "You're kidding, right?"

I shook my head. I'd been ready to begin my search in peace, but her tone made me pause. "What are they?"

She turned around, ignoring the mirror. "That settles it. You're coming with us."

"But—"

"It's an underground city."

I stared hard at her, trying to read her expression. She looked thrilled. "But I've never heard of it."

"Silly, not many tourists know about it yet. They're still excavating."

I stared at her blankly. "So why do you want to go there?"

"Ghosts. The vaults are bursting with them!"

My skin prickled, but I heard myself telling her, "Sure."

An hour later, I was trailing the two Kiwis toward the South Bridge. I'd been right last night; they were a few years older than me. Sandra was in college, but her traveling partner, Joan, was taking a gap year. The girls had been surprised when I hadn't know what that was; apparently, a lot of people they knew took a year off between high school and college to figure things out, but I'd never known anyone who did that.

Even though I was eager to get underway with my search for the other Red, I instantly liked Sandra and Joan, and hanging out with them in the unfamiliar streets of Edinburgh made me feel sort of cool. Sandra led the way down the crowded street, talking over her shoulder.

"It sucks that they give tours now, but I still want to see the vaults. My brother was here a few years ago, and he said only a few folks knew about this. It was much creepier then, I'm sure."

"How did he know about them?" I almost tripped on a raised cobblestone, but Joan steadied my arm.

Sandra smiled. "He's a ghost hunter. An amateur, but he loves it. If there are ghosts anywhere he goes, he'll find them."

Joan shivered. "That's so creepy. Do you really believe there are ghosts down there?"

We stood beneath the bridge, facing a dark opening that was shorter than a doorway. I peered into the darkness, my stomach twisting oddly.

Sandra laughed. "Of course not, silly! My brother's a bit addled is all."

Joan sighed in relief, and I glanced at the two girls, confused. "But I thought you wanted to come here because of the ghosts?"

"Ghosts or not, I like a good scare, and this place is guaranteed to deliver."

My uneasiness hadn't abated, and I could tell Joan was still nervous, too. She reached into her bag and pulled out a flashlight with shaking hands. Sandra took it from her and stepped into the vault. It was dark and damp, and the strange musty smell tugged at my memory, but I couldn't place it.

The beam of the single flashlight didn't cut very far into the darkness, and I paused for a moment to draw up a little Red magic. Even if Sandra said she didn't believe there were any ghosts down here, I wasn't so sure, and I didn't want to be defenseless. My fingertips tingled as I followed the girls, and red sparks caressed my arms. I stayed a few steps behind them, hoping they wouldn't notice.

Our footsteps echoed on the earthen floor of the passageway, and Joan crinkled her nose.

"It's all wet! I bet we're in the sewer."

Sandra laughed, dropping her voice a bit. "These are the vaults, all right. Can't you feel the ghosts?"

Despite her teasing, I felt something. But whatever presence was in the vault, it felt nothing like the dead in the realm of Hades. I shivered and glanced behind us at the receding doorway. The light from outside was almost gone, and the flashlight gave off an eerie, blue glow as we descended deeper into the vault.

"Why are we here again?" I called to Sandra.

"I told you! Ghosts!" She chuckled. "But really, this used to be a city, with shops and everything. I wanted to see it for myself." She moved forward as she spoke, and Joan and I followed her, watching the thin beam of the flashlight bounce along the corridor. My skin prickled along my neck, and I struggled to ignore the strange sensation.

"But why isn't it being used now?"

"I don't know, but it hasn't been used for centuries."

The light flickered.

"Sandy, be careful!" Joan's voice sounded tight.

Sandra laughed. "You girls are such drags. I thought you wanted an adventure."

I caught a whiff of sulfur. "Something isn't right."

"Not you, too?" Sandra sighed heavily. "How did I get stuck with two big scaredy cats?"

Joan whimpered. "I want to go out now."

The light moved ahead, and Sandra's voice called from further down the tunnel, "The only way out is through!"

The inside of my nose burned, and I suddenly identified the smell. Hecate always smelled of sulfur. Panic gripped me. "We need to leave. Now."

I stopped walking, and as soon as I was standing still, the earth beneath my feet began to ripple. A rumbling noise filled the air, and I lost my balance, tumbling into the rock wall.

"What's happening?" Joan's voice was far ahead of me, and I strained to see in the darkness.

"I don't know; we need to go back." Sandra's carefree tone had changed to one of fear, and the light began bobbing back toward me.

"Hurry. Seriously, I don't know what's happening, but this isn't good." I turned around to go back out of the tunnel. The ground moved again, and this time, there was a loud cracking noise. I whirled around in time to see a huge chunk of the vault ceiling crash to the ground, blocking the tunnel with the girls behind it. I was plunged into darkness as the flashlight disappeared.

Joan screamed briefly, and then went silent.

I reached out a hand and felt the wall. Cautiously, I took a step forward. "Joan?"

There was no answer. I felt something move in the dark beside me, and I yelped in surprise.

"Sandra?"

The only sound I heard was the faint trickle of water from somewhere far ahead.

I took a couple of steps back and raised my hands defensively. The presence I had sensed as soon as we entered the vaults seemed stronger, more pervasive. It felt like I was surrounded by thick, sticky air. I took a deep breath, trying to calm myself, but my nostrils filled with the smell of sulfur and I choked.

I conjured a small sphere of light, but my attention was too distracted to hold the spell. Before I was plunged into darkness again, I saw Sandra and Joan. What I saw terrified me.

The girls were lying, face down and motionless, a few yards in front of me. They were pinned to the ground beneath the massive boulder;

it looked like it had landed directly on them. Were they still alive? My stomach churned and I took a step forward, unsure of what to do.

I was forcibly reminded of the bodies inside the green car that I'd flipped; even though Hecate had said that I'd actually averted death, those two people were the first Nons I'd ever killed. Was I responsible for two more deaths? What if Hecate had caused the cave-in, trying to get to me? A shadowy presence brushed by my ear, and the sound of harsh laughter echoed in the cave. Recoiling in fear, I felt Red magic surge through me, and a blast of light filled the tunnel. Panicked, I turned and ran.

I emerged into a cold drizzle, gasping for breath. A few people glanced at me curiously, but I hurried across the street. I had just reached the other side of High Street when a sound like fireworks filled the air. Smoke poured out of the doorway to the vaults, and the bridge shook violently. Without looking back, I took off in the opposite direction, not caring if I drew attention to myself. *What the hell had I just done?*

A few blocks away, I stopped to catch my breath. I could still hear the muffled sounds of panic from the bridge. A high-pitched siren filled the air, followed by another. Doubling over, I felt sick to my stomach, and it wasn't just because of the image of Sandra and Joan's mangled bodies. I hadn't used that much Red magic since I faced Rochelle, and I wasn't prepared for the aftereffects.

"Easy there." A warm hand gripped my arm, steadying me.

I looked up at the tall man who had stopped to help, and I yelped in pain at the electrical charge that hit me. Energy coursed through my body unbidden.

Startled, he stepped back, dropping his hand. "What was that?" His voice was deep and sexy, and it had a slight Scottish lilt, but his tone was wary.

I closed my eyes for a minute, still tingling from the electricity that was sparking in the air. "Magic." The word was out of my mouth before I could think, and I wanted to curse myself for being so foolish. There was no chance this guy was anything but a Non, and it was unthinkable to get Nons mixed up in magic. It was too dangerous.

He raised a ginger eyebrow at me, but the rest of his face was an expressionless mask beneath his orange hair. "I think we need to talk. Over here." He gestured to a small pub sandwiched between a hotel and a bakery.

I glanced back in the direction of the vaults. It was probably better for me to be off the street in case anyone was looking for me. Warily, I followed him inside the low doorway. He sat down at a table in the back corner, under a dirty wall mirror. I slid into the chair across from him, tensed and ready to bolt if needed. My skin tingled with energy, and I made a conscious effort to hold a little Red magic, in case I needed to defend myself.

"No need for that."

Surprised, I looked at him, studying the sharp lines of his face. He tipped his head at my feet, pointing toward the exit. "You don't need to run."

I smiled at him, trying to cast a glamour. "Why would you think I wanted to run?" I asked sweetly.

He leaned back and crossed his arms, his mossy green eyes annoyed. "You'll have to try better than that. My little sister has a stronger glamour when she wants something!"

I almost fell out of my chair. "What are you talking about?"

His smile was blinding, but there was no humor in it. Instead, it was like looking at a hyena. Again, I felt the electric tingles I'd experienced in the street. His eyes widened a fraction before returning to normal. "You're a Witch." It wasn't a question.

I glanced around, checking to see if anyone was listening. No one seemed to be paying attention to us, so I leaned forward. "And how would you know that?"

"So am I."

I leaned back again, studying his hard face. His green eyes were intelligent, and he almost looked friendly, but a jagged white scar running down his left cheek made him look dangerous. This wasn't a guy I wanted to cross, but he *was* a Witch. Maybe he could help me find the other Red.

What the hell? "I'm Darlena." I stuck out my hand, but he kept his arms across his chest. After an awkward moment, I pulled my hand back and wiped it on my thigh. *What an ass!* He watched me carefully.

"What are you doing in Scotland?"

"I'm trying to find somebody."

His eyes bored into me. "Who?"

"Another Witch."

"You've found me."

I shook my head, trying to figure out how to get away from him. "I'm looking for a certain type of Witch. You never told me your name."

My abrupt change of topic didn't seem to throw him. "What kind of Witch?"

I hesitated. Hecate's spies could be anywhere. On the other hand, he was the first person I'd met who might know anything about the Red Witch I was so sure lived in Scotland. I didn't want to come right out and spill everything, so I hedged. "What types of magic are taught here in Scotland?"

He leaned back, appraising me. "Green. And White and Black."

"Any others?" I couldn't hide the disappointment in my voice.

"Of course. My sister's a Blue."

That surprised me. "I've never heard of Blue."

"Are the other three the only kinds of magic you know about?"

I stared hard at him, but his eyes gave nothing away. With a silent prayer for safety, I answered him. "I know about Red magic."

His eyes glowed brighter, but nothing in his expression or demeanor changed.

I leaned forward, wondering if this was such a good idea. "Have you heard of Red magic?" I asked quietly.

He nodded once, curtly.

"Maybe you can help me," I asked.

His hand darted across the table and grasped my wrist, sending another electric shock through me. "Maybe you can tell me what game you're playing."

"What do you mean?" I twisted my wrist, trying to pull it from his grasp, but his fingers were locked around me. Electricity shot through my arm, and I almost felt the way I did when I used Red magic. Almost, but this feeling was painful.

"Did you think I wouldn't notice that little stunt you pulled in the vaults?"

I stared at him, too surprised to say anything. His eyes flashed dangerously, and I cursed myself for making the mistake of talking to this guy.

"You don't use Red magic in my domain, girl. Not if you're smart." Searing pain shot up my arm from his grip, and I tried to shake him off. He didn't let go.

Slowly, my mind untangled his words. I gaped at him. "Do you mean you're a Red, too?"

His fingers tightened, and I squeaked. "You shouldn't be anywhere near me." His words were clipped.

"But you're the one I'm looking for!" The pain in my arm diminished somewhat, and I felt a thrill of excitement. I'd found the other Red!

He glared at me. "Do you really think I'll fall for something like that? Why would another Red seek me out?"

"I need help."

"Clearly. You trespassed in my realm. You used Red magic to do harm in my land. You need a lot of help, Darlena." He spat my name, digging his nails into my wrist. I finally twisted free, but there were bloody gashes where he'd raked me. A dull throb remained in my arm, reminding me of the strange electric current that had singed me. I didn't look at my wrist, but the scent of my own blood made me dizzy.

"I do need help. And you're the only one who can help me."

He snorted.

"Hecate wants me dead."

His eyes didn't flicker. "Why should that matter to me?"

"She wants me dead because I don't cause enough chaos."

"You've done plenty here already."

I raised my voice and narrowed my eyes. "But that was an accident! There was something in the vault with us, and it killed those two girls." He flapped his arms at me, and I lowered my voice. "It was coming after me. I didn't mean to do anything, but my reflexes kicked in. It felt like Hecate."

"Why would I believe a Red? You're just here to make trouble."

I pursed my lips. "Last fall, I went to the Underworld in Greece. I lived among the dead. All because Persephone thought it would protect me from Hecate."

"And why would a Red Witch need protection from her?" he

sneered.

I exploded. "Because I don't like the way she wants me to use my magic!"

The silence in the pub following my outburst was deafening, and the Witch across from me stood up quickly, a terrifying expression on his face.

"Move. Now. Outside."

8

I followed him, trying not to make eye contact with anyone in the pub. Once we were outside in the street, I opened my mouth to explain.

He shook his head. "Not here. Whatever it is you want to say, it's too dangerous to be said without wards. Follow me."

I crossed my arms and stood my ground. "Why should I trust you now?"

"You're the one who said you were looking for me!" He pulled his hand through his flaming hair, but the magical energy coursing through him had the effect of static electricity. He looked a lot less threatening with his hair standing on end. In fact, he almost looked hot.

I tried to hide my smile. "Maybe I was wrong."

The Witch snorted. "You've said too much to decide you're wrong now."

We stood motionless for a moment, glaring at each other. Finally, I turned my palms up.

"I'll follow you. If you promise that you won't do anything to me."

His eyes bored into mine, and again I felt electricity course down my back. I'd never had a similar reaction from being around any other Witch, and I wasn't sure I liked it. After a moment, he sighed. "You'll come to no harm in my dwelling place, Witch. But I won't have this conversation on the street."

I hesitated, but my need for information trumped my fear. Drawing a deep breath, I nodded. "Good enough."

His apartment was above a pharmacy a few blocks away. I followed the Witch up the stairs, but I paused when he opened the door.

"I said I wouldn't hurt you." His voice sounded exasperated.

"I know. But this is weird."

"Meeting a Witch on holiday, or going to my flat?"

"Both. Except, this isn't a vacation."

He grinned and held the door open. "After you, m'lady."

I hung back. "At least tell me your name. You've got the advantage: you already know mine."

He studied me and must have realized that I wasn't going any further until I had more information.

"Marcus. Marcus Welty."

I eyed him suspiciously. "What, like an old Roman?"

He shrugged. "My parents liked the classics."

I realized I had run out of reasons to stall. He looked at me, his eyes sharp.

"Okay. I trust you. For now." I brushed past him across the threshold, trying to summon up more confidence than I felt. As I came close to him, another zap of energy danced across my skin, and I heard him inhale sharply. I struggled not to react, but the electric transfer thing or whatever it was getting weird.

I looked around the tiny apartment. From where I stood just inside the door, I could see everything. Well, almost everything. "Where's your bathroom?"

"Why, do you need it?"

I glared at him. "I was just wondering. Everything else is out in the open."

He tilted his head toward a door beside the sink. "Through there."

I watched him lock the door and trace a star in the air. "May I?"

He stepped aside with a mocking bow, and I added a ward of my own. When I turned, he was watching me intently, and I suddenly felt self-conscious about the red sparks dancing on my arms. When he'd cast the ward, I hadn't seen any outward sign of Red magic.

I crossed my arms, trying to hide the fading sparks. "What?"

"You do that differently. What was the symbol you used?"

I shrugged, not wanting to reveal anything to him. I'd have to be more careful the next time I cast in front of him. I wasn't sure if he might be a potential threat, and I didn't want him learning any of my methods in case I ever needed to defend myself.

"Why did you bring me here?"

He crossed the room to a small fridge. "Want something to drink?"

"No."

He pulled out a beer and leaned against the counter. I realized that he wasn't as old as I'd originally thought. He couldn't be out of his twenties, but he carried himself as if he were much older. I was right, too; he was really good-looking, in a dangerous kind of way. Keeping the door at my back, I moved across the room and perched on a chair facing him.

We stared at each other for a minute before he took a swig of beer. The room crackled with electricity.

"Who are you?" His question surprised me.

"I told you my name."

He shook his head. "I don't mean that. Maybe I should have said, what are you?"

I bristled. "A Red Witch. Like you, I think."

"Maybe, maybe not. What else?"

"What d'ya mean, what else?"

He kept his eyes locked on my face. "Who do you belong to?"

"You mean my patron?"

His nod was brief.

"I don't have one."

The green eyes watching me narrowed. "I don't believe you."

"Well, it's true! I had Aphrodite for a little while, but then—" I stopped abruptly, feeling my cheeks heat up.

Marcus eyed me suspiciously. "But then what?"

I sighed, deciding that the only way to get anywhere with him was to trust him. "I ate a pomegranate seed. Persephone had given them to me."

I couldn't read his motionless face, so I pressed on. "After that, things changed. I was no longer bound to Aphrodite; I act for myself."

"And you said earlier that you need help with—the Queen."

The pause was barely audible, but I understood his hesitation. It wouldn't be wise to draw Hecate's attention by saying her name again. I shivered and nodded.

"When I first became a Red, she thought I'd cause a lot of destruction. But then I stopped a car accident, and I realized that if I could control my magic, I could maybe cause less destruction instead of more."

"An interesting idea."

I nodded, encouraged. "But then she decided I was too much of a liability. She tried to kill me."

"The gods can't kill mortals."

"I know that." Frustrated, I worked to keep my voice calm. "But she used another Witch." My voice broke, and I took a deep breath.

He eyed me warily. "And you defended yourself."

I nodded, not trusting my voice. I hadn't talked about what happened to Rochelle with anyone yet, and my chest felt tight. A cloud of guilt descended on me, and for a minute, I thought I would lose it in front of the irritating stranger. It took some effort, but I pulled myself together and tried to prepare for his next question.

Marcus took another swallow of beer. "So why Scotland?"

That wasn't what I'd been expecting, and I exhaled gratefully. "I had a dream. I wanted to find the other Red Witches. I'm not sure why, but I have this feeling that we're kept apart not because of our danger to humanity but because of the danger we pose to her."

He nodded thoughtfully. "And then you blew up the vault."

I stood up. "That was not my fault!" The sight of the girls' bodies flashed through my mind, and I shut my eyes quickly. I would *not* cry in front of him.

"Are you saying you didn't unleash Red magic today?"

I crossed my arms and compressed my lips.

Marcus smiled. He looked like a defense attorney going in for the kill. "So you did use Red magic. Here in my domain. Did you ever think that might cause problems?"

Mutely, I shook my head.

He pressed himself off the counter and took a step toward me. "I have a feeling you will cause a lot of problems for me."

"But will you help me?"

"Help you do what?"

"I need to find a way to stand against Hecate."

He made a quick banishing gesture at the sound of her name. "And what am I supposed to do?"

"Work with me! Help me try to balance chaos. You control a third of the world. Do you like being responsible for death and destruction?"

Marcus stood like a statue for a moment, not even breathing. I could see a faint red flush creeping up his neck.

"Of course not." His words were quiet and clipped. "I hate it. I've hated it for longer than you, I'd bet."

"So let's do something about it!"

He shook his head, his face fully flushed. "It's too dangerous."

"Not if we work together. Alone, yes, you're right, we make easy targets. But two Red Witches together—"

"No." His voice was sharp, but I ignored the warning in it.

"Do you like being her slave?"

He stiffened and turned his back to me. "I'm nobody's slave."

"If you let Hecate use you, you might as well be."

"I think you should leave."

I was stunned. "But I've come so far to find you!"

Marcus kept his back to me. "Clearly it was a waste of time."

"I don't believe that."

"Still, I want you to go."

"You can't tell me what to do." As soon as the words were out of my mouth, I realized how stupid I sounded.

He whirled around, his eyes flashing. "Actually, I can. You are in my domain. You've used Red magic here without my consent. I can do anything I want to you, and no one will stop me." A red glow surrounded him, and I scrambled to grab up my own magic as I took a step backward.

He didn't make a move toward me, but the air crackled dangerously between us. "But we could help each other!"

"I don't need your help. I've been a Red for longer than you can imagine, and you've been one for what, ten minutes? You can't help me." He spat the last words fiercely, and I took another step closer to the door.

"Why did you choose Red magic?" I softened my tone, hoping he would let me stay, but he just shook his head.

"Leave. Now."

I thought of one last thing. "I'm staying at the hostel on Princes Street. If you change your mind—"

"I won't."

"But if you do, come and find me."

He crossed the room in two wide steps and pushed me out the door. "You don't want me to find you," he threatened, slamming the door in my face.

I stared at the peeling red paint on the door for a minute, stunned. What the hell was I supposed to do now? I trudged down the stairs and headed back to the street, my thoughts churning furiously. I had come all this way to find Marcus, and I hadn't considered that another Red wouldn't want to help. It seemed like the obvious solution to me. Was I the only one who didn't want to destroy things?

I paced around the city, barely noticing the cobblestone streets lined with souvenir shops and pubs that had caught my attention before. What if this entire trip was just a big mistake? Two more people were dead because of me; what if something else happened? Guilt pressed into my thoughts, and I thought about Sandra and Joan with a shudder. Tears welled up in my eyes, but I clenched my teeth and inhaled sharply.

Forcing my thoughts away from the awful memory of the vaults, I pulled out my cell phone. Acting on impulse, I dialed a familiar number.

The phone rang once, twice, three times, but on the fourth ring it cut off abruptly and I heard a distant voice.

"Hello?"

I smiled despite everything that had happened. "Justin! It's me."

"I hoped you would call today."

"You did?" My heart swelled, and I fought to keep the silly grin off my face.

"Yes." He paused for a moment. "There's something I need to discuss with you."

I wanted to keep my voice light, but it quivered slightly. "Don't sound so serious!"

"I've been having dreams."

I paused. "Go on."

"Dreams about you."

"What every girl wants to hear." I fought back the surge of fear that rose in my chest. Did he somehow know what I'd done to those poor girls?

"Lena, I'm worried about you." His voice was full of emotion, and I almost started to cry right there on the Edinburgh sidewalk.

I forced a smile into my voice. "But there's nothing to worry about."

"Maybe. But you haven't made any bargains, have you?"

I laughed bitterly, thinking about Marcus. "Actually, just the opposite."

He exhaled loudly. "Good. Now is not a good time for you to try to make a deal."

"You can say that again," I muttered.

Justin continued talking over me. "You need to be careful. I don't know why, but I keep dreaming about you winding up trapped. I don't think you'll have pomegranate seeds to get you out of any bad choices."

The seeds had undone my bond to Aphrodite, but they'd also broken the love spell that I'd cast on Justin. I winced at the memory.

"Not expecting any other random seeds, thank you very much." I tried to sound confident, but my stomach clenched as I remembered that Persephone couldn't reach me now.

"But seriously, be careful. Please?"

"Fine." I closed my eyes for a moment, wishing I could lean my head on his shoulder.

He paused. "Is that a promise?"

I sighed. "It doesn't matter, because I'm coming home."

"What?" His voice sounded alarmed. "What are you talking about?"

"This whole thing has been a waste of time."

"Did you find the other Red?"

I grimaced. "Unfortunately."

Justin was silent for a minute. Then he surprised me. "I don't think you should come home yet."

I stared at the phone blankly. "Are you kidding? What's the point of hanging around here if I'm not getting any help?"

"Maybe you could enjoy yourself." His tone was so earnest; I could picture his warm brown eyes willing me to stay.

"But I miss you," I whispered. For a moment, there was silence on the line, and my stomach clenched. Had I crossed an invisible line? I so didn't know how to act around him anymore, but I needed him. I knew that much.

Finally, he sighed. "I miss you, too. But this is important. What if this is your chance to get out from under Hecate's thumb once and for all?"

"But what's the point if the other Red won't help me?"

"Be patient, Lena. Things might change."

I closed my eyes, trying not to cry. "I guess."

"Just don't make any deals."

"Fair enough."

We talked for a few more minutes until we ran out of things to say. Finally, as a joke, I asked about the weather.

"We're due for an ice storm. They're saying it's going to be the worst in twenty years."

I laughed. "They always say that, and it never is."

I could almost hear Justin shrug. "I don't know. Something's strange about this winter, but I can't tell what it is." Mom had said the same thing, and I felt a tingle of unease on the back of my neck. Something about the weather wasn't natural, but I didn't want to alarm Justin.

"You're imagining things. I have to go, but I'll call you later and let you know when I'm coming home."

"Give it a chance. Things may change!"

I smiled at the certainty in his voice. "Whatever you say."

After I hung up, I plopped onto a bench. Justin could always make me feel better. He might have been willing to date me again, despite the love spell and all the other craziness between us, but I wasn't sure I wanted to put him in that kind of danger. Hecate had already used my best friend to try to get to me, and I couldn't bear it if something were to happen to Justin, too. It really didn't matter, I realized; we hadn't talked about anything that had happened last fall, so I had no way of knowing if Justin thought of me as a friend or something more. He acted like he'd forgiven me for the love spell, but I couldn't be sure. For the moment, all that mattered was that he was safe, and he was more likely to stay safe if I stayed away from him. That thought gnawed at my heart, but I knew I was right. I wasn't safe to be around.

A squirrel chattered on the ground near my feet, breaking me out of my melancholy. It scampered off quickly, but I leaned back on the bench, thinking. I'd needed the simple reminder to just focus on the here and now. Sometimes, I got so overwhelmed with my problems that I forgot to enjoy things.

That had been happening a lot lately. I'd hardly noticed my surroundings in Iceland, and now there I was, sitting on a bench in Scotland, and I hadn't looked around since I'd landed. I shut my eyes and then opened them again, willing myself to really see what was around me.

Even in the depths of winter, I could tell that Scotland was beautiful. Surveying the street from my bench, I felt the irresistible impulse to look for Ebenezer Scrooge. Even though Dickens set his novels in England, something about the dark streets of Edinburgh made me feel like the Victorian era had never ended. I drew a deep breath, taking in the smell of pollution mingled with snow that hadn't fallen yet. It was strange and beautiful, and I started to relax a tiny bit.

Glancing up, I noticed the slate gray sky for the first time that afternoon. The storm looked like it wasn't far off. I pulled my old, green wool coat tighter around me and tried to get my bearings. I hadn't been paying attention to where I was when I followed Marcus to his apartment, and now I realized that I wasn't sure how to get back to the hostel.

I reached for the bag that hung over my shoulder and pulled out a shiny travel guide. My mom had traveled all over the Celtic lands when she was in college, and she'd offered me her beat-up guide book, but I'd opted to buy this new one. It had seemed silly at the time: I wasn't planning on doing any sightseeing, so why would I care if the guide was up to date or not? Still, now that I was lost, I was glad I'd listened to my impulse.

I had to turn the glossy map twice before I was able to orient myself, and I was surprised to see that I'd wandered much farther from my hostel than I thought. After another look at the looming clouds, I decided that I could afford to be spoiled. I flagged down the second taxi I saw and leaned back on the musty seat to think. Tall buildings rushed by, and I was overwhelmed by the surreal setting; Edinburgh was like nothing I had ever seen back home. A shiver of fear wormed its way into my brain as I thought about what had happened in the vaults, but I tried to push it aside and concentrate on the beautiful scenery going past. Still, the brief moment of relaxation I'd felt on the bench was gone, replaced with mounting anxiety. My thoughts drifted back to Marcus, and I frowned. It was pretty obvious that I needed help to deal with Hecate, but other than asking Marcus, I hadn't come up with any options. Maybe, I thought, I'd have to do something drastic. If Marcus didn't want to help me on his own, I was sure I could use magic to persuade him to become my ally.

9

When I stopped to pick up my key from the reception desk, a different man than the one who let me in last night was leaning behind the counter. He motioned for me to wait, and I realized he was on the phone. I looked at the photos that plastered the walls for a minute, just zoning out, but then his words penetrated my hazy mind and I felt a flash of guilt.

"They were staying here. That's right, New Zealand. I'll ask some of the other kids and let you know. Good-bye, officer."

I managed to keep my hand from shaking as he handed me the key, and I forced myself to smile at him.

He glanced at the key and paused. "Say, you're staying in dormitory 5C, right?"

I nodded, my throat too dry to answer.

"Did you get a chance to meet a couple of the other girls? Sandy and Joan?" He leaned forward expectantly, and I pulled the key away from him.

My thoughts racing, I considered the best answer. "They woke me up last night looking for a toothbrush." I clenched my fist, trying to keep my fingers from trembling.

If he thought it sounded lame, he didn't let on. "D'ya know their phone numbers or addys?"

I shook my head. He sighed and pressed his fingers to his forehead. "It looks like the girls got in a spot of trouble."

The sight of their crushed bodies in the vaults flashed through my mind, and I almost threw up. Taking a deep breath, I forced myself to ask, "Are they okay?"

He shook his head slowly, as if he wasn't sure how much to tell me. "There was a cave-in down in the vaults."

"Oh." I grimaced, sure I was turning green. "Hospital?" There might be a chance the girls had made it out okay, but his next word confirmed my worst fear.

"Morgue."

My stomach churned furiously; I needed to get upstairs before I was sick in front of this guy. I blinked a few times, trying to keep my face neutral.

He sighed again. "Ask the other girls in your room, if you see them. I need to get in touch with their parents, but when they checked in, they didn't leave any numbers besides their mobiles."

I nodded, not trusting myself to speak. As soon as he had turned back to the phone, I took the stairs two at a time, hoping I had the dorm room to myself. I was on the verge of losing it completely, and I didn't need an audience.

For once, luck was on my side, and I collapsed against the door of the empty room, breathing heavily. I climbed up to my bunk and sat back, closing my eyes and trying to think.

Were Joan and Sandra already dead before I'd used Red magic? I couldn't be sure. My stomach rolled as I thought about it. There was a chance that the cave-in had killed them, not my defensive blast of Red magic, but I had no way to know. Besides, the cave-in hadn't been natural; there was something in there with us, and I was sure Hecate had been behind whatever it was. Whether they died in the cave-in or after, when I used magic, the girls were still dead because of me. Just like Rochelle.

Hecate must be laughing somewhere. No matter what I do, I can't seem to stop killing people.

I collapsed into bed even though it was only late afternoon. Guilt threatened to overwhelm me, and my brain couldn't let go of the image of the girls' mangled bodies. Gods, how many more people would I kill? I told myself that if I slept, I'd be able to forget about what had happened in the vaults, but my sleep that night was plagued by even worse nightmares. Once more, I dreamed of Loki.

He was still bound in the same cavern, and his wife stood over him with her bowl. I wanted to pull myself out of the vision, but Loki crooked his finger at me and I felt myself moving forward against my will.

"So, Darlena. You have come back to hear my proposal."

"I can't do what you want."

His twisted face smiled. "I believe differently. You are quite the powerful Witch. Why limit yourself?"

I tried to step back, but my feet were welded to the floor. "I work against chaos. I don't want to cause more."

His laugh was raspy. "But it would be such a simple thing, child! No need to *really* cause chaos. The seeming is more powerful than the reality."

"What do you want?"

"A small boon. Make it seem as if the world is ending, and I will teach you how to bind Hecate."

I hesitated, stunned. "There is no way to bind a god."

The chains that held him rattled. "I of all people know that is not true. If you free me, you will have my bonds at your disposal. It is a simple matter, binding a god, once you have the right tool."

I stared at him. "Why would you work against the gods?"

He snarled. "What has any of them ever done to help me? I owe them nothing. But," he smiled, showing his sharp teeth, "I would owe the person who sets me free."

"But how would I free you?"

He jumped eagerly at my words. "We have a pact, then?"

I shook my head. "I never said that. I just want to know how you think it could be done."

"But you're considering it. Oh, yes, child, I can hear your thoughts turning. Trust me. It can be done, with my help."

The dream started to fade, but I called out, "I have not made any promises!"

"Not yet, child," he cackled. "But you will."

After that, disturbing visions of blood and broken bodies filled my dreams, and I woke up feeling worse than I had in a long time, which was saying something, considering how awful things had been lately. The dormitory was silent, and I felt a lump in my throat when I looked at the two empty beds that had belonged to Sandra and Joan.

I was only too happy to get up, pack my bag, and leave in search of another hotel. I did a finding spell before I left the hostel, and within ten minutes, I found myself standing in a marble and brass hotel lobby, checking in. The place looked expensive, but because I was alone, the woman behind the desk gave me the senior discount. After I forked over half my cash to guarantee that I'd have a bed for at least another week, I headed up to my new room.

There was a small balcony overlooking a back alley, but I was too tired to be charmed. Shutting the curtains, I unpacked my bag and plugged in my computer. Maybe a distraction would help me forget what I'd done in the vaults.

Nibbling on a battered-looking snack mix that I'd found in the bottom of my backpack, I scrolled through my inbox. There were four messages from my mom, and I realized with a start that I'd barely contacted her since arriving in Scotland. The emails didn't sound panicked, but they felt like someone had just flashed the Bat Signal; Mom wanted to hear from me, and soon.

As I composed an email, I thought about how to avoid anything that would get me in trouble at home. I told her I'd found another Red, and that I was "working on" forming a relationship. I would never tell my good, Green mother that I was thinking about messing with another person's will, even if magic was the only way to make Marcus help me. Sometimes, the methods of Red magic veered dangerously close to those little Black spells Rochelle had taught me before I was kicked out of Trinity, and I knew how my parents felt about Black magic.

They weren't alone. Even though Trinity taught White, Black, and Green magic, the emphasis was always on the kinder two forms of magic. I'd dabbled with Black magic because of my temper and my friendship with Rochelle, but that didn't mean I really understood this dark craft. According to my training, Black was almost always evil, White was good, and Green was of this world. And Red? Based on everything I'd done so far, Red was death and destruction. Firmly, I pushed the image of the bodies in the vault out of my mind.

After I emailed Mom back, I tapped my fingers, not sure what to do next. Something Marcus had said yesterday niggled at the back of my mind. Didn't he have a sister who practiced something called Blue magic? My limited experience with Red magic had made me question the balanced concept of the world that I had been raised with. If there were more than just four types of magic, what might I be up against?

It seemed like the only gods interested in acts of chaos were the Red patrons I had encountered so far. I knew that Green gods were generally related to nature and the earth, like my mother's patron, Demeter, the Greek goddess of the harvest. White and Black patrons were always harder to pin down. At Trinity, we mostly focused on the Greco Roman pantheon, and since they were a farm-based society, many of their deities practiced Green magic. There were a few who weren't ever identified in my classes as having any correspondence to one of the three magics—I remembered now that Hecate had always been described as being above the divisions of magic.

Suddenly, with a flash of intuition, I realized that I knew exactly how to get Marcus to listen to me without messing with his free will. I pulled up an Internet search engine and hit a few keys. In a moment, I had a photo and an address on the screen in front of me. It was time to expand my plans, and even though I felt a twinge of guilt at what I was about to do, I reminded myself of what was at stake. If Marcus didn't help me, I had a feeling that we'd both be vulnerable to Hecate. I was ready to do anything to stop her, and I knew I couldn't do it alone. I needed Marcus; I couldn't afford to be picky about how I got his help.

***

I found the school easily: it took up a full city block, and the old brick building pulsed with magic. It reminded me of Trinity, and I felt a pang of longing as I sat down on the curb across the street to wait.

I didn't have to wait very long; the website had mentioned older students having off-campus privileges for lunch, and the sun was high in the sky when I got there. Soon, girls in blue uniforms began trickling past me, laughing and joking. I scanned their faces, hoping that I would recognize her.

A girl with hair that was such a dark brown it might as well have been black emerged from the gate. She was walking slowly, carrying a book in one hand, her finger tracing the open page as she moved. Her lips moved silently, and I smiled. She was older than the picture I'd found, maybe thirteen or fourteen, but I was certain that was her.

"Isadora?" I stood up quickly and approached her. She paused and looked up, curious.

"It's Izzy. But yeah, that's me."

I stuck out my hand. "I'm Darlena. I'm a friend of Marcus."

She eyed my hand without moving, and then looked into my eyes. "No you're not."

Taken aback, I didn't know what to say. She went on, seemingly oblivious of my surprise.

"But you're like him, so I guess you won't be too bad."

"What do you mean?"

Surprise crossed her face. "You don't know?"

Confused, I shrugged. "What did he say about me?"

She giggled and flipped her hair. "He didn't have to say anything, silly. It's obvious you're a Red. What are you doing here?"

10

Dumbfounded, I stared at the girl. She laughed again.

"I only have an hour for lunch, so you'll have to talk fast." She continued up the street, and I rushed after her.

"If you know what I am, aren't you afraid of me?" I didn't want to ask that question, but this girl had caught me so totally off guard I'd forgotten what I'd planned to say.

She shook her head. "Nah. I'm used to Marcus. If he isn't dangerous, I don't see why I should be afraid of you. Of course," she smiled slyly, glancing at me, "he stopped teasing me the more I learned about Blue magic, so I guess that's some assurance."

"But what's Blue magic?"

Izzy gaped at me, stunned. "Seriously? You don't know anything, do you?"

I bristled. "I know plenty about White and Green and Black magic."

"And Red?" Her question irritated me.

"Of course." I thought I sounded confident, but she smirked as if she knew that I was lying. This girl was strange: maybe she did know.

I shook my head, irritated. "You haven't answered my question."

She smiled impishly. "Which one?"

Resisting the urge to strangle her, I said, "About Blue magic."

She fell silent, a serious expression on her face. When she stopped walking, I crashed into her.

"Sorry." She gestured to the food cart in front of us. "I always grab my lunch here."

At first I was annoyed at her change of topic, but then I shrugged. Maybe if we ate together, she'd be more willing to help me. I forced a smile. "What do they have?"

"Falafel. I love it. Want one?"

"I guess." Growing up with a vegetarian mother, I'd tried just about every non-meat food at one time or another, but I didn't remember what falafel tasted like.

"I'll order for you if you pay." Her smile had returned. "And then we'll talk."

Fishing around in my pocket, I dug out a few bills and she nodded, grabbing the money deftly and skipping over to the food cart.

I hung back while she ordered, watching her. I still hadn't figured out how old Marcus was, but his sister couldn't be more than fourteen. For just a moment, I felt guilty about my plans to use the kid, but I tried to shake it off. I didn't mean her any harm; I just wanted her to help me get her brother's attention. He might be willing to ignore me when I was just another Witch, but if I was his sister's friend, maybe he'd listen. It was a long shot, but I was desperate.

Izzy glanced back at me once, almost as if she could read the confused swirl of emotions in my mind, and I forced a smile and waved at her. She grinned back and turned her attention back to our food. Her braces flashed as she chatted with the tired-looking man at the food cart, and when she headed toward me I noticed he began to stand a little straighter and smile. Was she using magic to charm the guy? I almost asked when she got back to where I was standing, but something held me back.

The pocket sandwich she handed me was pleasantly hot in my hands, and I chewed carefully, afraid of burning my mouth. While I figured out what to say, Izzy took a huge chomp of her lunch and began talking around the food.

"So you want to know about Blue magic."

I nodded, chewing thoughtfully. The falafel tasted like unfamiliar spices, and I wasn't sure I liked it. "What is it?"

She rolled her neck twice and took another bite. "Well," she paused to swallow, glancing at me, "it's Water magic."

That made sense. Mom and Dad were Green Witches, and I'd always associated them with earth. Ever since declaring Red, I'd felt my own elemental pull. "Like Red is Fire magic?"

"Yup. Just like that."

"Okay." I looked at her expectantly.

She sighed. "It's hard to explain to someone else! Have you ever tried to explain Red magic to a non-Red?"

I thought about Rochelle and Justin. "Yes. I didn't do a very good job."

Izzy laughed mildly. "Right. Well, it's the same for me right now."

I thought for a minute. "If it's Water magic, what kind of things do you do?"

"I could mess with the weather, if I wanted to." She glanced up at the gray sky pressing down on us. "But I usually don't. I mean, if I change the weather pattern here, who knows what else I'm affecting?" Her words made her sound much older than I thought she was, and I studied her face, wondering if she'd be easy to manipulate. Maybe I had made a bad choice to use her to get to Marcus, but I had to see if it would work.

"My folks are Greens. I think they'd kill me if I ever did anything to the weather."

Izzy laughed. "Marcus doesn't seem to mind. He messes with the sun all the time." She paused and looked at me, intrigued. "I thought it was a Red thing."

I shrugged. "I guess Reds can be different." My voice was sharp as I thought about what Marcus had said to me yesterday, and I struggled to get my anger in check. There was no way I wanted to reveal to the kid that her brother didn't want anything to do with me; I needed her help.

Even though she fixed me with a stare that made me squirm, she didn't push me. She finished her lunch and continued. "Blue governs Water, which is elementally connected to things like love, creativity, and self-knowing." She glanced at me sideways. "What does Red govern?"

Surprised, I answered, "Chaos. I thought you knew that."

She shook her head. "Marcus doesn't talk about his magic much."

I nodded. That was something I understood only too well. "Red is Fire magic, like you said. That means it controls things like chaos, passion, and raw energy."

Izzy leaned back. "So it's a very active magic."

I snorted. "Very." *That* was an understatement.

"So is Blue." She laughed at my confused expression and went on. "It's a different kind of active, of course, but just think about the ocean.

Would anyone call it calm? Besides, water beats fire."

I shook my head, starting to see her point. "Why did you choose Blue?"

"Why did you choose Red?" she shot back.

"I—" I stopped. I didn't have an answer for her. "I'm sorry. I shouldn't have asked."

"That's okay. It's just not that easy to explain, y'know?"

I nodded and changed the subject. I knew I should try to bring the conversation around to Marcus, but I realized I was genuinely interested in knowing more about Izzy. "Do you have a patron?"

Her eyes danced. "Of course. Doesn't everybody?"

"Not a lot of the Witches at my old school did." I paused, debating how much I wanted to tell her. "I don't think my best friend had one."

If Izzy noticed that I'd said "had" instead of "has," she didn't let on. "That sounds like a weird school. We're encouraged to swear to our patron as soon as we choose our magical path."

"What kind of gods practice Blue magic?"

She stiffened her shoulders. "The best kind."

"I'm sorry." I realized I'd made her defensive. "I didn't mean that like it sounded."

She shrugged. "You don't know. I get it. Sorry I got ticked."

"It's okay."

"My patron is Isis."

I thought for a moment. "The Egyptian Goddess?"

Izzy nodded. "Queen of Heaven, Mistress of Magic, and Goddess of Ten Thousand Names." She stood up straighter as she recited the list, and I felt a subtle shift in the air around us. For a moment, my face felt warm, and I thought I smelled the desert.

I took a step back and the illusion dispersed. "Impressive."

She laughed. "She really is. She's been like a mother to me."

"How does that make your real mother feel?" I joked.

Izzy looked away abruptly. "I have to get back to class." She started walking back toward the school.

I followed her, surprised by how quickly the hour had gone by. "Can we talk some more?"

She looked at me, sizing me up, and again I had the sense that she was older than me. It was hard not to fidget as her eyes fixed on mine, and I smiled at her. It wasn't like she could read my mind or anything.

"I guess," she said after a moment. "Where?"

I thought about it. It seemed weird to go back to my hotel, but I couldn't think of anywhere else in the city where we would have privacy to talk. "I'm staying at a hotel uptown."

She grimaced. "Ugh. Boring."

"Well, what did you have in mind?"

For a moment, she scrunched her eyes shut, thinking. I wanted to laugh, but I kept my expression still. Finally, she looked at me with a smile. "Can you handle cemeteries?"

I stared at her for a minute. "Seriously?"

She grinned. "Well, I'm not following you back to your hotel, so why not?"

I shrugged. "I guess." I'd never made a habit of hanging out in cemeteries, but if that's where Izzy wanted to meet up, I wasn't about to give up the opportunity. I was certain she'd be my key to Marcus, even though we'd barely talked about him. And if I was being honest, I sort of liked talking with her.

She tapped her nose with her index finger. "Can you find Greyfriars?"

I nodded slowly, thinking back to my guidebook. "Isn't that one of the most haunted places in Edinburgh?"

The girl winked. "What's the matter? Are you afraid of ghosts?"

Sandra's voice echoed in my mind, asking the same question, and I shuddered, pushing aside the memory. "No, but I don't want to be one just yet."

Izzy smiled. "It's safe. Trust me!"

I smiled back at her, ignoring the flicker of guilt caused by her words. "Okay." I trusted her, but could the kid trust me? I wasn't sure.

11

After meeting Izzy, I headed back to my hotel to think. I lay on my back on the bed and stared up at the crackly ceiling. What did I want to get out of this trip? I thought about Marcus; it was obvious when I met him that he had a strong grasp of Red magic, but he was impossible to read. Could he actually mean what he said, that he didn't want to align with me? A little voice at the back of my mind whispered that surely he must want to shake off Hecate's control, too.

I used to think Reds were kept apart because of the magnified chaos we had the potential to cause together, but recently I had begun to wonder. What if we were really kept apart so we didn't challenge any of the Red deities? The gods I'd met were jealous of other magics, and carefully guarded themselves and their devotees with something approaching fanaticism.

Not for the first time I wondered if the training I'd received at

Trinity had been flawed. What if the things that I thought were laws of magic were actually just the laws of the narrow-minded faculty at my school? And why had the decision been made to only teach three magics? Most people at Trinity didn't even know there were any other forms of magic—I'd been one of them until Hecate showed up.

Shaking off my thoughts, I stood up and stretched. I had three hours before Izzy had promised to meet me. That should give me enough time for a shower and some food, I thought, heading for the small bathroom. While part of me was looking forward to hanging out with Izzy some more, I felt awkward. I knew I needed to use her to help me get to Marcus, but now that I'd met her, that idea felt a little sour. I liked Marcus's sister. She was a neat kid, and I had really enjoyed talking with her that morning. Maybe it wasn't fair to involve her in this mess.

I looked at myself in the steamy mirror. "All's fair in love and war." I smiled sadly at my reflection.

***

Even though I was on time, it wasn't Izzy I saw when I walked up to the gate at the graveyard.

Marcus didn't look thrilled to see me. That's an understatement; actually, he looked like smoke might start coming out of his ears at any moment. His jaw was clenched, and even from a distance, I could see the dangerous spark in his eyes. His presence set me on edge, but I didn't want him to know that. I squared my shoulders and tried to brush past him, but he grabbed my arm.

Jolted by the electricity I'd felt the first time we met, I lost my composure for an instant. Red sparks started dancing on my skin as I resisted the urge to lash out at him. A strange look flickered across his face, and he let go of my arm with a grunt.

"What are you doing here?" He growled the words, but I noticed he didn't touch me again.

"Here at Greyfriars, or here in Scotland?" I wanted to sound jaunty and unafraid, but my voice shook slightly.

"Take your pick. But more importantly, why did my sister call me to tell me she'd met another Red Witch this morning?"

I swallowed nervously. "She told you?"

He nodded. "I followed her here. She's inside, waiting for you."

I started to scoot around him. "Then I better get going."

"Not so fast." He shifted, blocking the narrow sidewalk.

"You said you didn't want to work with me. So why are you here?"

He raised his eyebrows. "I don't trust you any more than you should trust me. Would you leave *me* alone with your sister?"

I shrugged. "I don't know. I don't have a sister, so I can't tell you what I'd do."

Marcus nodded, staring at my face intently. "I don't think you mean her harm."

"I don't!" I rushed to assure him. "Nothing like that." I didn't mean to hurt her, but I did mean to use her; I hoped Marcus couldn't read my mind, but I felt a small thrill of triumph. Meeting Izzy had already brought me back into contact with Marcus. My plan was working!

"You don't mean her harm," he continued as if I'd never spoken, "but you're still raw, Red. You're more likely to cause harm even when you don't mean to."

The question that popped out of my mouth surprised us both.

"How long have you been a Red?"

His gaze turned wary. "Why?"

"Izzy said something this afternoon that made me wonder." That and his condescending tone whenever he talked to me. No one I knew in America declared their path before puberty, but both Marcus and Izzy seemed incredibly knowledgeable about their different magics for their ages.

"It doesn't matter. Let's just say I've been a Red a lot longer than you."

Defiance sparked in me, and I glared at him. "How do you know?"

"You declared, what, half a year ago?"

He laughed at my startled face. "If you weren't so new to this, you would never have come here. And if you knew what you were doing, you wouldn't have collapsed the vault."

I flushed. "You don't know anything about me, so stop pretending that you do."

His smirk irritated me, and I threw caution to the wind.

"I know more about Red magic than you think. I bet you haven't been to the Underworld for training. I bet the gods haven't fought over you." I hoped to elicit some surprise from him, but his stormy expression was not what I'd expected.

"You'd lose that bet, Darlena. I'd be careful what you say; you don't know anything."

He stepped around me and headed down the dark street. I watched his broad shoulders for a moment, and he spun around as if he could sense my eyes.

"If you do anything to hurt her, whether you mean it or not, I swear that I will find you. And when I do, you will not survive." He faded into the darkness, his threat hanging in the street like smoke.

Gods, what have I gotten myself into? Was working with Marcus even worth the risk? I tried to ignore the sinking sensation in my stomach and hurried into the graveyard to find Izzy. Marcus's threat was still ringing in my ears as I walked, and I hoped I wouldn't have to travel too far into the spooky graveyard to find his sister. I was too on edge to wander around the place, and I didn't want to make a fool of myself.

Luckily, Izzy was near the entrance. She was perched on a raised tomb, fiddling with her cell phone. "What took you so long?"

I started to tell her how annoying her brother was, but I hesitated. Sure, she'd told him about me, but he was the one who followed her here tonight. Maybe she didn't know he'd been outside. I decided to lie. "I fell asleep at the hotel."

She snorted. "Loser."

I shrugged. "I think I'm still jetlagged."

"That's not hard to get over. It's just like magic."

"What do you mean?"

She looked at me pityingly. "Whenever you do a lot of magic, don't you get that queasy lightheaded feeling?"

I nodded, not sure where this was going.

"How do you fix yourself?"

"I usually eat bread, or something else carby."

She smiled. "Anything else?"

"Tea?"

Izzy shook her head. "The best way to cure a magical hangover, or jetlag for that matter, is bread dipped in honey. Bread by itself is good, but the honey adds a kick that helps you feel better."

It sounded like it would work; I'd have to try it the next time I did a spell. "Thanks."

"Whatever. That's not why you wanted to keep talking."

I shook my head, trying to get my thoughts in order. I needed to make her trust me if I had any hope of getting to Marcus through her, but I wanted to hang out with her, too. "I don't really know where to begin."

"Who's your patron?"

I paused, unsure of how much to share with this girl. I'd told my parents and Justin about what happened with Aphrodite, but even that had felt weird. Why would I tell a complete stranger something so personal? *You told Marcus,* a sharp voice whispered in my mind. *Why not his sister?*

She crossed her arms, glaring at me. "I told you mine! At least be fair."

"I don't have one."

Her eyebrows raised in surprise. "Why not?"

"It's complicated."

"How?" She looked at me expectantly, her blue eyes open and bright.

I decided to trust her. There was just something about the kid that made me want to be her friend, and friends were honest with each other. Rochelle and I had told each other everything before she came after me. I sighed at that thought. Hopefully, Izzy wouldn't betray me once she knew me better. Besides, her brother already knew my story; if either of them were likely to use it against me, it'd be him.

"I had a patron. I swore to Aphrodite." The words felt heavy leaving my mouth, and they hung in the air between us as if I'd spoken a spell. I shivered, wondering fleetingly if Aphrodite would attack me someday. The vow I broke had pretty much guaranteed my destruction, but at the time, she'd seemed more hurt than angry.

Izzy scrunched her face up in confusion. "How … "

I held up my hand. "I said it's complicated."

"Sorry. Go ahead."

I took a deep breath. "I swore to her because, well, because I was desperate, I guess. She was the only Red goddess who seemed sane." I shuddered as I remembered the other Red gods who had sought me out; Pele hadn't seemed too awful until she followed me across the ocean, but Kali was terrifying from the start.

Izzy's eyes widened, but she kept her mouth shut.

"It was a mistake. I learned a lot from her, but not as much as I needed. So, um, well … " I trailed off, unsure. I scrambled up onto the tomb to join Izzy while I thought about what to say.

"What?"

I sighed. I had just told Marcus this story a day ago, but that didn't make it any easier. "I ate a pomegranate seed."

"What does that have to do with anything?"

"I'm not entirely sure, but it gave me kind of a redo."

"Where'd you get the seed?"

"Persephone."

Izzy whistled between her teeth. "Dang! How many gods have you met?"

I shrugged and her eyes got bigger.

"You don't even know?"

Thinking for a moment, I said, "Seven, I guess. No, wait, eight." I wasn't sure if I should count Loki or not, but I guessed I had met him, sort of.

"I've only ever met Isis." Her voice was quiet, and I glanced at her.

"I didn't mean to make you feel bad."

She shook her head. "I don't. It's just, well, you must be something pretty special if you've met that many gods."

"I don't think so. I think it's just that there are way more Red gods than there ever are Red Witches."

"So why isn't Persephone your patron?"

I sighed. "I wasn't ready to swear to a god again. It had helped me, the first time, but I'd also felt limited."

"I've never felt limited with Isis."

"You're lucky."

Izzy and I talked until midnight in the ghost-free graveyard, and everything she said made me feel like I still had a lot to learn about magic. How could someone so young know so much? It wasn't until I was walking back to my hotel that I realized I hadn't been cold all evening. As soon as I had that thought, I started shivering uncontrollably, and I hurried the last few blocks. Maybe Izzy's magic was more fiery than she let on, or maybe talking to her had just distracted me from the winter weather.

Because of the chill, it seemed like the city should have been deserted, but the streets were alive with people. Most businesses were closed, but every block I passed had at least two pubs, their doors open, spilling light and laughter into the cold, winter night. The holiday celebrations were in full swing.

I didn't feel much like celebrating, but the sound of the parties was enticing. Maybe I would be in a better mood once my plans were underway. I knew that the Hogmany celebrations in Edinburgh were legendary, but this wasn't a vacation. I had serious work to do. I'd made headway tonight with Izzy, but that still wasn't a guarantee that Marcus would help me. Maybe it was time for me to start considering other options. What was it Loki had said the last time I dreamt of him? That he'd help me bind Hecate if I freed him somehow? The very idea made the hair on my arms stand up, and I pushed the thought away. It had been a long day, and maybe I'd be able to think more clearly in the morning.

My room was dark, and I fumbled along the wall for a moment before my fingers found the light switch. Freya was sitting at the desk.

"What are you doing here?" I meant it as a straightforward question, but the goddess cocked her head to one side.

"I can move about all the north lands with ease, child. They worshiped me here as well as in Iceland."

I blushed. "I'm sorry. I didn't know that. But that's not what I meant. Why are you here, in my room, tonight?"

She sighed. "You have not listened to my advice."

"I don't know what you mean."

"You've spoken with Loki."

It took effort to keep my face neutral, but inside I was seething. What right did this goddess have to push her way inside my dreams? "Not intentionally."

Her eyes bored into me. "That doesn't matter. Did you not listen to my warning?"

The strain of the past months and the continued interference of the gods finally caught up to me, and I snapped. "I don't care what you're here to warn me about! I didn't ask for your help, and I'm sick of the gods using me as a pawn in their stupid games. I want you to leave. Now."

I opened the door, but Freya didn't move. She kept staring at me, and when I saw pity on her face, I looked away.

"You do not understand. I do not know if you will ever understand. But not all gods want to use you for their own gains."

I forced myself to meet her eyes. "How would I know that?"

"You will have to trust someone, Darlena."

I shook my head. "Not tonight."

Freya rose smoothly, gliding toward the door. "Then I hope that when you do decide to give your trust, you choose wisely. I fear that you may be the undoing of the world."

Her words echoed Loki's, and I stared at her, numb. Freya nodded once to me, her eyes stony, and then slipped into the hall. The door swung closed behind her.

12

The next morning, I woke up early. Even though I hadn't tried Izzy's trick with bread and honey yet, I felt restored, and for the first time since I left the States, my head didn't feel fuzzy.

I ordered room service and ate a big breakfast, lounging around in my pajamas and sipping my coffee. Since I didn't have anything better to do, I decided to check my email again. There was a response from Mom, which I'd been expecting, and also an email from Justin. Seeing his name in my inbox gave me tingles, but another email caught my eye before I could read what Justin had sent.

The sender was someone named "Dr. T. Farren," and the subject made me pause: "RE: Isadora."

I hesitated for a moment, but then I clicked on the email. My palms were sweaty by the time I was done reading, and my heart had started racing. Dr. Farren the director of Izzy's school, and she'd emailed me to discuss some "concerns" she had regarding my "relationship" with Izzy. She wanted to meet me in person this morning to discuss the "safety" of her students. How the woman even knew about me was a mystery. I'd only met Izzy for the first time yesterday, but evidently my dangerous Red reputation was all the woman needed to know.

Glowering at the computer, I typed the name of Izzy's school into a search engine. Although no magical school would put full information up on the Internet where Nons could find it, I was pretty good at reading between the lines, and I needed some information before I replied to Dr. Farren's pushy letter.

Izzy's school, like Trinity, hid behind a veneer of religious language: Lady on the Lake was an exclusive girls' preparatory academy where values and faith were taught side by side with the core subjects. I chuckled at that. Parents probably saw that line and got excited, envisioning science labs and literature classes, but I knew what the core subjects of a Witchcraft school were. I'd have to ask Izzy if her school offered divination; that was an elective at Trinity, but I'd never gotten the chance to take it. If they offered divination, it might explain why Dr. Farren knew about me so fast.

Without bothering to reply to the email, I bundled up and walked to Lady on the Lake to meet with the director. At least she was willing to meet me, I thought, as I glanced nervously up at the wrought-iron gates separating the school from the streets of Edinburgh. From the tone of her email, she might have rather just come after me in the night to boot me out of Scotland, but there was no way I was going to let her or her school intimidate me.

There was a pedestrian gate beside the towering gate, and it was unlocked. The fence reminded me of Trinity, and I faltered for a beat, feeling homesickness and anger wash over me. If I hadn't been kicked out of Trinity for declaring Red, who knows how much more I could have learned. When I was able to move again, my footsteps crunched across the frozen brown lawn; even though Edinburgh was far to the north, snow seemed an uncommon occurrence. In that way, I mused, it shared something in common with North Carolina. As I walked, I wondered fleetingly about the coming ice storm Justin had mentioned; maybe I would try to call home later in the day, just to check on everyone. I hadn't had a chance to read the emails he and Mom had sent, and I felt disconnected from them after so much time.

Lost in thought, I looked up and realized that I was standing in the foyer of the school building. Where Trinity felt like it wanted to be an old-world academy, Lady on the Lake had no pretensions: it simply was. The sweeping hallway around me reminded me of illustrations of cathedrals that I'd studied in my history class, and the black and white checkered floor beneath my feet had a shine to it that could only mean it was real marble. This school made Trinity look like a cheap imitation.

My boots squeaked on the glistening floor, echoing in the empty hall, and I paused, suddenly nervous. What if Dr. Farren had only asked to meet me to hand me over to Marcus for further questioning, or worse, to Hecate?

"You'll have to trust somebody sometime," I muttered to myself, recalling my visitation from Freya. *I might as well start now.* I couldn't do this on my own, and I sure wasn't ready to trust the gods.

A plain wooden door opened to my left, and a severe woman in a gray tweed suit stepped into the hall. Her heels clicked on the floor, and her steely hair was pulled away from her caramel skin in a perfect bun. I felt like a small child standing there in my ratty jeans and coat, and I jumped when she spoke.

"You must be Darlena. I've been expecting you. Come." She had a faint accent, but I couldn't place it. She turned sharply and I followed her through the doorway, not sure what to expect. Dr. Farren hardly looked like the kind of person who would run an eclectic, open-minded magical school; she looked more like the kind of principal who kept a paddle over her desk. Maybe I'd made a mistake in coming there.

Her office was a surprise: instead of a desk, she had floor pillows stacked at odd angles on a woven grass rug. She saw my expression and chuckled.

"The office will change to suit my needs at any given time. Today, we're just having a casual meeting, are we not?"

I nodded uncertainly, looking around. A tray sat on the floor, holding two mismatched porcelain cups, a silver kettle, and sugar. Dr. Farren sank gracefully to the floor, folding her knees beneath her, and tossed a red pillow to me. Not sure what else to do, I joined her, sitting across the tea service from the strange woman.

"Would you like tea?" She held out a small wooden box, and when I opened it, I was assaulted by a variety of smells. I grabbed a tea bag at random and set it in the cup she offered. She nodded and made her own selection, pouring steaming water out of the kettle with concentration.

Finally, she sat back. "Now it steeps, and we can speak. Why are you here?"

Her bluntness was surprising, after the polite tea exchange, but I realized that everything about this woman was going to surprise me. "I'm here to find help."

She nodded. "I had the sense that you were not here to do harm. But why contact Isadora?"

I shrugged, wondering how much she knew. "I thought she might be able to help me with a magical problem."

"Such as?"

I paused to stir sugar into my tea. "She knows someone I need to talk to, and he won't talk to me on his own."

Dr. Farren's jaw stiffened. "So you are using the girl to gain access to her brother."

When she put it like that, I sounded awful. I took a sip of tea and winced as it burned the roof of my mouth, and I hurried to set the cup down. "Yes. No. I don't know. It's not like that."

"You had better decide which truth you want to tell me, Darlena Agara, for I am fast losing patience with you."

"I'm a Red Witch."

The woman stared at me impassively. "So I gathered, if you seek help from Isadora's brother."

I gaped at her. "Look, how do you know so much about me? What did Izzy tell you?"

"She told me nothing. It was my patron who warned me about you. I want to know exactly what you're doing here, and what you want with my students. If you lie to me, I will know it."

I studied her face, and after a moment, I nodded. "I practice Red magic."

"You told me that already."

"I know. But that's why I'm here: I don't want to be the next Red Witch to die."

Her gaze was sharp, and I fought the urge to squirm when she looked at me. "Why would such a thing be your fate?"

My hands were shaking as I reached for the tea. "I've made a powerful enemy. I want to use Red magic to bring balance of chaos, and Hec—someone—doesn't like that."

Dr. Farren stared at me levelly. I had to admire the woman; I'd just dropped a lot of shit into her lap, and she didn't even flinch. "Why would the goddess you speak of want to stand in the way of balance? She is the keeper of the crossroads, the patron of travelers. Surely there is nothing that represents balance more than choice and movement?" Her eyebrows arched as she spoke, her disbelief obvious.

I was surprised that my issues with Hecate didn't faze her, but I tried not to show it. "I don't know. I just know that Hecate has tried to kill me before, and failed."

"The Queen of Witches does not fail, Darlena."

I paused, sipping my tea. I eyed her critically. "Then how do you explain what's happened to me?"

Dr. Farren leaned back against a gold cushion, stirring her tea with a faraway expression. "I am not sure. My patron told me a bit about you, and I have learned more by meeting you. But whatever the whole truth, it is clear that you are a Witch of some consequence."

I spilled tea onto my lap. "What makes you say that?"

She laughed. "Look at those who have found an interest in you! For that matter, look at the magic you practice: there are only ever three Reds in the world, and weak Witches never hold the post."

"But if I'm so powerful, why can't I seem to make anything work?"

"What is it you feel you cannot do?"

Frustrated, I pulled my long hair into my fist and started twisting it. "I can't work against the Queen alone! That's why I came here; if another Red Witch stands with me, we won't be vulnerable. Alone, I'm an easy target. I need to win, I need to beat the Queen, or more people will die."

"Power isn't about always winning. It's about wise use, weighing the costs and values of action before acting."

"I don't know enough about Red magic to do that." It was hard to admit that to her, but it was the truth.

Her eyes bored into me again. "You know a great deal more than you think."

I didn't know what she meant. It was clear that I knew nothing; every time I used Red magic, it ended with disaster. The room fell silent as I thought back on all the destruction I'd caused. I fiddled with my tea bag. It split, the leaves pooling quickly in the bottom of my cup. "Dang it!"

The director smiled slightly. "Give it here."

I looked at her. "What are you going to do?"

"Watch. Maybe learn."

I handed her my cup with the clump of tea in the bottom, and she cupped it with both hands, her long fingers encircling it. Her gray head bent over the tea, her eyes staring intently into the bottom of the cup. I watched, fascinated.

"I didn't know tea reading was still considered a magical art."

Her face was grim when she looked at me. "I realize now that there is much that you don't know. Even the small arts may prove necessary to you in your coming struggle." She set my cup down and frowned at me intently.

I stared back at her, twitching my fingers nervously. I wanted to ask what she'd seen in my cup, but part of me didn't want to know.

Finally, she nodded once. "I will not hinder your quest, although I don't agree with your reasons for using Isadora." She waved her hand to silence me, and I swallowed back my angry retort as she continued. "Just know that if you do anything to put Isadora or any of my students in danger, you will have to answer to me."

I glared at her, and she shrugged.

"It's the most I can offer. Take it or leave it."

I thought for a moment, and then I nodded. It wasn't like I had a choice. "I'll take it."

13

Even though I was still on the school campus, I called my mom once I left Dr. Farren's office. She picked up on the first ring. Her voice made my heart clench, and I had to fight back tears.

"How's the weather?" I asked, trying not to let on how affected I was to hear her voice.

"Lena? It's good to hear from you. The weather is cold. It's a bad winter." Her tone was serious, and I felt a twinge of worry.

"Have the pipes frozen yet?"

"Not yet, thankfully. But your dad and I haven't gone to work all week; the roads are iced over, and just about everything is closed."

North Carolina usually closed down at the first sign of bad winter weather, but a whole week was ridiculous, even in the South. "It's that bad?"

"It's worse. Something about this winter isn't natural."

I shuddered, remembering the hurricane Rochelle had created to kill me last fall. It hadn't worked, of course, but the storm had done a lot of damage. "Is there anything I can do?"

She paused. "I don't like the idea of you fooling with the weather."

"I know, Mom, but if there's something strange about the storm ..."

"You might just concentrate on sending good vibes to us. As long as the roads thaw soon, we'll be fine. Right now, it's too dangerous to go out."

I took a deep breath. "I guess that works out then."

"What do you mean?"

"I called to let you know when I'm coming home."

There was a pause. "When?"

"I'm not sure yet, but I know it won't be this week."

The silence that filled the phone was frigid, and I swore softly to myself.

I started to explain. "I found the other Red."

"Lena, that's great. It's just that I worry about you."

"I'm fine, Mom."

"I'm sure you are. But I've been having bad dreams lately."

Interested, I pressed the phone closer to my ear. "What sort of dreams?" Loki's offer flitted through my mind, and I forced myself to focus on Mom's voice.

She laughed, but it sounded flat. "Oh, apocalyptic things, fire and ice. Maybe I've just been reading too much poetry."

I knew the Robert Frost poem she was referring to—it had always given me the heebie jeebies. "Anything else?"

"No word from any goddesses on the home front, if that's what you mean."

I didn't want to ask, but I needed to know. "Not even Demeter?"

Mom sighed, and I felt a twinge of guilt. "I keep trying, but she doesn't seem interested in communicating with me right now."

Demeter was my mother's patron, but my deception last fall had damaged their relationship. I'd hoped it would be repaired by now, but that hadn't happened. Guilt gnawed at my stomach. "I'm sorry, Mom."

"You're doing what you think is right."

Her words made me bristle. "What's that supposed to mean?"

"Darlena, we support you. That's all that means."

I looked at the phone and tried to get my temper back in check. "Sorry. I'm on edge today." Meeting with Dr. Farren had left me feeling defensive, but there was no reason to tell Mom about that.

"Oh, sweetie. Can I do anything?"

I felt another twinge of guilt at her sympathetic tone. "I miss you guys."

"We miss you, too."

For a minute, we were both silent, and I brushed away the tears that prickled in my eyes.

When Mom spoke again, she sounded like she was trying to cheer me up. "Do you still have the herbs I sent?"

I smiled. "I do. I've used them for a few baths, too."

"That's what I was going to suggest. A nice hot bath with peppermint. Maybe you'll think more clearly when you're done."

"Why do you think I'm not thinking clearly?"

She paused. "Maybe it's the dreams I've been having. Either way, I'm worried about you."

"I'll be fine."

"Promise me."

I sucked in air between my teeth. Choosing my words carefully, I said, "As far as I can control, I promise I will avoid harm."

There was a pause. "We love you."

"Love you, too. Give Xerxes some tuna for me."

Mom chuckled. "That cat is already spoiled enough." She doted on him as much as I did, and we both knew it.

"Still. I'll be home as soon as I figure some things out here."

"I know."

When I hung up the phone, I was puzzled and tense. I had the feeling she wasn't telling me everything. Add that to the fact that Justin had mentioned dreams the last time we talked, and I was starting to feel uneasy. I felt the looming shape of Lady on the Lake behind me, but the building didn't offer me any comfort. I was on my own.

"Why are you standing here looking glum?"

I turned around, startled. "What are you doing here?"

Izzy shrugged. "Dr. Farren said she met with you, and I wanted to chat."

"What about?"

"The weather. What do you think? More about magic."

I sighed. "I'm tired of talking about magic."

"Did you just call your mum?"

I nodded. "She's worried about me."

Izzy thought for a moment. "Your mum's a Witch too, right?"

"Both my parents are Greens."

"Then maybe you should listen to her."

"But I think she wants me to come home right away, and I can't do that now!" As the words left my mouth, I inhaled sharply. I hadn't told Izzy what I was really doing in Scotland, and I was afraid that she was about to ask.

Instead, she fixed me with a wide smile. "So if you're here for a bit longer, come sightseeing with me."

"How?"

"Marcus borrowed a car. We're driving out to Clava."

Part of me felt like a sightseeing trip would just be a waste of time, but I was intrigued. "What's Clava?"

She laughed. "And you call yourself a Witch! You better come, just so you won't sound so dumb the next time you meet another Scottish Witch."

I eyed her, wanting to feel suspicious, but I was curious. "Won't Marcus mind?"

"Not at all."

***

An hour later, I was waiting in front of my hotel. I'd packed my camera and notebook in a small shoulder bag, and at the last minute, I'd stuck my athame and mirror in the pockets of my coat. I didn't usually take my tools with me everywhere, but then again, I didn't usually go sightseeing with a Witch who had made it clear he hated me.

When Marcus pulled up in a rusted black pile of metal, I grimaced. "What is that?"

Izzy popped her head out the window. "It's a Rover. Marcus borrowed it from a friend. Isn't it something?"

"It's something, all right," I said, as I slid onto the torn upholstery in the back seat. Stuffing was everywhere, and the brown fabric on the ceiling had come unglued in places.

"It runs." Marcus's voice was gruff, and I looked up to see him staring intently at me in the rearview mirror.

This was the second time my relationship with Izzy had brought him back into contact with me, and I decided to make the most of it. "Thanks for taking me along today."

He grunted wordlessly.

Izzy punched him playfully. "Now, be nice! We can't send her back to America thinking all Scottish boys are pricks."

"Where are we going?"

Izzy turned around, oblivious of the swaying car. I felt nauseous for her. "Clava Cairn. It's an old site from prehistoric Scotland."

"But what's there?"

"Don't you know what a cairn is?" Izzy looked surprised when I shook my head.

"A burial mound." Marcus's words were clipped, his eyes focused on the road.

"So we're going to an ancient burial mound?" I began to wonder why I'd let Izzy talk me into this. In the past few days, I'd had more than enough of haunted places and death.

"Oh, it's so much more than that! There are three mounds, each circled by standing stones. It's a really powerful place. Have you been to Stonehenge?"

I shook my head, and she smiled.

"Good! Then you won't try to compare this. Clava Cairn is different."

Absently, I fiddled with the stuffing seeping out of the back seat. "Why are we going there?"

Izzy glanced at Marcus and turned around in her seat. "You'll see."

I wanted to press her for answers, but I was walking a tricky line. Because of Izzy, I had another opportunity to convince her brother to help me, but I didn't think he'd be any more willing than before if I was a jerk to his little sister. I shrugged and leaned back against the seat, staring out the window as the misty Scottish landscape whirred by.

We wove through the countryside in relative silence for the next two hours. I was trying to figure out how to talk to Marcus alone; Izzy didn't need to know about my plans, but maybe he'd be more willing to listen now. I studied the back of his orangey-red head while we drove. If I shifted slightly, I could see pieces of his face in the rearview mirror. He met my eyes in the mirror briefly, and I shivered, looking away. True, I'd come to Scotland to find him, but something about Marcus frightened me. Maybe it was just because he was a Red; I seemed to scare people from time to time.

When he turned the car into a dirt driveway beside an old barn, I thought he was asking for directions. But Izzy opened her door before the car was even parked.

"Come on, it's this way!"

She set off, walking away from the barn into a wooded field. Marcus gestured to me, and I followed Izzy, trying not to glance behind me at Marcus. His long legs covered the terrain quickly, and he was practically breathing down my neck. I hurried after Izzy, but I felt a prickle of anticipation go down my spine. As we cut a path through the deserted field, I heard an odd buzzing in my ears. I shook my head to clear it, but the dull sound remained, like a machine running in another room.

Suddenly, we came upon the stones. Izzy was right: I wasn't expecting anything like this. Three mounds of stone rose out of the field. Each was surrounded by a ring of standing stones. The scale of the space was nowhere near what I had expected; when Izzy mentioned Stonehenge, I had been thinking of a massive monument, but the cairns and standing stones weren't much taller than my head. There was something familiar about the place, but I couldn't put my finger on it.

"It's a Bronze Age site," Marcus remarked quietly at my side. "No one is sure of the purpose, but they do know the doorway of that cairn," he gestured to the left, "lines up with the sunrise on the Winter Solstice."

"We're a few days late, but it'll still work." Izzy grabbed my hand, tugging me toward the cairn.

"What will work?"

"Why, contacting our patrons! The stones are a passageway to death, so the rules of geography don't apply."

Her face fell when I stared at her in fear.

"I thought you'd be excited! You said you felt cut off from Persephone here."

I nodded. "I do. But it's just, um … " I trailed off, uncertain.

Marcus glared at me. "Hecate must know you're here. She's choosing not to act for reasons of her own. Talking to your god won't hurt you."

I glanced at Izzy. "You said *our* patrons?"

She nodded vigorously. "Isis was everywhere in the ancient world, so I can talk to her easier than some, but she's like your Persephone: she's married to the lord of the dead, so this is one way I know I can reach her. Sort of like a hotline."

I turned to Marcus. "And who's your patron?"

"You can see me for yourself, Witch." The voice spoke from within the cairn to the left, and chills ran down my spine. Marcus hurried ahead, dropping to his knees in the passageway that led to the center of the cairn. Izzy hung back, but curiosity compelled me, and I stepped into the cairn. Frozen, I stood behind Marcus, staring at a face I'd seen before.

It was the woman from my cauldron dream. She was swathed in black robes like the Queen wore, but her eyes burned like emeralds and her wild hair looked more like vines and roots than cobwebs. However, the similarities were startling, and the goddess before me put me on edge.

"Who are you?"

Marcus, still kneeling, spoke in a powerful voice. "Hail to my lady, Cerridwen, keeper of the cauldron of life."

I racked my brain, looking at the goddess in front of me. "I've met you, I think."

She raised one eyebrow and said nothing.

Marcus glowered up at me. "Would you leave? I need to speak to my patron."

"She can stay, Marcus." Her voice was like a bell, but it held no warmth.

We both looked at the goddess in surprise, and he clenched his jaw. "Whatever my lady wishes."

"So, another Red Witch. What brings you so far from your realm?"

I backed up involuntarily. "I was seeking help."

"And have you found it?"

I glared at Marcus as he rose to stand beside me. "I'm not sure."

"A word of caution, then, Witch. The Red gods are rising. The help you seek may already be worthless."

"But I can't stop."

"Are you afraid?"

I paused, sensing some kind of trap in her words. "Not exactly. But I know that I'm not ready to do what I must. So I still need help, and I'll stay until I find it."

Her black eyes bored into mine for a moment, but then she waved her hand in dismissal. "I would speak to my Witch alone."

Angry, I bowed stiffly and walked out of the cairn. What was wrong with that goddess? She'd said she wanted to talk to me, but then after two minutes, she was done? Cranky, I started walking back toward Izzy. The buzzing in my ears became an unbearable roar, and I sank to the ground outside the circle of standing stones, clutching my head. Izzy came over to me and sat down glumly.

"At least you got to meet her."

"What?" My head hurt too much to listen. I closed my eyes, willing the strange pain to stop.

"I've never met his patron."

My eyes opened slightly. "Why not?"

She folded her arms around herself and shivered. "He says it's too dangerous for me. I've never come here with him before."

Despite the pain, I opened my eyes wide and stared at her. "Then why did he let you come today?"

She shrugged. "I guess I begged enough this time."

I felt a chill, and my head started to clear. "Who thought of inviting me?"

I knew the answer before she even spoke. "He did."

14

Despite the fact that I might be able to contact Persephone, despite my desire to meet Izzy's patron, I rushed back to the car. It offered little protection; Marcus had locked it, and the keys were in his pocket.

"How could I have been so stupid? I walked into this trap." I slammed my fist against the roof of the car, frantically thinking of some way to protect myself. If Marcus had brought me here, I was sure he had a reason, and after meeting his patron, I didn't want to wait around and find out what it was.

Something touched my shoulder, and I shot into the air. Izzy looked at me, startled.

"What's the matter with you?"

I drew a deep breath, trying to calm down. Izzy wasn't a threat ... was she? I looked at her intently, choosing my words with care. "Izzy, I don't think it was a good idea for me to come here."

Her eyes were wide and innocent. "Why not?"

I wanted to trust her, but I still wasn't sure. I ground my teeth and hedged. "I think Marcus's patron is a little too connected to Hecate. I might be in danger."

"We would never let anything happen to you!"

"I know *you* wouldn't."

"But neither would Marcus." She looked like I'd smacked her. I shook my head. "I don't know. I just know that I shouldn't be here." I didn't think now was the time to explain to her how I'd met her brother, although I realized she'd never really introduced us; did she already know everything? I stared at her, trying to read her mind, but I couldn't think straight over the buzzing in my ears. Weary, I pressed my hands to my eyes. "This was a mistake."

There was a loud crack from the cairns, and my eyes shot open. Before I could react, Izzy had shouted her brother's name and taken off running toward the stones. A red glow lit up the sky, and it looked like it was coming from the cairn where Marcus had been meeting with Cerridwen. For a moment, I hesitated. If something was happening out there, maybe it would be better if I used this as a distraction to escape. I tried the car door again, but it was locked. I knew I could have jimmied the lock with a simple spell, but I looked over my shoulder at the glowing cairns again.

"I hope I don't regret this," I muttered as I took off after Izzy. I drew on Red magic as I ran, and when I skidded to a stop in front of the largest cairn, red sparks were dancing up and down my arms. The ringing in my ears had turned into a dull throb, and I clenched my jaw, trying to force the headache away. Based on how much my head already hurt, I was on the edge of one killer migraine. With my arms up defensively, I crept into the cairn.

Izzy stood in the center of the stones, circling like a confused cat. The cairn was empty, except for her. Marcus and his patron were nowhere to be seen. Wary of a trap, I moved forward. I looked at the stones surrounding me and fought back images of mass burials behind the rock.

"Where is he?" Izzy's voice shook, but she didn't stop pacing. I wanted to laugh; she was acting like her brother might materialize out of the stones, but the panic on her face was real. Whatever had happened, Izzy hadn't known about it.

Someone behind me spoke softly. "He's gone."

Her voice hadn't changed, but I hadn't been expecting to hear it anytime soon. I jumped and spun around, wondering if this was a trick. Izzy stared at the shimmering image of Persephone, spellbound.

"What do you mean?"

The goddess smiled. "Where's your sense of formality, Darlena? Or haven't you missed me?" She spread her hands at her sides, as if waiting for me to embrace her.

I dipped my head slightly, but I didn't move forward. "I have. I've never felt so alone." My voice broke, and I drew in a ragged breath, struggling for control. I met Persephone's eye. "I didn't think I could reach you here."

She gestured to Izzy, who was still gaping silently. "The young one told you that you could. Why didn't you believe her?"

I shrugged. "I guess I didn't think it was possible. You hadn't shown up until now."

The goddess frowned. "You sound like you blame me for that. Surely you have learned of the geography that binds the gods."

My anger surged, simmering close to the surface. "It might have been nice if someone had thought to tell me before I traveled halfway around the world!" A blast of Red magic shot off of me, uncontrolled, and smashed into the stones beside us. Izzy gave a startled yelp and took a step back.

"I'm sorry," I hurried to tell her, trying to extinguish the red sparks on my arms, but she just stared at me, frightened. I sighed. "I'm sorry," I said again, this time to Persephone, "but it really wasn't fair not to tell me that I wouldn't have help here in Scotland."

The goddess glared at me. "Perhaps I would have, if you had thought to discuss your plans with me. But I cannot offer you assistance if you insist on keeping things from me."

"I've been keeping things from you? What about you? What else haven't you told me?"

"Darlena, you have no right to be angry with me. You undertook this quest. It was not I who sent you after the other Red."

Sullenly, I looked away from her. I wanted to ask her how she knew what I was doing in Scotland, but she kept talking before I had a chance.

"You have found him, but has he proved to be any great help? Would it not be better for you to return with me to continue your training?"

I didn't like her tone; it was as if she were sure I'd agree with her, no matter what she said. "Wait a minute. You just said that you didn't have anything to do with me being here. I didn't tell you anything. So explain to me why you suddenly seem to know so much."

Izzy let out a frightened squeak. "You shouldn't fight with her!"

I ignored the girl and faced Persephone with my hands on my hips. "Well?"

She sighed. "I have been watching out for you, Darlena. Have you forgotten my assistance last fall?"

"But then you went back to the Underworld for the winter, and you didn't try to stay in touch. What right do you have to keep spying on me?" My stomach churned, and I realized I was angry that the goddess had abandoned me. It felt almost too good to be true to be talking to her now, and I couldn't bring myself to tell her how much I'd missed her.

"Just because I was with my lord does not mean I gave up on you, child. Of course I have been watching you. There is much at stake, and much you could change."

I snapped at her. "But you have no responsibility to me. You aren't my patron. I don't have a patron anymore, and if I did, why do you think it would be you?"

Izzy inhaled sharply, but then everything went still. My words hung in the silence for a moment, and Persephone's face fell. She actually looked hurt.

"Darlena," she finally said, "just because you are not my sworn Witch does not mean you are not important. I recognize your power, even if you don't, and I know that you want to find balance. You matter to me, Darlena Agara, whether you want to or not."

Surprised, I dropped my arms to my side. "You aren't just following me to make me swear to you?"

"I am not like some of the other Red gods, Darlena. I will not force you."

I sighed in defeat. "I'm sorry." I rubbed my forehead. "I just don't know who to trust anymore. First Rochelle, and then—"

Persephone interrupted me gently. "Your time in the Underworld was short. There is still much for you to learn, and you know that you will always find sanctuary in my husband's realm."

I looked up and stared at her, feeling defeated. "What good is any of it?"

Her eyes hardened. "What do you mean?"

"It's like chasing smoke. Hecate hasn't shown herself since last fall. Well, not really," I amended, remembering the woman on the plane and the creepy presence I'd felt in the vaults. "I'm not even so sure I remember why I'm fighting her."

Persephone froze, her face like a mask. "Must I remind you of the blood she has caused? You of all people know how dangerous she is. Think of what she did to your friend."

I flinched. "But I haven't done anything to stop her. Look at this winter! Even nature isn't right anymore. Chaos is running rampant, just like Hecate wants. What good am I?"

The goddess took a step closer to me, but I backed away. She held out her hands, palms up. "Darlena, there is more at work than you realize."

"Then maybe you should tell her." Izzy's calm voice was a surprise; I'd almost forgotten that she was standing there the whole time. "And maybe," she continued sharply, "then you can tell me what my brother has to do with all this, and where I can find him."

Persephone glanced at the girl with pity. "He will play a much larger role than you think, child."

Izzy was quiet for a moment. Then she looked up, with tears in her eyes, and asked, "Is it too late for him?"

The goddess paused, considering. "I am not sure. You might do well to ask your patron."

Izzy nodded, her face puzzled.

I watched their exchange, perplexed. "Wherever Marcus is, he's with his patron. He probably went willingly."

"I would not be so sure." Persephone's words shocked me to the core, and Izzy started to weep.

I whirled to face the goddess. "You need to tell us what you know.

Everything," I added sharply.

Persephone raised an eyebrow. "Have you forgotten, Darlena, that you are speaking to a goddess? To the one who saved you? The one to whom you owe allegiance, yet you refuse to swear it?" She grew larger with each word until her head and shoulders rose above the mound of stones.

Trying not to show my fear, I stared up at her. "Maybe you're right. But how can I swear my allegiance when I know you've been keeping things from me?"

Her breath hissed like steam. "There are things that I am not sure of yet."

"Such as?"

In an instant, she was human-sized again, looking me in the eye. "I believe there is much more at work than the usual lust for chaos exhibited by the Red gods, and I believe you and the other Red will play a major part in the events to come."

I waited silently, trying to process what she'd said. Did that mean Marcus would help me after all?

Persephone paused, her head tipped to one side. "How much do you know of the creation of man?"

"Which time?" Izzy interjected, then blushed when the goddess looked at her and nodded.

"Exactly."

I looked at Izzy, and then I turned to the goddess. "I don't understand." It seemed like Izzy and Persephone were on the same page, but I was still miles behind.

Izzy spoke first. "Throughout mythology, whenever humans are created, it seems like the gods always decide they want a do-over at some point."

I frowned, remembering an old story I'd learned before enrolling at Trinity. "Like Noah and the flood?"

Persephone snorted. "That unoriginal tale was just echoing the times the gods destroyed their handiwork, again and again. But yes, like Noah and the flood."

Izzy chimed in. "Each time, the human race is made of stronger stuff, and each time the gods start over, it's because they feel like their creations don't respect them. But because the gods use better materials, it's become harder and harder to shake the etch-a-sketch."

"But that's just mythology. How does this affect us?" I had a nightmarish suspicion, but it was too horrible to voice. Even though I knew there was truth behind the old myths, I couldn't bear to believe that something so awful could happen again.

Persephone looked down at her hands. "I fear that some of my Red sisters and brothers have again grown discontent with humanity. They want, as the child said, a do-over."

I sat down on the ground, stunned. "So that means that Hecate ..."

"Wants to use you to destroy the earth."

Her words hung in the air like a curse. None of us spoke for a moment. My stomach roiled furiously, and the pounding in my head increased. I was going to be sick if we didn't leave the cairns. I put my head between my knees and forced myself to breathe evenly. It wasn't just the buzzing in my ears that was making me nauseous; it was the fact that Persephone had confirmed my worst fear.

Finally, Izzy spoke. "But what I don't get is why destroy the whole world? I mean, every time the stories say the gods started over, it was just one region, one group of people who got wiped out."

Realization dawned in my mind. "The world has changed, Izzy.

Before, getting rid of one pesky community was enough to restore balance. Now, the world is too interconnected. To get a true do-over, everything has to be destroyed." And the easiest way to do that was to let chaos take over. Had this been Hecate's plan all along, ever since she showed up in my living room last summer? I staggered to my feet, breathing heavily. I was sick of being a pawn for that crazy goddess. There had to be a way to stop her.

Izzy shivered. "So we're talking about the end of the world."

"Not if I can help it." I spoke fiercely, but my words felt hollow.

Persephone looked at me for a long minute, her face unreadable. "And how would you stop this?"

I drew a deep breath, my mind racing. It landed on Loki's strange bargain, and I shuddered. "What if there was a way to bind a god?"

15

I glanced between the stunned faces in front of me.

Finally, Persephone spoke. "Even if such a thing were possible, I do not think I could sanction it. You forget, Darlena, that I am also a god." Her voice shook with passion, and I realized I had to tread carefully.

"I'm not talking about binding you! Just Hecate."

Izzy looked at me like I'd gone crazy. "What good would that do?"

I floundered. "Maybe if she weren't free to use her power, we could bargain with her."

Persephone laughed harshly. "You would dare to bargain with such a powerful goddess? She would twist her words so that she still had the power to do as she pleased, and you can be sure that she'd be after you the minute her bonds were cut."

"But she's already after me, isn't she? Even though Rochelle is dead, I don't think Hecate will stop trying to kill me. So how does this change anything?"

The goddess paused, considering. "She hasn't come after you since the fall. Perhaps you are no longer her target."

I sighed, realizing I'd better come clean. "You haven't been watching everything. She's tried to kill me twice since I got to Scotland."

Izzy gasped, and I watched as realization dawned over her. "That's why you contacted me and Marcus, isn't it? You wanted help."

I nodded. "I thought that two Reds together would be able to face her."

The girl raised her eyebrow. "And a Blue?"

I shrugged uncomfortably. "I was trying to find a way to get Marcus to listen to me." Her face crumpled in anger, and I hurried to add, "That was before I met you! As soon as we met, I realized that I liked you—"

Izzy crossed her arms over her chest and interrupted me. "You liked me enough to drag me into this mess, right?"

"I'm sorry," I whispered.

She didn't say anything, and Persephone cleared her throat. "I did not realize she had been actively hunting you since we parted, Darlena. I'm sorry I wasn't able to intercede."

I glanced at her, surprised at her apology. "It's okay. I've managed to survive so far. But I don't think binding her could possibly make her hate me more."

The goddess nodded slowly. "You have a point. But I still don't think it is possible to confine a god. If it were, it would have been done before now."

But it has been done. If Loki was trapped, wasn't that proof that the gods could be caged? "Leave that to me." I hoped I sounded more confident than I felt. "If I can find a way, I think it may be our best option."

Izzy spoke up quietly. "But to catch Hecate, you'd have to face her, right?"

I cringed. I hadn't really thought about that part.

Glancing at Persephone, Izzy continued. "So there's a chance that she'd kill you before you could control her. And then we'd be even worse off than we are now."

I put my hands up. "But what other choice do we have? I had hoped Marcus would help me, but he won't be helping anyone now."

Tears welled up in Izzy's eyes, and I realized I'd been too harsh. I reached out to put my hand on her shoulder, but she backed away.

"Since you mention him," she sniffed, "how are we going to get him back?"

Persephone and I exchanged a glance. I clearly had a very different idea of what had happened to Marcus than Izzy had, but I couldn't help but feel relieved that Izzy was still talking about "we." Maybe she'd forgive me for using her to get to her brother.

"What do you think has happened to your brother?" Persephone spoke gently, and Izzy stopped crying.

"Why, he's been taken!"

"Izzy, he was here with his patron. She wouldn't harm him." I meant to match the goddess's tone, but my words were still sharp.

Izzy shook her head frantically. "She wouldn't harm him, but don't you see?"

We looked at her blankly.

"Hecate must have him!"

Her words rang with certainty, but I wasn't so sure.

"Why would she want him?"

Izzy frowned. "The reason you said! You were counting on his help."

I snorted. "But he wasn't going to help me." Exasperated, I realized I had conjured up Red magic again, and I forced myself to let it go. "He'd already told me he didn't want to have anything to do with me."

"Maybe he changed his mind." She looked so determined, but I knew better.

"Izzy, has Marcus ever changed his mind about anything?"

She frowned stubbornly and didn't answer my question. "He brought you here! I'm sure he wanted to help."

Persephone spoke gently. "If we can, we will look for Marcus. I will keep my ears open among the gods and see what I can discover. But you two," she glared sternly at me, "need to work on a plan. I'm still not sure I agree with you trying to bind Hecate, but until you think of something else, I suggest you start working on spells to see what might work." Her form started to shimmer like smoke, and I realized she was leaving. "Just remember, Hecate is not acting alone. Confining her may be a start, but it might not be enough." She faded until she was translucent.

"How can I contact you again? I don't want to do this alone."

She smiled sadly. "It is still the winter. Any place of death will let you reach across to my husband's domain."

Izzy's eyes grew wide. "I completely forgot about Hades!" She shivered.

Persephone chuckled. "Don't worry, child. My husband is on friendly terms with your friend. He finds her amusing."

She faded, her laughter still ringing in the cold air, and I shivered. True, I liked Hades, but did I really want a god like that to find me "amusing"? I sat down, drained. Izzy knelt on the cold ground beside me and sighed.

I didn't look at her. "I'm sorry about using you."

"Did you mean what you said?"

"About what?"

"About actually liking me, stupid."

Cautiously, I met her eye and nodded. "I think you're cool, and it's been fun hanging out with you. But I understand if you never want to see me again after all this."

Her eyes flashed. "First, we have to get Marcus back. You aren't getting off that easy."

I dropped my head, ashamed. "You're right."

After a pause, she put her hand on my shoulder. "I'm just kidding. What you did sucks, but I sort of understand. And I think you're cool, too."

I smiled at her awkwardly. "So you don't think I'm a monster?"

Izzy laughed. "I don't think you're any worse than my brother."

That thought sent chills down my spine, but I knew Izzy hadn't meant to sound threatening. I bumped her shoulder with mine and stood up. "We better figure this all out, and fast."

Izzy nodded. "Can you drive a manual?"

Her question surprised me. "What are you talking about?"

She gestured out of the cairn. "The car. It's manual. Can you drive it?"

I shrugged. "Maybe. My mom's car is a stick. I can try."

"Good." She fished in the pocket of her hoodie for a minute and then handed me a key ring.

I raised my eyebrow. "I thought I saw Marcus put these in his pocket."

Her shrug was eloquent. "Maybe you did. But I never said I didn't like to pinch things. Guess it's a good thing, this time."

I eyed her cautiously. What else didn't I know about Izzy? A slow smile spread across my face. "Glad you did."

She grinned in response. "But now you know, so you better check your pockets."

My hands went involuntarily to my backpack, and Izzy laughed. "You don't trust me?"

Her tone was suddenly serious, and I studied her face. "Actually, I think I do."

"That's good. Darlena?"

"Yeah?"

"I think I trust you, too."

I gave her a quick hug. "Thanks." It had been a long time since I felt like I had a friend.

Her eyes flashed impishly. "Just don't screw it up."

I rolled my eyes. "Are you ready to leave now?"

"Give me ten minutes to try to contact Isis."

"Can I stay?" I was really interested in Izzy's patron, especially since I remembered that Izzy had said Isis was similar to Persephone.

Izzy hesitated, but then she shook her head. "I want to talk to her alone. No offense," she hurried to add, "it's just that today has been so much. I need her advice."

I nodded. "I understand. I forgot you said she was like another mother."

"Yeah." Izzy looked down at her feet. "So I'll meet you at the car?"

"Make sure you don't disappear, too." I tried to joke, but her face crumpled when I spoke, and I felt like an ass. "I'm sorry, Izzy. We'll find him."

She nodded, tears streaming down her face. "I'll be done in a few."

I walked back toward the car, watching the frozen patterns my breath made in the air. Today hadn't been anything like I'd imagined.

While it had been sort of a relief to see Persephone, her news horrified me. True, I wasn't surprised to know that Hecate wanted to destroy the world—she'd never struck me as the nurturing type. What did surprise me was something Persephone had said about the other Red gods. If Hecate wasn't acting alone, would binding her do any good?

Opening the car door, I slid into the tattered driver's seat. Who had Marcus borrowed the car from? If Izzy didn't know, I wasn't sure how we would get it back to its owner. As the thought flitted through my mind, I started to giggle. I had just found out the world might be coming to an end, and I was worried about getting a trashed car back to its owner? My laughter grew until I was doubled over, clutching the immobile steering wheel for support. By the time Izzy came back to the car, my fit of hysterics had passed, but I was still hiccupping from time to time.

She shot me a look but didn't say anything, and I turned the key in the ignition, forcing myself to calm down. "Any good news from Isis?"

Out of the corner of my eye, I saw Izzy shake her head. "Nothing that helps us."

I fumbled with the clutch and the car lurched into motion. "That sucks."

"Yeah." She hesitated.

"What?"

Izzy's voice was small. "Isis warned me about something. She thinks I may be in danger."

I risked a glance at her as the car ground down the road. "From what?"

"She wasn't sure." Izzy paused and then met my eye. "But she thinks it has something to do with Red magic."

16

The drive back to Edinburgh was tense. I didn't really know how to drive a stick, so between the grinding and thumping sounds coming from the car and Izzy's warning from Isis, we were both on edge when we finally made it back to the city that night.

"Drop me near the school, okay?" Izzy didn't look at me, and I wondered what she'd been thinking.

"Okay. I don't mind taking you home, though."

"It's fine. The school is good enough."

I shrugged. So much for trusting each other; she didn't even want me to know where she lived. I pulled up to the curb outside the looming gates, and the car jerked to a halt. "Do you know who Marcus borrowed the car from?"

Izzy shook her head. "No, but I can do a spell to find out."

"Okay." I turned the car off and handed her the keys. "I'll leave it here with you, then."

I got out of the car and headed off in the direction of my hotel. Izzy cleared her throat. "What's our next step?"

I turned and looked at her, surprised. "After what your goddess said, I figured you didn't want to help me."

"We need to get my brother back." Her voice shook, but I couldn't read her expression in the faint glow from the streetlamp. "And," she added dryly, "I don't fancy the end of the world."

"Me, neither." I took a deep breath and crossed my fingers. "Should I meet you back here?"

She nodded. "We have to figure out how to bind a god."

"I have a few ideas." The words slipped out, and instantly, I wished I could take them back. I wasn't ready to tell Izzy about Loki yet, but luckily, she didn't ask.

"So do I."

Her words surprised me, and I smiled. "I'll see you in the morning, then?"

"Sounds good."

We stood there awkwardly for a minute, and finally I turned around first. I was glad she still wanted to help me, but the fact that she didn't want me to follow her home grated on me. What did she think I'd do to her?

I was in a pretty awful mood by the time I got back to my hotel, and I ignored the blinking message light on the room phone. Even if Mom or Justin had called, I was too drained to talk to them right now. Instead, I fell into the bed with my clothes on and passed out before I realized that I should at least brush my teeth.

***

The next day, I met Izzy in front of Lady on the Lake. She was already there, sitting on the ground with two cups of coffee.

"How'd you get here so early?"

She smirked. "Wouldn't you like to know?"

I accepted the second cup she passed up to me, but I stayed standing. "No, seriously?"

She shrugged. "I thought you'd figured it out by now; this is a boarding school."

I almost choked on the steaming coffee. "You're kidding. So you're, what, a snobby boarding school brat?" I laughed at the words.

She didn't. "Sure. Something like that." Izzy stood quickly and headed for the building.

"I'm sorry." I rushed to keep up with her. "You just have to understand: I've never met anyone who goes to a boarding school. Trinity was exclusive, but we still went home at night."

Izzy remained silent, but her pace slowed considerably. I walked beside her in silence until we were inside the foyer, standing on the polished marble floor. Then I stopped and put a hand on her shoulder.

"I'm sorry. Really. Can I see your room?"

A slow smile spread across her face. "I thought you'd never ask!"

She trotted up the stairs, chugging coffee as she went. I followed quickly, feeling awful for the way I'd teased her. I'd never had a sister, so I hadn't really realized what a big difference there was between fourteen and sixteen. I had to stop treating her like a girl my own age. Rochelle would have laughed at my snarky comment. That thought stopped me cold. What was I doing, comparing Marcus's sweet kid sister to someone as warped as Rochelle? I shook my head and took another swig of coffee.

"Here it is." Izzy stood proudly beside a thick wooden door.

I hesitated for a moment. "Do you have a roommate?"

She shook her head. "Nope. The school believes that magical practice is best done with relative privacy."

I glanced up and down the massive hall. "How many students go here?"

She shrugged. "It depends. But there are always enough rooms, even if they aren't all the same size. I've been here awhile, so my room isn't too bad."

That was an understatement. When she opened the door, I thought I'd just entered a ritzy hotel suite. "Not too bad? Are you kidding? This is huge!"

She blushed and perched on the edge of her bed. The bedspread was a brilliant blue batik pattern, with gold swirls and stars scattered across it.

"That's really cool." I pointed to her bed, and she blushed again.

"Thanks. I designed it."

I stared at the bedspread. "Did you Witch it?"

She laughed. "Nope, it's not magic. I found the fabric in town at a market, and I got the girl in the next room over to do the sewing. Totally mundane."

"But it's really gorgeous. Izzy, you have a great eye for color!"

She shrugged. "Just for blue."

I nodded, and sat on the rag rug in the center of the room. "What else did she say yesterday?"

Izzy fiddled with her coffee cup. "Who?"

"Isis! Who do you think?"

She took a long sip from her coffee cup. "She said she'd heard about you."

I bristled. "I hate it when the gods think they know me just because they've heard about me." I wanted to ask Izzy if Isis had told her to be afraid of me, but I sort of didn't want to know the answer.

"It wasn't like that! She'd spoken with your old patron."

"Aphrodite?" I was surprised. "What are she and Isis doing palling around?"

Izzy leaned forward eagerly. "When Isis's followers spread, lots of people compared her to Aphrodite."

I frowned. "But Aphrodite is a Red goddess. How'd they make the comparison?"

She shrugged. "It wasn't just Aphrodite. Isis got compared to every major goddess, wherever she went. It's like people realized she was super important, even if they didn't understand her."

I thought about that for a moment. "What did Aphrodite say about me?"

Izzy creased her brow. "I'm not sure. Isis just said she'd heard about you from her."

I must have looked skeptical, but Izzy continued.

"She had more to say about what I need to focus on right now."

"And what's that?"

Izzy looked at her hands again. "Balance. Isis strives for balance, and she reminded me that I need to, too."

"Balance." I sighed. "Izzy, I think maybe you need to remind me to focus on that, too. That's how this whole mess started."

"Have you given up on finding balance within Red magic?" Her question was tentative, and when I glanced up, she was staring intently at me.

"No. But I'm worried."

"What about?"

I hesitated, not sure how much I could say to her. "Is it really balance," I asked, choosing my words carefully, "if a Witch gains power over a god?"

Izzy was silent for a moment. "I don't know," she whispered.

"Me, neither. But I don't know of any other way to stop Hecate. We have to bind her."

She stood up. "I know." She looked at me and raised an eyebrow. "You said you had an idea?"

"It's not one I like."

She nodded. "Me, neither."

We were silent for a moment. Finally, I said, "We just need to know more before we do something."

Izzy looked thoughtful. "Let me show you the school library. It's the whole top floor of the building; if there's a safe way to bind a god, we'll find it there."

I nodded, throwing my coffee cup into the trash. I followed her into the hall, wondering what ideas she'd had that she wasn't telling me. Maybe there was another way besides making a bargain with Loki. I hoped we could find it if there was.

***

The library was massive. Rows and rows of shelves stretched to the ceiling, and here and there ladders leaned against the stacks, inviting you to climb up and have a look. I stood, gaping at all the books, while Izzy marched up to the librarian's desk in the center of the room.

No one was in sight, so she rang a small brass bell on the counter. The sound was musical, and a tall man appeared almost immediately from behind the desk. It was as if he had been crouching down, waiting to spring.

"Yes?" He peered down his long nose.

Izzy glanced at me before she spoke. "We're looking for books about the gods."

He frowned slightly. "Can you be more specific?"

"Stories about control," I chimed in.

He glared at me. "Control over the gods?"

"Just myths about different times the gods were, um, incapacitated." Izzy smiled, batting her eyes innocently.

The stork-like man glanced between us and finally sighed. "There are such stories. But they are not collected in one volume." He eyed Izzy for a moment. "You follow a god of Egypt?"

She nodded. I took a step back, hoping he wouldn't try that trick on me, but he didn't even look at me.

"We'll start with Egyptian stories, then."

He led Izzy to a shelf near the wall, and pulled down a thick, dusty volume. It looked heavy; she sagged a bit when he put it in her hands.

"This cannot leave the library. You see how old and precious this book is."

Izzy nodded reverently, and I leaned in to have a closer look. The dust on the book made me sneeze loudly, and the librarian glared at me.

"Something for you to look at, too, I suppose." He scrutinized me, and then his expression turned to pity. "You haven't taken a patron?"

How in the world did he know? I raised an eyebrow but stayed silent. Clearly, this weird man knew his way around the massive library. We needed his help, and I didn't want to risk offending him by getting into an argument about the supposed value of taking a patron. Besides, he kind of gave me the creeps, and I figured the less I said to him, the better.

He tapped his cheek in thought. "Perhaps a compilation, to help you choose. I have just the thing—it's written by one of our own faculty members." He led the way to another shelf, catty-corner from the one where he'd found Izzy's book, and handed me a slender green book. "You can sit over there to look at these." He gestured to two wing-backed chairs facing a window.

"Thank you." Izzy smiled at him, and his expression softened as he looked at her. Even the grumpiest people seemed happier around Izzy, and I wondered again if that was because of her magic, or just her sweet personality.

"Just be careful with these books. You wouldn't be able to replace them if you damaged them."

He retreated to the desk, and we crossed over to the chairs he'd suggested.

I flipped through the book he'd handed me. It talked about different gods and the elements, but at a glance, none of the stories spoke of confinement.

"This may be something." Izzy's quiet voice was hopeful, and she pushed her open book at me.

I skimmed the tale of Isis and Osiris while Izzy watched me intently.

"So," I said slowly, still reading, "his brother Set made a coffin to his measurements. And he covered it in gold, and offered to give it to whichever god would fit in it?"

Izzy nodded.

"And Osiris fell for it?"

She glared at my tone. "He wasn't the only one. All the gods wanted that coffin! If Set had wanted to, he could have trapped them all."

"But he didn't. He just wanted to get his brother out of the way."

"And when Osiris climbed into the coffin, he couldn't escape."

I exhaled loudly. "Well, that's great, except for a few things. One, how would we build a coffin like that, and two, how am I supposed to convince Hecate to try it on for size?"

She looked hurt. "Have you thought of anything better?"

Loki's offer was on the tip of my tongue, but I shook my head. "Not yet. I'm going to get another book."

I handed the book back to Izzy and left her happily buried in the myths. I thought about stopping at the librarian's desk, but frankly, he gave me the creeps. The way he knew that I hadn't taken a patron was unnerving, almost like he could read my mind. Craning my neck, I wandered around reading the neatly labeled shelves, skimming for something that would help us.

There didn't seem to be any system of organization in the library. I found "Divination: Tarot" on the shelf below "Gods: Native American." Despite the weird filing system, I felt better walking through the library than I had since leaving North Carolina. Libraries had always been calming places for me, I guess; when you're surrounded by books, it's like nothing else is real. But my fight with Hecate was real, and I needed to focus.

I paused in front of a shelf labeled "Divination: Flame." Without thinking, I reached up and pulled down a thick leather-bound book. Kneeling on the floor beside the shelf, I began to turn the waxy pages. I was getting absorbed in the book when someone tripped over me.

"Ouch!" I tried to keep my voice down, remembering the stern librarian around the corner, but I was startled. I stood up quickly, clutching the book in my hand.

Dr. Farren looked surprised to see me. "I hadn't heard anything from you since our meeting yesterday. I thought you might have returned home." She glanced at the book in my hands, her frown deepening.

I shook my head. "No. I think I have a plan." I paused, but before I could continue, she cut me off.

"Then maybe you and I should speak somewhere more private." Her gesture took in the handful of people browsing through the library shelves.

I nodded. "Let me tell Izzy."

"You're here with her?"

I ignored her surprised tone. What did the woman think I was, a leper? "Yes. She's helping me." I headed toward the chair where I had left Izzy, but it was empty.

Dr. Farren looked around in consternation. "Does she know about you?"

"I've told her everything." *Well, not everything*, I mentally amended, but Dr. Farren didn't need to know that.

The book Izzy had been looking at was still on the chair, flipped open to a different page. This one was illustrated, with a red hippopotamus devouring a boat. I looked more closely at it, confused. I didn't really know much about Egyptian mythology, but the caption said it was a picture of Set attacking Horus.

"Horus was Isis's son, right?" I asked Dr. Farren, pointing to the illustration curiously.

She nodded, glancing at the book. Suddenly, she gasped. "Good gracious!" She stared at the picture, panic flashing across her face. Her eyes darted around the room and she grabbed my wrist.

"We must act. Now."

Before I could struggle or protest, she dragged me from the library.

17

Dr. Farren hustled me into her office, shutting the door behind us with a slam. I watched her seal it with a ward I didn't recognize, and then she moved clockwise around the room, tracing the ward in each corner and in front of the two tall stained glass windows.

Instead of the floor pillows, the room was now furnished with a massive oak desk. A throne-like chair sat behind it, and a rough wooden stool was placed in front. It was totally different than the office I remembered. The first time we'd met, she'd been friendly and her office had felt welcoming. Now that she was pissed, the office seemed like the setting for an inquisition.

Dr. Farren sat on the throne, her back straight. With a gesture, she indicated that I should sit down, so I perched awkwardly on the stool.

"How well do you know Isadora?" Her voice shook slightly, but her face was an emotionless mask. Still, I felt the tension in the room increase with her question.

"She's got a brother who practices Red magic, like me." I paused. What did I really know about Izzy? "She's a Blue Witch, and dedicated to Isis. She, um, she likes street food and cemeteries," I finished lamely.

Dr. Farren nodded slowly. "What do you know of her parentage?"

I shrugged. "Nothing, really, except she said Isis was like a mother to her. I wish I felt that way about a god!" I laughed ruefully. "The ones I know are mostly out to kill me."

The director didn't smile. "Your friend is an interesting Witch. Do you have any idea where she might be?"

Startled, I almost slipped off the stool. "You think she's missing? But she was just there a few minutes ago. Maybe she went to grab another book or something."

Dr. Farren sighed. "You must understand, Darlena, I am still not sure how far I can trust a Witch like you. And there are things that you should not hear from me."

"What are you talking about?"

She reached for the old-fashioned black telephone on her desk. "I need to contact Isadora's brother. Maybe he can tell you."

I swallowed. "You won't be able to reach him."

She set the phone down and glared at me. "All right, young lady, it seems that you have some things to explain to me."

"Marcus is gone."

"Gone where?"

I hesitated. "I'm not sure. Izzy thinks Hecate took him, for some reason. I think he left willingly." I paused. "I don't trust him."

She eyed me shrewdly. "Why is that?"

"I came here for help, but he didn't seem concerned with what I told him. Either that," I added bitterly, "or he'd like to see chaos take over."

She looked at me intently. "Where did you last see him?"

"At the Clava Cairns. He and Izzy and I rode out there yesterday. We thought that—"

"It doesn't matter what you thought! I know you haven't had the same kind of training, but I'd expect those two to know better than to go prancing around such a powerful site unescorted."

I looked at her in surprise. "Why is it powerful?"

"As a Red, you of all people should realize the power of death. Those stones were built to symbolize the passage to the afterlife. They embody the power of death, and all that that entails." She tapped her fingers on the desk, staring at me. "Clearly, we have to act."

I held up my hands. "I'm really confused. What's going on?"

She picked up the phone again, ignoring me. "Hello? It's Tali. Yes. I know. Sooner than we thought. Now."

Dr. Farren hung up the phone and sighed. "You better come with me." She rose swiftly and left the office. *What the hell is going on?* After a moment, I followed her.

It was hard to keep up with Dr. Farren's wide strides. Luckily, her car wasn't parked too far away from the school. I waited until she'd pulled the BMW into traffic before I started asking questions.

"What's this all about? And where are we going?"

She maneuvered the car through the thick holiday traffic. "The first question will take a while to explain. But we're going to the countryside."

"Why?"

Dr. Farren glanced at me. "To stop what's started, if we can."

I grimaced. "I still don't know what's going on. But why do we have to go to the countryside? Can't we do whatever we need to do here?"

"My Coven is based there. We need all the help we can get."

"Your what?"

She looked at me, surprised by my tone. "Don't they teach you anything in America?"

"The only time I've heard the word 'coven' was in one of those trashy horror movies. It was a group of Satanists."

She snorted. "That's an improper use of the term. A Coven is a group of Witches."

"Isn't that what your school is?"

"A magical school and a Coven are two very different things. A Coven is a group of Witches who practice together. They swear vows to the group, as well as to their own patrons. In that way, they gain strength in their magic.

I looked out the window at the frosty landscape whizzing by. "But isn't that dangerous? To work so closely with other Witches?"

Dr. Farren looked at me in surprise. "Why would it be? We've all sworn allegiance to each other. That vow is just as binding as a dedicancy to an individual patron. No one breaks that kind of vow."

I didn't want to correct her. "But how does working as a group make the magic stronger?"

"Our group has members from three of the magical paths, so we each contribute our strengths and weaknesses. It means our spells are more well-rounded, shall we say."

"Which three?"

"Pardon?"

"Which three paths are in your Coven?"

"It's not up to me to share information about my Coven sisters and brothers. You'll have to ask them when you meet them."

"I still don't understand why you need your group right now."

She sighed. "Because if I'm right, the end of the world might become a reality really fast."

My heart sped up as I stared at her, startled to hear my own suspicions voiced.

She smiled thinly. "My Coven has been watching events for some time, keeping an especially close eye on the gods who foster chaos. Not just the Red deities," she added, looking at me quickly, "but any of the gods who enjoy a good disaster now and again."

"Who's your patron?" I asked abruptly.

She glanced at me, but then lifted her chin proudly. "Hera."

That made so much sense; the woman was queenly and powerful, even when she was angry. "So you're a White?"

She nodded.

"How do you contact her?"

"I beg your pardon?"

I paused, and worded my question without bringing Freya into it. "I thought that the gods are bound by the places they were worshiped. So how do you talk to Hera here in Scotland?"

She laughed. "Museums are excellent places: artifacts from all over the world now make their home here in this land." Her eyes flickered to me and then back to the road. "I'm surprised to learn that you do know some things."

I tried to ignore her tone. "Trinity taught three paths: Green, White, and Black. I never knew anything else existed until I made my declaration to Red."

She nodded. "That's the American system. For some reason, when Witchcraft crossed the ocean, the Puritan fathers chose to eliminate half of the magical paths."

"So there are six paths altogether?" I paused, ticking off on my fingers as I went. The gray landscape whipped by the window, but I ignored it. "There's Red and Blue, Green and Black, and White." I looked at her curiously.

"The sixth is the Yellow path."

"Is that the path of Air?"

"Once more, very good!"

I shrugged. "Izzy and I talked a little bit about how the elements come into it." I paused. "Do you really think she's gone?"

Dr. Farren ignored my question. "The American system is incomplete. Together, the six magics represent the five elements that govern the planet: earth, air, fire, water, and spirit. To only teach spirit and earth is like amputating the legs from a man: horrible and wasteful."

"There must have been a reason they stopped teaching the other three paths."

Dr. Farren snorted. "The reason is obvious! Your forefathers liked things to be black and white, if you'll pardon the expression. It was easier to build a magical system that dealt with good, evil, and mundane. Less complicated than the reality."

"I guess I don't understand. I mean, cutting out Red makes sense."

"Does it?" She looked at me for a long instant, but just when I was starting to worry that we'd crash into oncoming traffic, she turned her eyes back to the road.

"Well," I struggled to find the words, "it's dangerous, isn't it? I mean, look what's happened to me! My best friend tried to kill me because of Red magic."

She sighed. "Not all Witches are as power mad as your friend was."

I nodded. "But still, having a path that only three people can practice, I can see why they wouldn't talk about it much. It's like the most exclusive party around—people are sure to get jealous."

"I don't believe that's true. Especially if Witches were taught early on to respect all six of the paths, I don't think even the exclusivity of the Red path would cause jealousy or conflict. Each path has dangerous elements."

"But sometimes it feels like Red is the worst."

She smiled sadly. "You bear a heavy burden, but you chose it for yourself. Some Witches are not so lucky."

"No one can be forced to choose a path. That's against the Rede."

Dr. Farren stared straight ahead at the road. "Laws can be broken."

***

Dr. Farren parked in front of an old, white farmhouse when we reached the countryside. I counted three other cars parked in the driveway.

"Darlena, there are many things you are about to learn. You won't like all of them."

"I don't care. I need to understand what's going on, and I want to find Izzy."

"And Marcus?" Her question was gentle, but I detected a hint of sharpness in her tone.

"I guess I'm not sure if he's worth finding."

She smiled sadly. "You may change your mind."

I glanced up at the farmhouse looming before us. It looked old and abandoned to the naked eye, but my senses were tingling: magic had been done here, frequently. The residue made the house almost glisten. "Is it okay for me to go in there? I mean, I haven't sworn an oath to your group or anything."

"That's a chance I'm willing to take. I think everyone will

understand." Despite her words, she looked nervous. I wondered idly what she hadn't told me about the Coven.

"Crawck!" A loud scream came through the front windows of the house, and I jumped.

"What was that?"

Dr. Farren smiled. "Julia's parrot. She never travels without him. You'll get used to it."

The bird screeched again, louder, as the door opened. I was startled to see the stork-like man from the library standing there in the doorway, and I recoiled behind Dr. Farren for a moment.

She patted my shoulder. "Good afternoon, Samuel. You must have left immediately to beat us."

He nodded, glaring at me. "As soon as the girl vanished. I didn't think you'd bring this one, though."

Dr. Farren pulled me forward gently. "It concerns her."

He didn't respond, but stepped aside so we could enter the house. The door swung shut silently behind me, and I felt a moment of fear. I glanced at Dr. Farren for reassurance, but she looked away.

18

Despite what I'd been afraid of, the Coven seemed like a normal group of Witches. I guess the horror movies Rochelle and I had watched for years had really warped my mind. I was expecting evil rituals and human sacrifice, but from what I could tell, I might as well have wandered into a book club as a magical group. Besides Dr. Farren and the man from the library, three other Witches were waiting: Julia, the woman with the parrot, Frederick, a short old man who reminded me of my Grandpa Agara, and Frances, his wife. It was their farmhouse.

Sitting on a plush loveseat, I surveyed the Witches around me.

"Is this everybody?"

Frederick shook his head. "Our group is made up of nine members, but we're only waiting on one more."

I glanced at Dr. Farren questioningly.

"Not everyone could come out on such short notice."

"Oh." I sat back against the cushions, thinking.

Frances offered me tea, but I shook my head.

"What does this girl have to do with anything?" Julia and her parrot glared at me, and I sank further back in the seat.

"When we are all here, we can discuss it." Dr. Farren's voice was firm, and the other Witch shrugged gracelessly.

I'd never liked being around adults, and sitting there on display for this strange Coven was starting to grate on my nerves. Abruptly, I stood up, and the parrot let out a piercing shriek.

"Could you tell me where the restroom is?" I spoke to Frederick. Of all the Witches, he seemed the least threatened by me.

"The W.C.? Top of the stairs to the left. Mind the seventh step— the board's loose."

I nodded and left the room quickly. Once out of their sight, I slowed down, climbing the stairs carefully. It wasn't just the seventh step; the entire staircase looked like it might crumble if you breathed on it. Miraculously, I made it to the second floor. The bathroom was easy to find, and I locked myself inside.

I wasn't sure why I was so angry; hadn't Dr. Farren offered to help? But the longer I sat in the living room downstairs with those Witches, the more annoyed I became. I splashed water on my face from the pedestal sink, trying to calm down. When the water hit my skin, I shivered. Glancing at the mirror above the sink, I bit back a curse. For just a moment, I thought I had seen another face in the mirror besides my own. When I checked over my shoulder and didn't see anything, I shook my head. Looking back at the mirror, I only saw my own ragged face.

"Better not start hallucinating," I told my reflection. I stood there for a minute, studying myself in the mirror. I'd been eating since I came to Scotland, but not enough to make up for the months when I barely touched any food, and my cheeks were still unnaturally hollow. My eyes looked haunted, and I didn't think that was just because of the start I'd given myself. The people in the car, and then Rochelle, I ticked off on my fingers, feeling guilt rest heavily on me with each death. Sandra and Joan in the vaults, and now maybe Marcus and Izzy? Even though I wasn't sure Marcus was in any danger, I knew that it was my fault if he were. I'd caused so much disaster since declaring to the Red path; would I ever be able to make it right?

Trying to shake off my melancholy thoughts, I ran the water over my wrists, chilling them until my fingertips felt numb. I couldn't let myself mourn; I had to keep moving, had to keep trying to do something about the chaos I'd caused. After an extra splash of water on my neck, I headed back downstairs to join the Coven.

The stairs felt much sturdier going down, and I paused. What if the rickety steps were just an illusion, like a glamour? Intrigued by the thought that had popped into my head, I jumped once on the stair I was perched on, and the wood felt solid beneath me. I stared intently at the stairs, and I was finally able to discern the glimmer of magic resting like powder on the steps.

I looked back upstairs, thinking. Why would a Witch enchant something in his home, unless he was protecting something? What was the Coven hiding? I listened for a moment, but the voices in the front room droned on calmly: no one seemed concerned by my absence. Yet.

Deciding quickly, I turned and went back upstairs. Ignoring the bathroom, I passed down a long hallway. The floor looked like it sloped like a cheap funhouse, but if I walked carefully, I found it was flat. Another glamour! I pushed open the door at the end of the hallway and gasped.

Izzy was lying bound and gagged on the floor. Her eyes flashed when she recognized me, and she thumped her heels twice.

"What do we have here?"

I jumped, startled by the old man's sudden appearance. Firmly, Frederick closed the door and steered me back to the stairs.

"What are you going to do with her?" I stepped away from him, wondering if I could run down the stairs, but he kept his hand on my shoulder. I fought back the rising panic that filled my throat.

He clicked his tongue. "Silly child. Able to see the other enchantments, and not that one?"

I stopped on the stairs and blocked his way. "What are you talking about?"

"Coven secret. But things are not as they seem."

Forcefully, he prodded me down the stairs and back into the front room.

"Even if Jewel hasn't arrived yet, we'll have to do something. The girl has seen the room."

If I thought I was unwelcome before, I wasn't prepared for the looks on their faces at Frederick's announcement. The parrot clicked his beak in agitation.

I sank back down on the loveseat. "I think I deserve some answers."

They stared mutely at me, but then a rusty voice began to speak.

"Things are not as they seem." Everyone swiveled around to look at Samuel, the sharp-nosed librarian, leaning against the old brick fireplace across the room. He met my eyes, and I shivered. "What do you know about the siblings you seek?"

I huffed, "Well, one of them is tied up in that room upstairs!"

No one twitched.

"First, she is not." Samuel's voice was firm. "Second, answer my question."

What did he mean? I knew what I saw, but the look on Samuel's face warned me not to push it. I frowned. "I know Marcus is a Red, and Izzy's Blue. Otherwise, I guess I don't know a lot."

"You know their patrons, I thought?" Dr. Farren's voice was insistent.

I nodded. "Cerridwen and Isis."

"But do you know how they came to serve those gods?" Frederick's voice was harsh, and Frances crossed to him, taking his hand. Confused, I shook my head.

"It's not a pretty story." Julia laughed harshly and her parrot echoed her.

"But it's one the girl needs to hear in order to understand," Dr. Farren interjected. Frances nodded, but the other three Witches showed no change of expression. For a moment, no one breathed.

Finally, Samuel sighed. "Does the Coven agree to share this information with this Witch, even though she has sworn us no oath and owes us no allegiance?" His words reverberated through the room, and the other Witches straightened as he spoke. Simultaneously, they nodded once, and I wondered for a minute if Samuel was in charge of the group. That thought made me shiver; it was pretty obvious that he wasn't my biggest fan.

"Very well. It has been agreed. But the consequences of our actions may reach farther than you suppose." Despite his threatening words, the librarian looked sad.

"Their story begins over twenty ago, long before Isadora was born."

Dr. Farren closed her eyes as if she was in pain, but Samuel kept speaking.

"When she was pregnant with her son, Marcus's mother was overtaken with fear of her own mortality. She made a foolish bargain, breaking magical law to protect herself. She vowed her unborn child to the service of a powerful goddess, Cerridwen. The Witch thought that with a son in service of the Goddess of Death, she would never know the gruesome fate that her heart feared."

I stared at him in horror. Even though I sometimes bent the Rede, I couldn't imagine a Witch who would be willing to break the strongest of magical laws. Poor Marcus! What would it have been like if my mom had promised me to a goddess before I was born? With my luck, she would have given me to Hecate. I gulped nervously.

"But," Julia took up the tale, "she didn't think it through. To make a vow for another Witch goes against the Rede, for Marcus should have been allowed to choose his own patron and his own path. His mother did him harm in this."

Gods, how awful! "So Marcus didn't swear to the Red path?" My question broke the spell of the story, and Samuel glared at me.

Dr. Farren shook her head. "It was chosen for him. He never wanted it, but no Witch can unbind a vow to a patron, once made, even without his consent."

She gave me a hard look, and I shook my head slightly. There was no way I wanted to discuss my own vow-breaking history in this room full of strange Witches; I wasn't sure how Dr. Farren had figured it out, but maybe she'd read it in my tea leaves. I kept my mouth closed, and she relaxed and looked at Frances.

Frances had tears in her eyes when she began to speak. "Marcus did not choose his path, and his training—" She paused and glanced around the room. "His training also did him harm. The boy has had a hard life, all thanks to his mother."

"What happened to her?" I sort of hoped Marcus's mom had been punished for what she did, but the tense expressions on the faces around me said otherwise.

Frances took a deep breath. "The woman did not die, but felt great remorse when she realized what fate she had given her son. When she was pregnant a second time, she tried to soften her error."

"But she was still selfish." Samuel's voice was harsh. "Still, she bound her unborn child to a path and a patron, but this time, she chose more wisely. She offered the goddess Isis the service of her child."

"And she didn't live through Isadora's birth." Dr. Farren looked pale as she spoke.

No one said anything for a moment. Frances wept against her husband's shoulder, and the librarian turned, staring blankly out the window.

"But," I hesitated, not wanting to break the stillness, but needing to understand, "why is your Coven involved? And how does this explain what's happened to them?"

Julia was the one who answered me. "She was one of our group. We each have ties to her, and a responsibility to her children."

"But where are they? I saw Izzy upstairs."

Dr. Farren shook her head. "That wasn't her. It was a Seeming."

Something jiggled at the back of my memory. "What's that?"

"A powerful Witch can create a Seeming of herself. It's a sort of double."

I looked at Dr. Farren, confused. "Why would Izzy do that?"

"Izzy didn't. Those who have her sent that Seeming. It's a warning." Frederick sat down heavily, still holding his wife's hand. "They want us to know she's still alive for now."

"That's awful! It's like a really nasty ransom note, isn't it?"

Samuel laughed sharply. "That's exactly it."

"But who has her? And what do they want?"

"We aren't sure yet who has taken her. Still—" Frances broke off nervously. Five sets of eyes stared at me in pity.

The parrot shrieked knowingly. "They want you!"

19

Panicked, I stood up. My hands crackled with Red magic, and I prepared to defend myself.

Frederick raised his palms slowly in a gesture of peace. "We aren't the ones who want to harm you. You came here for answers, and we're trying to give them to you."

I didn't release the power. How stupid did he think I was?

Dr. Farren spoke. "Darlena, think. If we wanted to turn you over to Izzy's captors, we would have done so already. The situation is delicate, especially now that Marcus is missing."

I looked around the room, studying their faces. Other than Samuel, none of them seemed openly hostile. In fact, Frances and Julia both looked afraid. I lowered my hands slightly, but I didn't let go of Red magic.

"Why?" I demanded.

They glanced at each other, nervously.

Dr. Farren cleared her throat. "Darlena, it would seem that you have made some very powerful enemies. It's possible that Izzy may be released if you are sent in her place."

"So why haven't you given me to them? I mean, it's obvious Hecate has her, right? Why haven't you tried to sacrifice me? Everyone would be happy then." I laughed bitterly, and the red sparks shot up my arms to my elbows. My skin was starting to singe from holding all that magic and not using it, but I wasn't ready to trust the Coven yet. It would be easier for them to just hand me over and be done with it, but that didn't mean I'd let them take me without a fight.

"And as to who we're dealing with, perhaps it's better if you don't know." Samuel spoke from the fireplace, not looking at any of us.

"I already know. It has to be Hecate."

A ripple of tension flowed through the room at my statement. I noticed Frances turn quickly to the window and trace a protective symbol over the glass.

"Why would that be your assumption?" Dr. Farren's voice was guarded.

"Oh, I don't know, maybe because she's spent the past few months hunting me down!" My voice rose at the end, and the parrot let out an indignant squawk.

Frederick looked at Dr. Farren. "I thought you said the girl had some measure of sense."

I felt an irrational desire to blow something up. The red sparks surged up my arms, covering me from fingertip to shoulder. My skin was smoking, and I realized that even if I needed to defend myself, I couldn't hold that much Red magic for that long. Annoyed, I knelt to the floor and pressed my palms to the boards, picturing the earth beneath the house as I let the magic seep out of my hands. When I looked up, everyone was staring at me.

Dr. Farren smiled slightly. "She does. See how she didn't just blast us to smithereens?"

Frederick snorted. "But she could. She's a loose cannon, Talia."

"Look, stop talking about me like I'm not here. Who has Izzy, if not Hecate?"

Dr. Farren looked down at her hands, refusing to meet my gaze. I glared around the room, but no one answered my question. What were they hiding?

"Do you know what Hecate plans to do with you, child, should she have you in her hands?" Frances's voice was soft, and I thought I saw a tear in the corner of her eye.

"When she had Rochelle try to kill me in the fall," I began unsteadily, "Rochelle said she'd been promised that she'd become the next Red Witch to take my place." Glancing around nervously, I went on, "I would assume that she wants to replace me with someone who suits her purposes."

"Ah, yes, her purposes." Samuel stood straighter and took a step toward me. "And just what do you believe she wants, Darlena?"

I glanced at Dr. Farren, who nodded slightly. "I think she wants enough chaos to end the world." I licked my lips.

Their stunned faces made me feel like I'd just said the most ridiculous thing, but thankfully Dr. Farren came to my defense.

"We have been worried about such an event. There are many cases throughout mythology of different gods wishing to cleanse a civilization and start over. Usually when those gods are feeling neglected."

I jumped in. "But civilizations don't exist in isolation anymore, so for this to have any effect, they need to attack the global society as a whole." I thought about the strange winter back home in North Carolina. "Has the weather been odd here lately?"

They looked at each other, and after a moment, Dr. Farren nodded. "There have been more rainstorms than usual, even for Scotland."

I nodded. "It's an unusually cold winter in North Carolina, too. My mom says she's never seen anything quite like it."

"So the weather might be a sign that things are out of balance." Her eyes met mine, and I felt a rush of relief that at least somebody was willing to listen to me.

"Izzy and I were trying to figure out a way to bind Hecate. We hadn't thought of any other way to stop her, and now she's missing." My throat caught, and I realized that I was more worried about Izzy than I'd let on. This wasn't just about stopping Hecate anymore; the Blue Witch had begun to be my friend, and I couldn't sacrifice another friend.

Samuel frowned. "First, you tell us that the gods are plotting an apocalypse. Then you toss off the suggestion that trapping Hecate would be the solution to all this. Do you have any idea how irreverent you sound?"

I shrugged, nonplused. "If Hecate can't influence events, maybe I can work to stop any chaos she sets in motion. Otherwise, she just keeps getting in my way."

Julia leaned forward. "Is that how you use Red magic? I always thought it was about destruction and fire."

I shook my head. "It can be, but I've also been able to use it to bring a sort of balance. Death will still happen; chaos is just a part of life, like it or not. But if the Red Witches used our magic to spread out the natural effects of chaos, we might be able to find a more positive balance." I took a deep breath. "Last fall, I stopped a hurricane from making landfall."

They gaped at me for a moment. "That was dangerous," Dr. Farren finally said.

"I know. It's what made Hecate turn on me for real."

"I begin to understand why you sought help from Marcus, but how did you get Isadora mixed up in all of this?"

Frederick's question made me look down at my hands. In a quiet voice, I confessed, "I thought Izzy would help me get closer to Marcus. He'd been pretty clear that he didn't want anything to do with me, but Izzy, well ... "

I risked looking up. Frances stared at me pityingly, but Samuel had a look of rage on his face.

"So you used the girl. Just like a Red," he spat.

Gods, I wanted to blast him and show him what a Red could really do. I struggled to get a grip on my anger. "I didn't mean to! I mean, yes," I amended, "I meant to use her to get to Marcus. But Izzy was so funny and smart, and the things she said about Blue magic! I never knew there were any other magics. I didn't even know Red existed until I made my declaration."

"Ignorance is no excuse." Samuel's words felt like a death sentence, but none of the other Witches moved.

I glared at him. "Besides, I need all the help I can get. And Izzy was willing to help me."

"Until your presence threatened her. You're disgusting, Miss Agara." Samuel's words hung in the air, and I risked a glance at the rest of the Coven. Most of them were expressionless, but Julia wore a matching expression to Samuel, and Frances wouldn't meet my eyes.

I gulped. "What I don't understand," I said, turning to Dr. Farren and trying to ignore the rest of them, "is why did Hecate take Izzy? I mean, she was helping me, but this seems a little ... extreme."

"How much do you know about Izzy's patron, Isis?" Julia interrupted.

I shrugged. "Only what Izzy told me."

"Do you know, for example, that Isis spent years searching for her husband's remains?"

I wrinkled up my nose. "No, I didn't."

"Or," Julia continued, "that her husband was murdered by Set, her brother, who is also a Red god?"

I shuddered, starting to understand. "I don't know the story."

Dr. Farren sighed. "Isadora is unique. Remember that we told you she was sworn to Isis before birth?"

I nodded. Marcus and Izzy's mother had really screwed things up for her children.

"Well," Dr. Farren hesitated, and out of the corner of my eye, I saw Samuel shake his head. What was that about? Dr. Farren cleared her throat and continued. "Your friend is a uniquely powerful Witch. Let's just leave it at that. She is very precious to her patron. If there's a war brewing between the gods," I bristled at the emphasis she placed on the word *if*, but she went on, "then Isadora would be a valuable hostage. Whoever has her doesn't want her to get involved in this fight."

Or they just don't want her to help me. My certainty that Hecate was behind Izzy's disappearance strengthened, and I clenched my fists in anger. "Do many of the other gods know about Izzy's relationship with Isis?"

There was a tense silence, and then Dr. Farren nodded. "Isis made no secret of the love she bears for your friend. Their relationship has angered gods in the past, but none have ever acted on it."

"Until now." Julia's voice was mournful.

"So Izzy is powerful, and now she's gone." They stared at me like

I was an idiot, and I sighed, exasperated. "Don't you think that's even more reason for us to get her back?"

Dr. Farren stared at me levelly. "As a hostage, it is likely that whoever has taken her has done everything in his power to isolate her from her patron. It will be nearly impossible to rescue her if she can't access her own magic."

Frances sniffled. "That poor little girl. As good as dead."

I could only stare around the room for a moment, but then I recovered and glared at the Coven. "We have to help her!" I stood up, waiting for the other Witches to agree with me.

No one spoke for a moment, but then Frederick shook his head.

"It's too dangerous. Isadora will either escape, or not." Frances looked ashamed of her husband as he spoke, but she nodded after a moment.

"But that's not fair! She needs help. I don't care how much Isis loves her; she won't be able to fight the gods." I couldn't add Izzy's death to my conscience; I had to persuade them to help me.

"No," Samuel said, his eyes steely. "Only a Red would dare stand against the gods. So you can see why you must stay out of it." He paused, thinking. "Marcus's disappearance makes a certain amount of sense, now."

I started to argue, but he cut me off.

"If, as you say, Hecate wishes to upset the balance of the world, don't you realize that rushing off to rescue your friend would be a gift? She'd have you then, with no struggle."

"So you admit that Hecate probably has Izzy!" I glared at him triumphantly. "All the more reason we have to save her."

"Slow down, girl. I admit nothing; it is merely obvious that whoever has taken Isadora could use her as a bargaining chip with

Hecate. If you rush off after her, her captors would claim an even richer prize. Do you think for one minute that you would be safe in the hands of any of the gods of chaos?"

Something about his words made me pause. "Gods of chaos?" I looked around the room, but no one met my eye. "You know who has her!"

"Perhaps. And perhaps not. But we will not share that knowledge with you."

Dr. Farren glared at Samuel like she wanted to argue with him, but she didn't say anything. Once again, I got the feeling he was the leader of the Coven, and his decision would bind the rest of them. I ignored him and appealed to Dr. Farren. "I can't let Izzy ... I have to help her."

"Very noble, but also very foolish. Think before you act, Darlena." Dr. Farren looked at me sternly.

I stayed silent, but my mind was made up. I would find Izzy. It was my fault she was in this situation, and I'd get her out. Whichever gods of chaos had her would be no match for me. Red sparks surged up my arms for a moment, and I felt Samuel's eyes on me as I stalked out of the farmhouse.

20

When Dr. Farren dropped me off in Edinburgh that evening, she hesitated like she wanted to say something. I didn't want to hear more of her cautious lecturing, so I slammed the door and waved as fast as I could. She shook her head, but she drove off without speaking.

As I passed the reception desk, the clerk stopped me.

"Miss Agara, there have been three messages for you."

Messages? "Are you sure?"

He nodded politely and handed me three crisp sheets of hotel stationary, folded in half. I thanked him, and headed to the privacy of my room.

The first note was from my mother. She'd called the hotel earlier that day, and the only message she left was that she'd call back. My heart clenched with loneliness, and I realized how homesick I was. I really wanted to talk to Mom about everything I'd learned in the countryside, but I should probably read the other two messages first.

One was from Justin. It was short and to the point: "We need to talk." I wondered what the hotel clerk had thought when he wrote down that message! I'd obviously neglected everyone the past few days if even Justin was calling the hotel looking for me. The thought of hearing his voice again was comforting, and I debated for a minute between calling Justin before I called Mom. I glanced at the last message as I picked up my phone, and my skin started to tingle.

"Meet me there, same place, same time, tonight." There was no name signed to the message, but I was sure it must be from Izzy. Who else had I met anywhere while I'd been in Scotland? Maybe she'd managed to escape! For a minute, my pulse sped up. Where would she want to meet? It must be the cemetery, I reasoned; I hadn't met her anywhere else, other than the school, and I doubted she'd invite me there. If the message was a trap, I'd just have to be careful, but my instinct said the message was genuine, and I felt giddy with relief.

Ignoring the other messages, I donned my coat and scarf. I debated calling Dr. Farren and telling her where I was going, but then I decided not to. I wanted to see what was going on before I involved the Coven, and somehow, I didn't think Dr. Farren would approve of me running around Edinburgh in search of Izzy. The entire Coven had made that pretty clear; they didn't want me involved, period.

I grabbed my backpack and headed out into the street. Partiers surged around me as I walked. With New Year's Eve a night away, everyone was getting into the spirit of the season. I had to step carefully to avoid the broken bottles that littered the street, but luckily none of the partygoers paid me any attention. The bells of a church were chiming as I rounded the corner to the cemetery gate.

It was locked. I rattled the gate, glancing around to see if anyone was going to come yell at me for trespassing. I was alone. It wouldn't take much for me to open the gate, but I hesitated. Marcus had already flown off the handle at me for using Red magic in his land.

Marcus isn't here, I reminded myself harshly. *He's the least of your problems.* With a deep breath, I held the lock in my hand and summoned a burst of Red magic. The lock started to heat up, but I held on until I was clutching the melted remains of the padlock. I unwound the chain from the gate and slipped inside.

The last time I'd been here with Izzy, I'd been too wrapped up in our conversation to notice how creepy the graveyard was. Smooth, gray stones, worn down by the weather, lined the twisting path, and here and there large marble statues of angels sprouted up among the simpler headstones. The cemetery was surrounded by a high wall, and the sounds of the city were muffled. In the distance, a siren started to wail, but I ignored it. My ears began to buzz, and I shivered, recalling the afternoon at the Clava Cairns. I shook my head, hoping that nothing dangerous was waiting for me in the shadows.

"Izzy?" I whispered, but my voice bounced off the headstones. The graveyard was silent. I moved through the cemetery slowly, checking the shadows for Izzy, but I didn't see her. After a half hour, I had traversed the main path that looped through the graves, and my head was pounding. The buzzing sensation had been increasing, and I was miserable. Had I been wrong about the note? I was about to turn and leave when I felt the air around me tremble.

Suddenly, Izzy was standing next to me, looking confused.

"Where'd you come from? I've been looking all over for you!" I rushed to hug her, but she stepped back, putting a finger to her mouth to silence me.

"Izzy, I don't feel like playing games—" I started to argue, but the pleading look in her eyes seemed sincere, so I stopped talking and followed her to the steps of a looming mausoleum. It didn't have a door, just a gaping opening, and the blackness of the grave slipped around me as I followed her inside. I hesitated, unsure, but Izzy moved forward into the tomb. Whether she was real or not, I needed to find out where she'd gone.

"Here goes nothing, I guess." Warily, I entered the tomb.

My steps echoed off the marble floor. As I walked, the floor began to slant down gradually until it was more like a ramp. I realized that I was walking into the earth, descending away from the tomb and Edinburgh. I paused, frightened. This was feeling more and more like a trap. I'd lost sight of Izzy almost immediately, and the back of my neck prickled in warning. What waited for me at the end of the ramp?

"Izzy?" I whispered, but my voice was magnified in the dark chamber, and it sounded like something was mocking me by repeating my words. The darkness felt threatening, and I clutched my backpack to my chest like a shield. A faint glow emanated from the bottom of the bag, and I dug out the crystal sphere that Hades had given me in the fall. It was glowing weakly. With the ball in my left hand, I gathered up a burst of Red magic to hold in my right. Now that I had light and protection, I felt a little calmer, and I continued to move with care down the sloping tunnel.

The tunnel had been growing lighter as I walked, but the crystal sphere was still burning dimly. The sparks dancing on my arm weren't bright enough to give off more than a faint red glow, and I paused to let my eyes adjust to the new source of light. A carved stone gateway was standing at the end of the tunnel, filled with blinding white light.

"Izzy?" I called hopefully. "What is it?"

"The door to Annwn. The living can pass through it, if they can find it. All Otherworlds lead to each other." Her voice came from behind me, and I jumped. When I turned around, I couldn't see her.

"Izzy? Where are you?"

"I need you to find me! He—" Her voice cut off abruptly, and I spun in a circle, confused. I was alone in the tunnel.

The stillness almost swallowed me after her voice was gone, and I shivered. A human couldn't just vanish into thin air, and she'd left in mid-sentence. Maybe Izzy had sent the message, I thought, trusting that I could help her. After all, she was a pretty powerful Witch; who's to say she couldn't have reached out with a Seeming to show me the way to rescue her? I glanced back the way I had come, then I looked at the doorway, deciding.

It wasn't a choice, not really. I had to find Izzy. But one thing held me back.

I racked my brain, but I knew next to nothing about this place, Annwn. I assumed it was another Underworld from what the Seeming had said, but I had known more or less what to expect when I found myself in Hades' domain last fall. If I walked through that doorway, I'd have no knowledge to protect me. It would be like being blind. For a moment, I lingered in the dark, staring at the glowing doorway. I gripped the sphere tighter and made my choice.

"'Unto the breach,'" I quoted with a sigh, as I stepped into the light.

The air changed as I walked forward: the cold clamminess of the graveyard and the tunnel were replaced by warmth. If I didn't know better, I would have thought I was stepping into the most perfect springtime ever.

I began to feel too warm in my coat and scarf, and I pulled them off absently, stuffing the bulky fabric into my bag. The tunnel wasn't sloping down anymore; it tilted gently up, toward the surface. Suddenly feeling claustrophobic, I hurried forward. A pink glow became visible far up the tunnel, and it grew as I rushed toward it.

21

Without warning, the tunnel dropped away and I burst into sunlight. I plunged forward, rolling head over heels. My fall knocked the wind out of me, and I came to rest face down in a soft patch of moss. Taking a deep breath, I staggered to my feet and looked around. Soft, rolling hills covered with clover were set against the purple cliffs of far distant mountains, making the place look like a painting. It was beautiful, and nothing like the dark tomb I'd just emerged from. I breathed deeply and was surprised at the rich, sweet scent that filled the air. It was like I had wandered into fairyland.

"Don't think you haven't."

The voice came from behind me, where the tunnel should have been, but when I turned, I saw a wide tree stump instead. Sitting on it, with his legs crossed, was the most gorgeous guy I'd ever seen. His skin reminded me of a triple latte, and his curly black hair hung charmingly over his eyes. And his eyes! I couldn't pinpoint the color, but his eyes were some perfect blend of grass and ocean waves. Nervously, I pushed my hair out of my own eyes and stared at him. He smirked at me and winked.

"Another live one! This is certainly turning into an interesting morning!"

I frowned at his words. "Morning? But it's not morning." I thought for a moment, calculating how long I'd been in the tunnel. "It can't be after ten o'clock at night!"

He grinned. His teeth actually sparkled. "Suit yourself. But here, it's morning. Can't you feel the sunrise powers?"

I paused, reaching out my hands and sensing the air around me. He was right: it felt like dawn. "But that's impossible!"

"This is Annwn. Nothing is impossible."

I looked around again. If this were an Underworld, it was nothing like I'd been expecting. "You said 'another live one.' Will you tell me what you meant?" Maybe he'd seen Izzy! If she were here, I knew I'd need help finding her; the verdant field around me was beautiful, but other than the mountains in the distance and the stump the guy was sitting on, there were no landmarks in sight.

"Maybe I'll tell you. But nothing is ever free, especially not information."

I glanced at him warily, and his teeth flashed. "What do you want?"

"Just a dance. With you." His voice was like honey, and I felt my body beginning to sway in anticipation.

He laughed at my startled expression. "Be careful, Darlena, you'll catch flies that way!"

I shut my mouth quickly and looked harder at him. "How did you know my name?"

"You told me when we met."

Confused, I thought back. "No, I didn't. I just met you." My head started to throb again, and I raised my hand to cover my eyes. The sunlight was so bright!

He slapped his chest with one hand like he'd been shot. "How can you say that? Have you honestly forgotten me?"

My mind was fuzzy from the heat and the wonderful perfume in the air, but I knew that I'd never met him before. I would have remembered someone that gorgeous. "I'm sorry, but I think you're trying to trick me."

He snarled and I backed up a step, wary.

"I hate when Witches wander through! You're no fun."

He shimmered, and suddenly the hunk was replaced with a tiny, mean-looking man. Even standing on his stump, he didn't clear my waist.

"What are you?" I blurted.

His once beautiful voice turned raspy. "I am Fey. You knew I was tricking you, so now I have to answer three questions truthfully. Well, two questions, now. That was one."

I glared at him. "That's not fair."

He shrugged. "Magic never is."

I thought for a moment. "Okay. My second question: how do I find my friend?"

He scrunched up his face. "Walk until the mountains disappear. Then you'll be a few steps away."

"That doesn't even mean anything!" Angry, I flexed my fingers. Maybe a zap of Red magic would make the creature behave.

Screeching, he leaped off his step. "Didn't anyone tell you the rules? You can't use magic in Annwn."

"Why not?"

His eyes glistened wickedly. "Because Annwn has its own magic. And that was your third question."

With a sound like a suction cup being ripped off a window, he vanished, and I snarled in exasperation.

"I hate fairies!" I screamed at the vacant stump.

"Just because you hate us, doesn't mean we like you more!" a chorus of voices taunted.

I spun around, but couldn't see anyone. The disembodied voices giggled. It was like wandering through a nightmarish Munchkinland.

"Are you going to help me?" I called to the empty field.

More giggling.

"Fine." I pulled out my athame. Even if I couldn't use magic here, it wouldn't hurt to appear on my guard. There was a collective gasp in the air, followed by the sound of a million suction cups being pulled off a window at once.

After a moment of stillness, I called out, "Are you still there?"

There was silence. The fairies were gone.

Nervously, I looked at the blade in my hand. It glinted dully in the bright sunlight, and if I looked at it carefully, I could see a faint glow edging the knife. I moved it in the air, and the color around me faded for a minute. Whatever had just happened, it was clear that my athame held some power here in Annwn. I glanced around uncertainly, but I kept the unsheathed knife in my hand. Looking at the mountains in the distance, I started to walk.

The air stayed sweet-smelling and hot, and it was easy to forget that I'd left behind a bitterly cold winter. As I walked, I shed my sweater, balling it up in my bag with my coat and scarf. I looked down at my jeans, wishing I could transform them into shorts, but the creepy Fey man had said magic wouldn't work here. I rolled up the cuffs, though, and kept moving.

I must have been walking for almost an hour, but the mountains hadn't shifted at all. Not only were they still visible, but they didn't appear to have gotten any closer. It was hot and sticky, and I realized I was thirsty. I desperately wanted a drink, but of course I hadn't packed any water in my bag. Just then, I came up on the edge of a burbling stream.

It startled me; it was as if the water had appeared in response to my thoughts. I knelt eagerly to scoop up a handful of water, but something stopped me. Maybe it was a flash of intuition, or maybe I had remembered something I'd learned in school about the Fey, but I paused. Sitting back, I looked hard at the shimmering surface. I could almost see smoke rising off the water, and I shivered.

I wasn't thinking clearly. Just because I didn't know anything about Annwn didn't mean I didn't know anything about magic. I'd been so cautious about eating in the Underworld before until Hades promised me he meant me no harm. Why wasn't I being as cautious now?

Fishing through my bag, I pulled out the pill container of herbs. Thinking for a moment, I pulled out a peppermint leaf and a dried chrysanthemum flower. Mom had said something about that combination of plants being good for breaking enchantments, and I hoped they would keep me safe. Cupping my hands again, I reached into the stream, letting the water run over the herbs in my palm. After a few seconds, I lifted my hands to my face to drink.

The water was cool and crisp, and it didn't taste like anything except water. I hesitated a moment, waiting for something to happen, but when nothing did, I took another drink, filtering the water over the herbs in my hands before sipping it. After three long gulps, I felt refreshed and less bitchy. Standing up, I picked up my bag and continued walking toward the mountains.

When I had jumped from rock to rock across the stream, I looked up to find that the mountains were gone. I stumbled and almost slipped, but I steadied myself and looked around again. There were no mountains in sight. There was also no sign of Izzy.

I turned in a slow circle. "All right, what do I do now?" I asked the empty air.

A silky voice came from behind me. "If you sheathe that blade, I will tell you."

I whirled around to see a young woman dangling her feet in the stream.

"Why do I have to put this down?" I gestured with the knife and she flinched.

"Iron is too firm, too grounded for Annwn. The Fey cannot stand this metal."

That was good to know. I looked at her carefully, studying her beautiful, delicate features. "Are you another fairy?"

"Put the knife away and we can speak more freely."

I wondered if it might be a trick, but since I'd never intended to use the athame as a weapon anyway, I didn't see the harm in doing as she asked. Once the blade was sheathed, the young woman shimmered for a moment. Her image settled into place again, but she was more defined. Her black hair was shiny, and the gauzy blue dress that hung on her body seemed more solid somehow.

Standing warily a few feet away, I asked again, "So what do I do now?"

She shook her hair, sending droplets of water across the stream. "That is not the right question. The question is, what do you want?"

"What do you mean? I came here to find Izzy."

The fairy looked sad. "What if you knew that your friend was beyond your reach?"

I sucked in my breath. "Is she?"

With a shrug, the fairy studied my face. "What if she were?"

I thought for a moment, sorting through my jumbled thoughts. "Then I guess I need to find Marcus. He might be able to help."

The fairy looked at me sideways. "But is this what you truly want? To help the one who threatens your power?"

"How do you know any of this?"

She laughed, a tinkling sound like an antique music box. "What I know does not matter. What you want is all that is important."

I gave her a hard look. "I want to help my friend. And I want to stop Hecate from destroying the world."

The stream grew turbulent, and the sun dimmed. When I looked up, I saw threatening clouds blotting out the blue sky.

"You must take care with your words, Darlena. What mortal has the right to question the gods?"

I was so shocked by her words that I barely registered the fact that this fairy knew my name, too. "You can't possibly want the world to end, can you?"

Combing her hair with her fingers, the fairy stared off into space. "Once, my people walked above ground. We were driven beneath the earth by your kin, by the mortals who have since destroyed the world they took. So you are wrong," she stared hard at me and I backed up a step, "to assume that the Fey would not wish to see mortals fall."

Nervously, I looked around, but we were still alone. "Then why did you offer to help me?"

She smiled. Her teeth were wickedly sharp. "I never said I would help you. I said I would tell you what to do now."

The fairy didn't move, but I held up my athame, still in its sheath. She winced slightly.

I forced my voice to sound strong, but I was frightened. "Tell me how to get out of here, and then leave me in peace."

"Look behind you for a count of one hundred. Then you will see the way."

Skeptical, I glanced over my right shoulder. "How can I trust you enough to turn my back?"

She bared her teeth. "You can't."

Right. I didn't trust the creature, but I didn't have any other choice. Taking a deep breath, I turned my head and began to count slowly. My voice shook, and when I reached "ten" I unsheathed the knife. This time, the sucking sound was loud and directly behind me, and I had to fight the urge to turn and look for the river fairy. She'd gotten awfully close to me while I was counting, but I thought that with the knife I should be safe.

I kept counting, even though the fairy was gone. I didn't want to spoil whatever spell she'd started, especially if it was my one chance to get out of here. When I reached ninety-nine, the air around me shimmered like campfire smoke, and when I said, "One hundred," there was a low chime like a distant church bell. Slowly, I turned around.

Where the stream had stood was a stone gate. Unlike the entrance to Annwn, this was freestanding in the field. It had a square lintel, and the two columns supporting it were carved to resemble flames.

Vaguely, I remembered that Izzy's Seeming had said something about the Otherworlds being connected, and I had a feeling this gate would transport me out of Annwn. Where it would take me, however, was a mystery. Holding my athame in my hand, I stepped toward the gate. I closed my eyes and whispered a prayer to Persephone that this gate would serve me better than the last one.

22

The gate took me to a dark, subterranean chamber. I could still see the fairy hills of Annwn behind me through the gate, but the image was fuzzy, as if I were looking at an unfinished painting. When I turned around, darkness stretched ahead of me. I pulled out the crystal sphere once more and let my eyes get accustomed to the dim glow before I started to walk into the darkness. The sound of dripping water echoed off the rocks around me, and my footsteps sounded loud in the void. Gradually, I became aware of a red flash in the distance, and I sped up.

The dark chamber gave way to a huge cavern., and everything in the cavern was bathed in red light. I blinked for a moment, and then I realized that my eyes weren't playing tricks on me. My senses tingled, and I groped blindly for Red magic, but it was out of reach. I could feel it, but it was like trying to catch a fish: it kept slipping out of my grasp. Panicked, I unsheathed my knife and took a deep breath, trying to calm down. I hadn't been able to use magic in Annwn, but I hadn't felt as threatened there as I did now, even with the crazy Fey.

The cavern pulsed with power, and what I saw almost made me turn and run back the way I had come. In the center of the cave, Marcus was perched on a stalagmite. The tip of the rock dug into his lower back, and his spine curved like a beach ball. He was bound and gagged, and his head lolled dangerously to one side. I moved quietly across the vast cavern, my eyes darting around to see if this was a trap. I couldn't see anyone besides Marcus, but I was wary.

For a moment, I stood beneath him, wondering what to do. Marcus was unconscious, his breathing low and heavy. I reached up to try and pull him down, but my fingertips barely grazed the edge of his body. The soft sound of water filled the cavern, and I gritted my teeth, trying to focus.

I noticed a large rock sitting near the stalagmite. I hopped up on it and leaned forward. Grabbing hold of Marcus's feet, I tugged gently. I thought I could move him an inch at a time, slowly. Instead, I was crushed under his sudden weight as his body flew off the tip of the stone. Electricity flowed through me, zapping my skin everywhere Marcus's body touched me. I struggled to get out from under him, but the tingling sensation took a minute to fade. Gingerly, I poked his stomach with my finger.

He groaned, but didn't open his eyes. I leaned forward.

"Marcus," I hissed in his ear, "wake up!"

"Izzy?" he mumbled, his eyes still closed.

"No. Darlena."

He cracked his eyes and glared at me. "Why aren't you dead?"

Rattled, I stared at him. "What do you mean?"

"She said you would be dead if you entered. That, or you'd be too much of a coward, and that you'd go home in defeat."

His words made no sense. "Who said?" Quickly, I untied the ropes that bound his wrists.

"Cerridwen."

I felt a chill run down my arms at the mention of his patron. "She did this to you?"

He struggled to sit up. "Remove the desire, and the problem will disappear. You wanted me. We thought if I were gone, you'd go."

"We." My voice was flat. "You've been working against me all along."

He hesitated. "At first, yes."

"This is how she rewards good behavior?" I gestured to the rock and snorted. "I'm glad she's not my patron!"

Marcus glared at me. "She has every right to punish my disobedience however she chooses." He rubbed his wrists, trying to get his circulation back, and I watched him intently.

"How did you disobey her?"

He didn't look at me. "It doesn't matter now. You're here, and I owe you. Although I'm not sure how you even got here."

"What do you mean?"

"You shouldn't be able to move through the Otherworld. You haven't been trained."

Ignoring him, I gestured to the rock. "What else was she going to do to you?"

He grimaced. "I don't want to talk about it."

"Were you going to help me?"

He looked away, but his silence spoke volumes.

"Well, now you can. I'm trying to find Izzy."

His eyes flashed. "What happened to my sister?"

I sat back on my heels. "I don't know. But we'll find her."

He shook his head, mumbling something I couldn't make out. "What?"

His eyes opened and met my gaze. "I said if she's hurt, you're dead."

"You already said that. Back in Edinburgh." I used my athame to cut the bonds around his ankles. "In fact, you said it more convincingly the first time."

Marcus flexed his muscles and grunted. "We better move."

"Can you even stand up?"

He wobbled a bit, but he stood in one try. "We have to leave. Now."

I nodded and turned toward the tunnel, but I froze. Passageways led off in every direction like the spokes of a wheel, and they all looked exactly the same. Marcus saw my expression and turned pale.

"You don't know the way out, do you?"

"Don't get arrogant with me! I rescued you, didn't I?"

He snorted. "Some rescue. Did you have a plan at all, or are you just winging it?"

I studied the tunnels, trying to spot something that would guide us. "Stop complaining. We have to get out of here. Then you can go back to hating me."

Finally, he shrugged. "Then let's get out of here."

"Do you have any suggestions?"

He stared at the tunnels. "This is the Otherworld, right?"

I nodded.

He closed his eyes and creased his brow in concentration. "I think I remember learning something about the different worlds. How they're layered."

"What, like a cake?"

He chuckled. "Sort of. They all exist simultaneously, and it should be possible to travel from one directly to another."

I didn't want to tell him I'd already done that. I balked at the idea of going back to Annwn. "How is going to another Underworld going to help us?"

He lifted his eyebrow. "You did an awful lot of bragging about the Greek Underworld."

Realization dawned on me. "You think Hades would help us?"

"He's helped you before, right?"

I nodded slowly, thinking about it. "So we have to get from here to the Greek Underworld." *How in the world am I supposed to do that?*

Marcus shrugged. "Unless you have another suggestion."

I shook my head and looked around for another gate. *Idiot.* Of course it wouldn't be that easy. With a sigh, I took out the crystal sphere that Hades had given me. Marcus looked at it and took a step backward. He licked his lips nervously.

"What?" I looked from him to the sphere. "It's just a rock."

"It's powerful. Can't you feel it?"

I shook my head, confused. "What do I do now?" I asked, hating the helpless tone in my voice.

"I don't know. Maybe if we both focus on Hades?" He glanced at me curiously. "What's it like there?"

"It's underground, like this, but not warm. There are gems in the walls, raw, uncut gemstones, and precious metal like graffiti on every surface. And there's a river." I spoke slowly, my voice dropping into the low tones of trance. I was barely aware when Marcus reached out his hand and covered the crystal with it. The cavern spun, and we were plunged into blackness.

***

I blinked, confused. We were in a dark cave with a sluggish river, but I knew right away this wasn't the Greek Underworld.

Marcus looked around expectantly. "Shouldn't that three-headed dog be around here somewhere?"

A voice laughed. "Not here, boy."

We turned to face a beautiful woman leaning beside a wooden door.

Marcus looked at me. "That's Persephone?" he whispered.

I shook my head, and fear began to spread over his face.

"Where are we?"

The woman snorted, not looking at us. "You could ask that of me, boy. The girl does not know. It would be wise to be gracious toward your host."

His Adam's apple bobbed as he swallowed. "I'm sorry; I didn't mean to be rude. Where are we?"

"You are in my realm. It and I share a name. Can you guess that name?"

I stared at the woman. Was this another fairy playing a trick on us?

She snarled, reading my mind. "Do not compare me to those flimsy folk. My people are much stronger, much more powerful, than a fairy could ever hope to be."

Okay, not a fairy. Probably a goddess, then; Aphrodite had been able to read my mind, and it seemed like Hecate could, too. I stared at the woman intently. There was something familiar about her, but I couldn't put my finger on it.

"Who are your people, Lady?" Marcus asked respectfully.

The woman cackled. "Ask the girl. She knows."

Marcus glanced at me, his eyes clouded. "What is she talking about?"

"I have no idea! I thought we were going to Hades, but this isn't right."

"This isn't right," she mocked. "How right you are, girl! It isn't right that I am disrespected at my own gate. You dare to travel in my realm, and yet you refuse to answer my question?" She swelled in size, towering over us, and for the first time she looked straight at me. I shuddered. Half of her face was the beautiful face we'd seen, but the other half was carved with age like a ragged crone. Her fiery eyes blazed at me, and I felt my memory stir.

"Have I met your family?" I asked cautiously.

"My father offered you a bargain. A bargain which you refused. I do not like it when my family is insulted." Her eyes burned into mine, and I took a step back, feeling cold.

"He didn't mention your name."

She laughed wildly, still looming before us. "Why should he? All men know my name. I am Hel."

"Hell indeed," Marcus muttered to me, pulling me back another step. "Who's her father?"

I looked at him, frightened, and whispered, "Loki."

23

Hel laughed and both sides of her face contorted. "That's right, boy; my father is the master of chaos. And this girl dared to spurn his offer of friendship."

My stomach twitched in fear, but I couldn't help myself. "He didn't offer me friendship. He offered a bargain, like you said."

The goddess stepped closer to me. I couldn't take my eyes off her wrinkled skin.

"Give me one reason why I should not destroy you this moment?" she hissed.

Marcus jerked my arm, pulling me back. "We don't mean you any harm!"

At the same moment, I said, "Because I want to take your father up on his offer."

Marcus stared at me and Hel laughed, but her eyes looked

uncertain. "A fine lie, girl, but not good enough."

"Do you know the bargain we discussed?" I asked cautiously.

She bared her teeth. Half were perfect pearls, and half were rotting in her mouth. I swallowed back bile and forced myself to look at her.

"I know that he was most disappointed," she hissed, "when you turned him down."

"He didn't say I had a time limit. I've been thinking about it."

She stared at me. "And what of the boy?" She jerked a finger toward Marcus.

I took a deep breath. "He's my friend. I need his help to do what your father asked."

Thankfully, Marcus didn't speak. He turned away, crossing his arms, and studied the wooden door. His shoulders were tense, and I knew he was going to question me later, but at least he was going along with it for now.

The goddess glared at me. "If you are tricking me, Witch girl, you will not see the light of day again."

"I'm not. I need to speak with your father."

Hel gestured away from the door, into the darkness of the cavern. "You will find him there. The bowl is about to be emptied. You might want to hurry, unless you want to be caught in a cave-in."

With those words, she vanished, leaving a swirl of black smoke in the air.

I started to walk in the direction the goddess indicated without looking at Marcus. "Are you coming?"

Marcus's words were clipped. "What bargain?"

I turned, meeting Marcus's eye. "What do you mean?"

His fist smashed into the stone and I jumped, startled. He hit the wall again. "Don't screw with me, Darlena. What bargain are you going to make with Loki, and why am I involved?"

I looked down at my hands and whispered, "He said he can help me bind Hecate." Thinking quickly, I added, "Maybe he would even help us find Izzy."

"And in exchange?"

"Nothing major." I started walking again, and Marcus followed after a second.

"If you lie to me, I won't help you."

"What if you don't like the truth?"

"I'll decide for myself once I hear it." He crossed his arms and glared at me.

I tipped my chin up and faced him. "He wants me to free him." We had come into the cavern I remembered from my dreams. The god was still bound, and the same woman stood over his face holding the bowl. I thought about what Hel had said about the bowl being emptied, and hurried forward. I didn't want to be underground when Loki started thrashing around.

"I knew you'd come." Loki's smile was twisted, but I forced myself to smile back.

"Will you still help me?" I tried to keep the eagerness out of my voice, but Loki's eyes glinted as if he'd won.

"You remember the price?" he rasped.

I glanced at Marcus, who shook his head slightly. "Yes, I do."

"And you are willing?" He tried to sit up, but his chains prevented it. They rattled mournfully as he moved, and I looked at his bonds for a minute before I answered. They were strong enough to hold Loki; I had to believe they'd trap the Queen, too.

I took a gulp of air. "Yes. To stop Hecate, yes."

He cackled. "Very good. When I am free, I will help you." He swiveled his head around and looked at Marcus. "And with your help added to the pot, boy, I'll even free your sister."

I stared at him in surprise. I had planned to ask for his help, but I hadn't got around to it yet. Loki chuckled sharply. I glanced at Marcus, but his face was expressionless.

"Husband," the woman at his side spoke urgently, "I must empty the bowl."

Loki's eyes locked with mine. "See that you don't fail." His wife moved the bowl, and a drop of venom plunged into his eyes.

I turned away just as he started to scream. The rock walls shivered and the ground rolled under my feet. Running, I grabbed Marcus, ignoring the electricity that shot through my hand.

"What's happening?" Marcus yelled, following me.

The tunnel grew unbearably hot, and I ran faster. "We have to get out of here!"

Jets of steam pressed through the rock around me, and with sick certainty, I suddenly knew where we were. I skidded to a halt and Marcus crashed into me.

"What the hell is going on?"

I looked at him, petrified. "I think we're inside a volcano."

Steam shot past me, punctuating my words.

"What?" Marcus stared at me in disbelief.

"'When Loki shakes, the earth quakes!'" I quoted something I'd read on the Internet. "We're so screwed."

The tunnel filled with a roaring sound. "We have to do something!" Marcus was yelling, but I could barely hear him over the sounds of the mountain.

"What?"

"Magic!" He extended his hand to me.

I shook my head, frustrated. "It won't work!"

"Different Underworld, different rules. We have to try."

The heat was overwhelming. At any moment, the mountain would erupt. "Okay!" I took his hand and felt Red magic coursing into me. Sparks covered our arms, and my skin glowed.

"Now!" he screamed, raising my arm into the air. With a blast, we released magic into the ceiling above us. The rock crumbled, blown away, and in the hole above us I thought I could see daylight. The cavern around us was still rumbling dangerously, and I turned to Marcus.

"Boost me up."

He slipped his hands under my raised foot, and I practically flew into the air. I grabbed at the rock and scrabbled toward the opening. Marcus pulled himself up after me, grunting with effort.

Below us, the mountain groaned and rumbled. With a burst of adrenaline, I heaved myself up and landed face down on a sheet of ice. Marcus panted beside me.

"Come on!" I staggered to my feet and attempted to run down the slope of the mountain. Marcus crawled behind me, but an explosion jolted him to his feet. I turned to look back and I froze.

The mountain was erupting behind us. Flames shot up through the ice, spewing rock and molten lava at least a hundred feet into the air. I watched the destructive force of the volcano, feeling Red magic tingle in my fingertips. I wasn't aware of the sparks covering my skin, but my hands started to lift of their own volition. Magic surged through me as I raised my arms toward the mountain. I could taste the chaos; it was within my reach!

Marcus grabbed my arm and pulled hard. "We have to move!" he shouted, dragging me with him down the face of the mountain.

I dropped my hands, instantly losing the connection to Red magic, and ran. I didn't know what I'd almost done, and I didn't want to stick around and find out. Panting, I followed him as we slipped and slid down the icy mountain.

Smoke filled the air, and flaky pieces of ash rained down on us. Even as we skidded on the ice, the air around us felt thick and warm. It was like a sauna. I didn't look back again at the geyser of flames, but I knew the mountain was still spewing lava. When we reached the bottom of the cliff, I crumpled to the ground in a dead faint. The last thing I saw as I fell over was a sharp black rock rushing up to meet me.

24

Fuzzy memories of Annwn, Hel, and Loki began to dance through my mind, and I turned to the side, retching. When my stomach was empty, I wiped my mouth and looked around.

Marcus was sitting beside me, his head in his hands. He didn't look up, even when I nudged him with my toe. Shapes swam in front of me, and I closed my eyes for a moment. When I opened them, it was almost too dark to see.

"What happened?"

Marcus glanced up, and I was startled to see that his eyes were swollen. It looked as if he'd been crying.

I drew a deep breath and looked around. In the inky darkness, I could barely make out the towering shapes of trees. Confused, I turned my head. There was no sign of the mountain.

"Marcus," I fought to keep the panic out of my voice, "where are we?"

He shrugged. "I had to do something. We were drawing a crowd at the volcano."

I looked at him, frightened. "Where did you take us?"

He looked up at the trees again. "The Black Forest."

"What?" I sprang to my feet. Well, I tried to: I almost toppled over, but I managed to stand there, swaying, glaring down at Marcus.

He rose swiftly, his dark eyes piercing. "That volcano wasn't natural. It wasn't safe. And when you passed out, I didn't know what to do."

"And the first thing you thought of was taking us to rural Germany?" I clenched my fists, fighting back another wave of nausea. A thought occurred to me, and I stopped shouting. "How did you even get us here?"

He glared at me, his lips pressed into a thin line. "Magic. How else would I have done it?" he snarled.

Confused, I wavered on my feet. "Even some of the gods I've met can't transport a human through time and space like that." I looked at him out of the corner of my eye. "What spell did you use?" Clearly, Marcus was way more powerful than I'd realized. I wondered if freeing him from the cavern had been such a good idea.

His eyes hardened. "Now is not the time for a lesson." He strode through the trees.

"Are you really that powerful?" I rushed to keep up, trying hard not to focus on the way the ground still seemed to be swirling.

"No!" He whirled around so fast, I almost bumped into him. "If I were powerful at all," he rasped, "none of this would have happened. Izzy wouldn't be gone, and I wouldn't be stuck traipsing around the woods with a Witch like you!" His face was red, and a vein in his forehead pulsed.

"It's not my fault Izzy disappeared." I glanced around the trees nervously. Something moved out of the corner of my eye. I caught a flicker of wings, and I looked around. I spotted an owl and froze.

Marcus didn't see the bird behind him. "I think it is! If you hadn't come around, talking about fighting Hecate—"

I pushed him to the ground with a thud just as a tangle of feathers passed overhead. The owl squawked indignantly and flexed its claws, preparing to dive again. "Don't draw her attention!" I stood slowly, never breaking eye contact with the bird. It was like watching Hecate: the same predatory, yellow eyes. The bird froze, watching me as I whispered a spell to bind it in place. The eyes followed me with malice as the body hung awkwardly, poised for flight but not moving.

I kept my gaze on the bird. "We have to get away from that thing. It's one of her spies, and I can't do much more than bind it."

Marcus touched my shoulder. "How long will the spell hold?"

"As long as I don't break eye contact with it." I stepped backward cautiously.

Suddenly, Marcus was in front of me. "You can't walk backward in this forest," he said as he lifted me easily over his shoulder.

Electricity surged through my stomach where I was thrown over his shoulder, but I was getting used to the strange sensation whenever I touched him. Still, I didn't want to be airborne. I fought him for a moment, but he had a point. This way, I could look at the bird and continue to travel away from it. "Fine. Just be fast."

The minute the words left my mouth, he began to run. Branches whipped my eyes, but I glared at the bird without blinking. My eyes started to water, and just when I was sure I wouldn't be able to maintain the spell much longer, there was a blinding flash, and then blackness descended around us.

At first I thought I'd passed out again, but I could hear Marcus panting beneath me. I blinked once before I realized that my eyes were open. The forest was enveloped in blackness darker than night.

"What was that?" I called over my shoulder.

"Stop squirming!" Marcus tightened his grip on my torso, and I drew in my breath quickly.

I kicked my legs, and he grunted, but he kept running and he maintained his grip on me.

"I can't see the owl. You have to put me down!"

Unceremoniously, he dropped me like a sack of potting soil. I landed on my ankle, wrenching it painfully.

"You said to put you down, m'lady." Marcus smirked as I rubbed my foot.

I ignored him, looking around. My eyes hadn't grown any more accustomed to the blackness: I might as well have been asleep for all I could see. I could barely see Marcus; he cast an eerie red glow in the gloom.

"Do you know where we are?" He looked around, sniffing the air like a dog. Finally, he nodded.

"I know my territory. Don't you know yours, Witch?"

I shook my head. "Why is it so dark?" When he didn't answer, I pressed on. "I don't know if I would recognize any of my territory in this darkness, but we aren't in my land, we're in yours. So you better figure something out."

He moved so quickly I didn't realize it until he was right in front of me. If I'd leaned forward just a fraction of an inch, my nose would have brushed his throat. I swallowed nervously and looked up at him.

"I could just kill you and be done with all this." His voice was low, and I forced myself not to shrink from his threat.

"What would that solve?"

He laughed coldly. "Your corpse might buy me my sister."

I swallowed. "I want to help you find her."

"But this might be easier."

I drew Red magic into my body and pushed him forward. He flung across the clearing and smacked into a tree, his red glow barely visible in the gloom. Before I could bind him with a spell, I found myself suddenly whisked into the air.

I dangled there like the Hanged Man in Rochelle's old tarot deck, suspended above the earth in terror. When I thrashed and tried to draw on my magic, I dropped dangerously toward the ground. Forcing myself to breathe, I grew still.

Marcus walked under me and looked up into my face. "You can't fight me, Darlena. Give up. It'll be easier."

With a flick of his wrist, my invisible bonds snapped and I plunged toward him. My scream stuck in my throat and turned into a sob when I stopped moving, my face inches from the rough ground.

"Stop! Please. What do you want me to do?" I gasped, hating myself for begging but too afraid to do anything else.

I fell the last few inches to the ground and sprawled on my back. Gradually, the forest around me lightened until I could once again see the tops of the trees.

"Save my sister."

I scrambled to my feet. "I'm trying! I don't know where to look."

He considered me for a moment. "You aren't really trying."

We glared at each other, unmoving.

Finally, I opened my hands, palm up, and reached toward him.

"Couldn't we help each other?"

Marcus considered. "I don't know how much you can help me. You've proved you're no match for my magic."

"Without me, you'd still be tied up on a boulder!"

He shrugged, but I saw a flicker of something in his eyes, and I pressed my advantage. "We can do this together. You heard Loki: he'll give us both what we want."

Marcus closed his eyes. "All right," he spoke quietly. "I will help you until I have what I want." He opened his eyes and glared at me. "Only until I have my sister back."

"Swear it." He might try to kill me as soon as we found Izzy, but I hoped it wouldn't come to that. Maybe Izzy could talk him out of it. I wasn't sure what I'd done that had pissed him off so much, but Marcus wasn't someone I wanted as an enemy. I didn't want to be his friend, either, but I didn't know what else to do.

Without hesitation, he started speaking calmly, weaving a binding spell. He reached out and clasped my hands, and the spell snaked around our wrists like smoke. Red sparks surged up my arm, and his hand let off a red glow. When Marcus had stopped, I finished the spell, adding to our agreement that he would help me bind Hecate, regardless of the wishes of his patron. He raised an eyebrow at that, but nodded, and the spell sank into our hands with a sigh. For a minute, my hand felt like dead weight, and then a crackle of energy rippled through me.

I started to let go, but Marcus tightened his grip and leaned forward. He brushed my left cheek with his lips, then my right. Shivers raced down my spine at his touch, and I started to pull away.

"This is how I was taught to seal binding spells." His voice was close to my ear, and it tickled.

Hesitantly, I kissed each of his cheeks, and we squeezed our hands tighter. I didn't meet his eyes, trying to hide my confusion over my reaction to being so close to him.

"So mote it be." We spoke the final words in unison, and our hands glowed bright red for an instant before they looked normal again. I flexed my fingers, feeling the spell tingle as it settled into my being. Like it or not, I now owed Marcus loyalty, and he owed me the same. Glancing at the hard-faced Witch beside me, I remembered that Justin and Mom had both warned me about making bargains. I looked away, not ready to think about either of them right now, especially Justin. For some reason, he was the furthest thing from my mind.

25

I looked around at the looming trees and shuddered. "Tell me why you whisked us here, of all places?"

He started to speak, and then paused. His brow furrowed as he thought about my question. "I'm not sure, actually. All I could think of was getting away from the eruption, and as far from Hel as we could possibly get."

Goosebumps prickled my skin, and I rubbed my arms quickly. "But wasn't Germany one of the places invaded by the Vikings?" If it was, Hel could still reach us. And so could Loki.

"I didn't think of that. I told you, I didn't pick the place. I just willed us somewhere as far away from immediate harm as I could."

"Fair enough." I paused, looking at the pine needles that covered the ground in irregular patterns. I wondered if I could get him to teach me that traveling spell. Maybe he'd be more willing to now that we were partners. "Thank you for taking me with you."

He snorted. "You're dangerous, Darlena. I'd rather have you where I can watch you. Besides," he added, "I think you know where Izzy is."

"I told you, I have no idea. I followed something that looked like her into Annwn, but then she was gone."

He frowned. "That sounds like a Seeming."

I nodded. "But I haven't seen her—er, it—since."

"We will find her." His voice was firm, and I didn't argue.

Instead, I looked around the forest. Even though it was hard to tell, the woods seemed to be getting darker as we spoke. "Shouldn't we find a place to sleep? We can discuss this more once we're settled."

He nodded. "If we're going to sleep, we'll need shelter."

Before I could ask what he had in mind, Marcus turned away from me and raised his arms. Blistering heat sprang up behind me, and I spun around. The trees surrounding us were engulfed in flames. Before I could act, Marcus lowered his arms and the flames licked down, turning into embers. In an instant, they were extinguished.

"What did you do?" Aghast, I stared at the charred trees.

"What needed to be done. I can't make something out of nothing. This will shelter us."

I gestured at the burned patch of forest. "How?"

He smiled sharply. "Easy. Watch and learn, Witch."

With a few deft flicks of his hands, Marcus tipped the charred trees to the ground. Too quickly for me to follow his motions, he wove a complicated spell, and the next thing I knew, a small lean-to stood before me, made out of blackened wood.

"Couldn't you have just chopped the trees down? Why did you have to use fire?" I was upset thinking about how casually he had almost destroyed this old forest. My parents would have been mortified by such careless Witchcraft.

"Fire is the most powerful tool for any Red Witch, something you'd know if you didn't insist on denying who you are." I opened my mouth to argue, but he plowed on. "Besides, I did the forest a favor. The new growth that springs up after any forest fire is healthier than those old trees have been in a long time. Fire is a way to cleanse and bring renewal."

I thought about that, and I nodded grudgingly. "I still don't think you needed to be so extreme."

He laughed and headed toward the structure. "I provided shelter. Shall you provide the food, partner?"

Sitting cross-legged on the cold ground, I dug in my bag, which had mercifully made the journey from Scotland with me. I probably had a few granola bars left. My fingers brushed against something cold and sharp, and pain shot through my hand. I yelped in surprise, jerking my arm back.

"What is it?" Marcus was on his feet instantly, his hands clenched in a defensive pose.

Cautiously, I pulled a shard of mirrored glass out of my bag and held it up.

He looked at my stricken expression, puzzled. "So what? You don't really believe that old tale that a broken mirror brings bad luck?"

I shook my head. "No. But that was a mirror from a goddess. Breaking it can't be a good sign."

Marcus reached out, and I placed the fragment of Aphrodite's mirror in his hands. He turned it over slowly, examining it from every angle. "Who gave this to you?"

"Aphrodite. When I first chose her as my patron."

His eyes stayed on the glass. "And when you changed your mind?"

"She said I could keep it. I've never really used it. I'm sure it's magic, but there wasn't time to find out what it does."

"And now it's broken." His voice was quiet.

I nodded. "I wonder what it means."

"One thing is pretty clear," he said, looking at me with a stern expression, "you can't waste the gifts of the gods again. You should never carry a magical tool without understanding how to use it."

I thought of the crystal Hades had given me, and my mother's athame. I must have glanced at the bag, because Marcus reached for it.

"What else do you have in here?"

I tugged the bag reflexively, jerking it out of his grip. His eyes turned hard.

"I want to make sure you don't blow me up without intending to."

Nettled, I clutched the bag tighter. "Don't worry. If I do anything to you, I'll mean it."

He glared at me for a moment before he chuckled. "Fair enough. But remember, we have a bargain."

I nodded. "I won't be the one to break it."

"Neither will I." His dark green eyes held mine, intense and powerful. I tried to keep his gaze, but I finally had to look away.

I fiddled with my bag, pulling out a granola bar and handing it to him. "I have other tools, but I know how to use them. The mirror was the only thing I never bothered with."

Instead of answering, Marcus reached into the cargo pocket on the side of his pants and pulled out a crooked twig a little shorter than my forearm. He held it out to me.

"It's my dedicancy gift. A birch wand."

I looked at it with interest, but I didn't touch it. I didn't want to give him another excuse for hating me.

He smiled slightly. "You can hold it if you like. You have my permission."

Gingerly, I took the wand from his fingers. It was bent near the tip, and the length of it was white and smooth with age. Energy rippled through the wand and into my hand, and for a moment, it was like I was still holding Marcus's hand. I shivered at the unexpected pulse of electricity. "I've never used a wand."

He looked surprised. "I thought all Witches did!"

I shook my head. "My school focused more on internal magic rather than using objects to manipulate energy."

He snorted. "That's a load of horse shit. You must have realized that a tool can make you more powerful." He reached for his wand, and I felt it grow hotter under my fingertips as he took it. When my hand was empty, I felt suddenly cold.

"But is it a good thing for Witches like us to be more powerful?"

Marcus put his wand away. "Why shouldn't we be strong? Did you ever think that's why Hecate is after you, because you're the weakest of the three of us?"

Eagerly, I leaned forward. "Do you know the third?"

He shook his head. "Not likely to, either. We each have our own realms to govern. Only a crazy person would go looking for another Red Witch." He smiled tightly at me.

"I'm crazy? Just because I don't want to fight Hecate alone?" My anger rose.

"Easy. We're partners, remember? Put it down."

I glared at him. "What are you talking about?"

He gestured slightly toward my hands. "You just grabbed a ball of energy. I don't want you to throw it at me."

I looked down, startled by the red sparks pulsing around my

fingertips. "I didn't mean to do that."

"You're quite the loose cannon, aren't you? No wonder the Queen wants to use you."

The red sparks dissipated, and I stared at him. "What's that supposed to mean?"

"If she is out to reshape the world, like you said, what could be better for her than an untrained Red Witch wreaking havoc in a third of the world?"

Confused, I shook my head. "But she's trying to kill me!"

Marcus looked skeptical. "Are you sure of that?"

The events of the past six months played through my mind, and I snorted. "If she isn't trying to kill me, she sure has a funny way of showing it."

He pressed on. "But think about it. A goddess like that should have no problem killing you. So why are you still alive?"

"Because the gods can't directly harm us," I argued. "That's why she sent my best friend against me!"

I couldn't read Marcus's expression. "I didn't know that. When?"

"Last fall." I looked down, fighting back an overwhelming urge to cry.

"What did you do?"

"What could I do? If she lived, she would have become the most destructive Witch since Caracella and his slaughter at Alexandria." My words felt heavy, and my heart clenched. I hated talking about Rochelle.

"So you killed her."

I nodded, unable to speak.

"Publicly?"

I glared at him. "I'm not that stupid! We had a fight at night, at the school. No one but my family knows."

"Interesting. So Hecate tried to have you killed once, and you're convinced she's still out to get you?"

I turned my back on him and lay down. I didn't want to have this conversation. I was afraid that if I kept talking about Rochelle, I might have a meltdown, and I didn't want Marcus to see that. "We should sleep. We need to figure out what to do, and I'm too tired to think."

Marcus was silent for a moment, and I concentrated on my breathing. When I had almost lulled myself to sleep, I heard his voice again.

"There is so much you still need to learn about our path."

26

The next morning, Marcus refused to move.

"We need time to regroup. And we're safe here."

I shook my head. "Did you forget that owl?"

"No, but has anything bothered us since then?"

"But it's only been a few hours!"

He shrugged, surveying the charred landscape he had created. "Still. I feel like this place is safe."

"And I'm just supposed to trust your feeling, is that it?" I asked sarcastically.

Marcus looked at me for a long moment. "Yes," he said simply.

I stared at him in disbelief. "But there's no reason I should trust you!"

He held up his hand, and I saw the remnants of the binding spell flicker for a moment in the early morning light. "No reason?"

I blew out a loud breath. "Fine. Fine, I have to trust you. You're right."

He looked self-satisfied for an instant before his face smoothed out.

I ignored his expression. "But I want to set the wards."

"We'll set them together."

By the time Marcus and I had circled our campsite three times for added strength, my head hurt and I didn't think I could stand much longer. When I sank to my knees, Marcus handed me my bag. Wordlessly, I grabbed a granola bar and devoured it. I offered one to Marcus, but he shook his head. While I ate, I looked around at the forest. If I tilted my head at just the right angle, I could make out the shimmering bubble that marked the protective wards we had cast that morning.

I looked at him sideways. "So why did you want to stay here?"

He thought for a minute before answering. "I said it last night. You have a lot to learn for a Red."

I fought back the urge to laugh at him. "Tell me something I don't know!"

"We're in this together, for now. I figure that if I don't want you to accidentally blow off my head, I should teach you some things. Besides," his face hardened, "whoever has my sister is going to be hard to beat. You need to be able to fight."

I stared at him for a moment. "I'm not sure I want to learn from you," I finally said.

He nodded. "I'm not sure I want you to, but it seems necessary. Right now, you're dangerous to be around."

"How did you learn to control your magic, anyway?"

He was silent for a moment. "I was pledged to the goddess I follow at a very young age."

"You were pledged before you were born."

His eyes burned with anger. "How did you find out about that?"

I fought the urge to shrink away from him, suddenly aware of how close his hard face was to mine. "The Coven that Dr. Farren is in."

"I should have known they'd get mixed up in this. Did they also tell you," he continued in a bitter voice, "that my mother was more to them than just a member of their little group?"

I shook my head. "It was clear they were worried about her, though."

He snorted. "Not worried enough, considering the group is run by her parents."

I thought back to the farmhouse in the countryside. "Frederick and Frances are your grandparents?"

His expression grew harsh. "Not that they ever acted like that. They let my mother do what she did, and they never moved to intercede. Twice! Seeing me bound wasn't enough; they let her do it to Izzy, too."

"Maybe they couldn't interfere."

"They should have! I don't care about any of the laws that govern Witchcraft. They were my family, and they abandoned me."

"How did they abandon you? I get that you're mad that they didn't stop your mom, but they're still really concerned about you and Izzy!"

Marcus laughed humorlessly. "Oh, they're concerned about Izzy, all right. But not about me. They let my mother bind me to a powerful goddess, making me a Red Witch against my will, and they never lifted a finger to help me."

I didn't know what to say. He went on, talking as if he'd forgotten I was there.

"Mother still went to the Coven meetings, even though they disproved of what she'd done with me. But they never allowed me to come. They never offered any help."

"Maybe they just didn't understand how to help a Red Witch.

There aren't many of us, you know."

He glared at my attempt at a joke. "I don't care if they understood or not. They left me to my patron for training." His eyes bored into me. "Do you have any idea what it's like to learn magic from a goddess who governs death and rebirth?"

I shuddered at his words, but then I stopped. Hadn't I done something similar when Persephone sent me to her husband? "I don't know," I began slowly. "I mean, I learned from Hades."

"Cerridwen and Hades are two very different figures. I would imagine he's a pretty mild, impartial man?"

I thought about the way his voice broke when he spoke of his wife. "In most matters," I said dryly.

Marcus nodded. "Cerridwen is anything but mild. The Celtic gods make the Greeks look playful and kind."

He was certainly right about that: Freya was nothing like her sister goddess of love. There was some harshness to her, and to each of the Northern gods I'd met, that didn't seem to be there with my former patron. Only Hecate seemed as terrifying as Loki, and for completely different reasons.

"How did she teach you?"

"My goddess believes in learning by example. And since she and I both deal with chaos, well, her best example was the battlefield."

I thought for a moment, struggling with my current events. "But there aren't any wars going on in lands that she would have access to."

"Not in our time, no."

His words made me go cold. "Are you saying that she trained you, what, out of time?"

He shook his head, his smile bitter. "Oh, no, we were very much a part of every time she selected." He shuddered. "I had seen more slaughter by the time I was ten than most veterans will ever live through."

"Why?" I hated to ask, but I couldn't fathom what would make his goddess subject him to such horrors.

"She wanted me to understand the power of Red magic. I saw it firsthand, thousands of times. Red Witches aren't indestructible, but we can destroy entire civilizations before anyone stops us."

We were silent for a moment. His words made me think of Hecate, and what I thought she might be planning. I shivered and wrapped my arms around me. Marcus's eyes gradually lost the haunted look, and he shook his head a few times before looking at me again.

"Well," he got to his feet, "enough of that. You need to learn how to use your power." He held out his hand to help me up.

I hesitated. Did I really want lessons from this man who'd been trained in such a brutal way? What if he wanted me to suffer through the things he had seen? *But we're partners now*, I told myself firmly. *He won't harm me.*

My mind whispered the word "yet" as I got to my feet to face the other Red Witch.

Marcus and I spent the rest of the morning drilling. He wanted me to create a blaze like he had the night before, but I refused.

"I think we've done enough damage to this forest!"

"But remember, Darlena, every forest fire—"

"I know," I snapped. "Forest fires lead to fertile growth, blah blah blah."

He glared at me. "Did you know that some plants can't reproduce without the heat of a fire?"

"What do you mean?"

"There are certain pine trees that have evolved to respond to fire.

They won't open their cones unless they're subjected to intense heat."

I thought about that for a moment. "I didn't know that. But I still don't want to cause a forest fire today! Your burn was pretty big last night; the woods need some time to recover."

He laughed. "I think you're just worried about it getting out of control," he taunted.

"Maybe. But I'm still not doing it."

Marcus lowered his hands, looking resigned. "I get that. But eventually, you're going to have to face the fire aspect of Red magic, and if you're unprepared, it won't be pretty."

"I'll risk it. What else can you show me?"

We moved through the elements. First, he taught me how to make the earth ripple and reshape itself. He demonstrated by opening a chasm in the forest floor and pushing the earth up to create a sheer cliff face. If I just looked at it without taking in the surrounding woods, I would have been convinced we were standing on a rocky shoreline.

"Now you try."

My attempt was far less grandiose, and I was almost embarrassed of the little mound of rock I managed to move. Marcus smiled encouragingly.

"Remember, I've been doing this my whole life. That wasn't too bad for your first time."

I gritted my teeth and tried harder, but all I managed to do was widen the chasm in front of us a fraction.

"Surrender to the magic, Darlena. Let it flow through you. You are Red magic."

Marcus's words were soothing, like listening to a yoga instructor, but my mind rebelled. I didn't want to be Red magic: I had chosen to wield it, wasn't that enough?

"You aren't concentrating," he murmured when a spasm of rock slid off my mound to the earth.

"You're making me nervous!" I complained.

"I think you're making yourself nervous. You still haven't fully accepted what you are."

I glared at him. "I don't care how you were taught, but I believe that I'm more than the magic I practice. Just because I'm a Red Witch—"

"You'll have to find your own balance then. That's nothing I can help with."

I sucked in a deep breath. "I know." I'd been looking for balance ever since I declared to Red magic. Gritting my teeth, I focused on the chasm. "Should I try again?"

He paused, considering. "If you want balance, why don't you try to heal what we've both done?"

"How?"

"That's the question, isn't it? You said you wanted to use Red magic to mitigate chaos. Well, start by cleaning up after yourself."

I glanced up at the cliff he had made. "Show me how."

"Nope. Figure it out."

It took me an hour, and I almost crushed us under a rockslide, but eventually I had forced the earth back together. There was still a slight rise where Marcus's cliff had been, but otherwise, the forest floor looked flat and undisturbed.

Marcus clapped sarcastically. "Not bad for your first lesson. Now air."

I glanced up at the still branches overhead. "What am I supposed to do with it?"

"A breeze would be nice."

Hesitating, I wiped my hands on my jeans. "Isn't that an awful lot like Weather magic?"

"So? What are you afraid of?"

I ignored his tone. "My parents are both Greens. They taught me that Weather magic has unintended consequences."

He snorted. "You sound like a stuck-up old grandmother."

"Don't you ever worry about it? Consequences of your spells, I mean."

Marcus stilled for a moment, thinking. Finally, he said, "I suppose I try to be mindful. But when you've felt the power of Red magic pulsing through your veins for close to a quarter of a century, it gets harder to think cautiously. The power," he whispered, "can be intoxicating."

I took a wary step back, but Marcus went on as if he didn't notice me.

"Red Witches have reshaped the world. What concern did they have for their actions? Why should I question myself when I have so much power just waiting to be used?"

"The Rede," I spoke loudly, trying to break his trance-like stare. "The Rede says that we can act as we like, as long as our actions do no harm."

"Who knows what really causes harm?"

"And just because it's hard to figure it out, you'd rather not think about the ramifications of your magic?" I was getting angry, but I couldn't help myself. Marcus was a powerful Witch, but it seemed like every other thing out of his mouth was a direct challenge to the beliefs of my family.

Marcus ignored me, his face turned to the sky. "Interesting."

"What?" I snarled. "Have you had a change of conscience?"

"No." He pointed to the canopy, and I looked up, startled to see the trees violently swaying. "Your magic is sharper when you're angry."

Struggling to calm myself, I sent a silent apology to my mother for accidentally interfering with the weather. "Isn't yours?"

He paused, thinking. "I don't really know. Although if anger does make magic more powerful … " A dark look crossed his face.

"What? What are you thinking?"

"Nothing important."

I paused, thinking of the brutality he had witnessed. "I'm sorry."

He shrugged. "It doesn't matter now. But that is something to think about: anger and Red magic."

Eager to share my own knowledge for a change, I told him, "When I was fighting Rochelle, I realized that anger might make my power stronger, but other emotions also had an effect. Love was … " I trailed off when I saw the hard look in his eyes.

"Back to work. We've wasted too much time talking. I'll count that for moving wind, even though you did it without thinking."

"What's next?" I tried to sound enthused, but the truth was, I was tired. We'd been working all morning, and Red magic drained me more than basic spells. I felt woozy, and my stomach grumbled loudly.

Marcus glanced at me. "Maybe we should take a break. You look like you're about to fall over."

He looked like he hadn't even broken a sweat, I noticed with chagrin. "I can keep at it if you can."

"Still. I want a snack. Do you have any more food in that bag?"

I nodded and crossed to the lean-to. "But I'm running low. We're going to have to move on soon."

Marcus looked at the shadows around us. "One more night here. Then we'll move on."

"And then what?"

His eyes met mine. "And then it's time to make good on your promise to Loki. Let's see if he keeps his end of the bargain."

27

Dawn came a lot sooner than I wanted, and I groaned when Marcus tapped my shoulder.

"Darlena, get up. We need to move on."

I refused to open my eyes. Instead, I rolled over and pulled my arms over my head. But then I heard Marcus gasp.

"Darlena! They're here!"

The panic in his voice rocketed me to my feet, despite my headache, and I rushed to draw up as much Red magic as I could. The clearing was empty. Confused, I looked around, my arms tingling with magic.

Marcus stood a few feet to my left, trying not to laugh. "At least I know you'll be ready in a crisis."

"That was so not funny," I growled at him. I wanted to throw the Red magic at him and teach him a lesson, but I knew I was no match for his powers. Angry, I released the magic.

Marcus was still fighting his laughter. "I beg to differ. Come on, Sleeping Beauty, help me clear the area."

Working silently, we erased all trace of our presence and released the protective wards. Even though it was just a campsite, it felt strange to leave it behind. It had been nice to feel safe for a short amount of time.

As we trudged through the forest, I thought about the magic Marcus had taught me. I wasn't sure how any of his spells would help, and I wondered if he was deliberately teaching me useless magic so he would have the upper hand.

As if he'd heard my thoughts, Marcus stopped and turned to look at me.

"Where should we go now?"

Surprised that he had bothered consulting me, I paused. "I don't know Germany at all. Where do you think we should go?"

He frowned, looking up at the watery sunlight that slipped between the trees. "I can transport us somewhere, but I'm not sure where we should go."

"Back to Scotland?" Even as I said it, I realized that was wrong. There was nothing we could accomplish there.

Marcus seemed to agree with me. "I don't know how that will help us."

"Well, maybe we need to figure out our plan. Then we'll know where to go."

"I assume you don't actually want to destroy the earth, so how can we make it seem like the world is ending?"

I flinched. I should have known Marcus would decipher what our bargain with Loki really meant, but I'd been avoiding it as long as I could. "I'm not sure. So much crazy shit happens everywhere now.

What would be extreme enough to convince anyone that the world is ending?"

He shook his head. "I don't know. The things that used to make people panic—comets passing, solar eclipses, earthquakes and other disasters—barely get a reaction from most people anymore."

His list of disasters gave me an idea. "What about several small disasters all at once?"

He looked at me intently, so I went on.

"What if we could cause simultaneous disasters all over the world? Between the two of us, we control two thirds of it, right?" If we could do that, this might just work.

He nodded thoughtfully. "That's true. But how do you suggest we do this without really destroying anything?"

I sighed loudly and closed my eyes. "What we need," I mused, "is a harmless disaster."

Marcus snorted. "When are disasters ever harmless?"

"I don't know, but I don't want to be responsible for a lot of death. People can rebuild after destruction, but there's no turning back death."

There was a long pause while we thought. Marcus finally broke the silence with one word. "Nuclear."

When he spoke, I felt as if I'd jumped into a frozen lake. I opened my eyes and stared at him in terror.

"It's perfect, really," he went on, ignoring my expression. "Massive nuclear meltdown. If we're careful, there won't be any deaths, and we can take care of cleaning things up after you've bound Hecate."

"I can't poison the earth!" I was aghast. "Marcus, I was raised by Green Witches. If anyone is a true tree-hugging hippie anymore, it's my family." He opened his mouth, but I pushed on. "My parents used to go to all kinds of protests, and as far as they're concerned, the biggest evil in the world is nuclear force. Not just warfare, but the energy, too. Mom's always said that so much power comes with an un-payable price." My hands were shaking, and I stuck them in my pockets, hoping he wouldn't see.

"But think, Darlena. It's the only way we can guarantee that no one is harmed. We could clean everything up before any radiation leaked out into the atmosphere. Unless you just want to say the hell with it and set off volcanoes and earthquakes right and left."

"You know I'd never do that. The whole reason we're even having this conversation is because I want to stop Hecate from destroying the world."

He stared at me levelly. "Do you have any other suggestions?"

My silence answered for me.

"It wouldn't be too bad," Marcus wheedled. "Just a few plants would have to go on the blink. Not that many, really. One on each continent would do."

"We don't control all the continents." My words were dismissive, but my voice asked a question.

"I control Europe, from the mid-Atlantic all the way to the Russian coast. And you control the Americas, right?"

"And Japan and Polynesia." I answered without thinking, but when he smiled I felt a sinking sensation as if I'd already agreed to the plan.

"That's plenty of space to make it seem like the world is ending. And then you'll have the bonds, and I'll have Izzy. Piece of cake."

"I don't like this! I don't want to set off any nuclear reactors." I tried one last time to argue with him, but he glared at me coldly before turning away.

"That doesn't matter. We have to get my sister back."

***

We slept in the forest that night after setting up temporary wards and pitching another lean-to. When Marcus started the forest fire to get wood for our shelter, I turned away feeling nauseous.

How was I even considering something like this? On the one hand, Marcus was probably right: in the short term, this was the safest way to meet Loki's demands. The gods would surely free him if the world seemed on the verge of a nuclear collapse. On the other hand, I knew that even if we did no immediate harm, our actions could have consequences for generations, maybe even centuries.

I fell asleep still wrestling with the decision, and my dreams echoed my fears.

I was walking in a dark field. At first I thought it was night, but then I realized that everything around me was charred black from fire. The sky was so thick with ash that it looked like storm clouds hung over the earth. As I walked through the desolate landscape, I stumbled and nearly fell. When I looked down, I realized with horror that I had tripped over a woman.

Her flesh hung in strips from her body, and her skin was cracked and burned. When she opened her eyes, I felt like I could see the entire world. Her lips moved, and I knelt beside her.

"What did you say?" I asked frantically, desperate to help her if I could.

"You have done it." Her voice was faint, but her words were clear. With that, she closed her eyes and melted into the black earth. I watched her vanish in horror.

"You have destroyed my grandmother."

I spun around and found myself facing a huge man chained to a rock. At first, I thought he was Loki, because of the chains, but there were no other similarities.

"Who was she?" Frightened, I eyed his bonds. He seemed securely trapped, but if he thought I had killed his grandmother, I didn't want him to come any closer to me.

He laughed sadly. "Mother to us all. She existed before time began. But you have done the unthinkable."

"Please," I whispered, holding out my hands, "I don't know what I've done."

He nodded at the blackened wasteland around me. "The gods have tried to destroy her. For years they have crushed her creations and her spirit. But no one has succeeded until you."

I stared at him, trying to understand. "Who are you?"

He smiled sadly. "I was once Prometheus, the fire-bringer. But now I am just another lost child. Without her, we are nothing."

"But I don't understand. Who was she?"

"That which sheltered you. She was Gaia, the earth."

At his words, I turned and ran. Blindly, I flew through the charred field. My feet splashed through a stream, but when I looked down, the water looked like melted lead. There was no color anywhere in the landscape; everything was charred and blackened. When I looked at my own hands, all I saw was bone.

I woke up with a start to find Marcus's face looming over mine in the darkness.

"Are you all right? You were crying out in your sleep."

I shook my head, trying to clear the images from my mind. The horror of my nightmare was still fresh, and I squeezed my eyes shut, willing myself not to think about the destruction I'd seen.

"What's wrong?"

I couldn't form words, so I shook my head again. I let out a stifled sob, but I was too worked up to care. Marcus sat down cautiously beside me and reached his arm across my shoulders, turning me to face him. I barely noticed the electric current that rushed through me as I fell against his chest. The tears I'd been holding back came, like a dam bursting, and I sobbed against him.

Awkwardly, he patted my back. I kept crying, and his hand stopped patting. Instead, he rubbed soothing circles up and down my spine, and warmth spread through my body. Gradually, my tears slowed, and finally, I was still. For a moment, Marcus still held me, and I gripped his back, pressing closer against his comforting warmth. Despite my horrible nightmare, I felt strangely, suddenly safe. Marcus stiffened, but then he tipped my face up so I was looking at him.

"It was just a dream."

I started to shake my head, but he held my chin firmly. "Dreams are only that. Don't mistake them for reality." I froze, staring at his eyes. They glistened strangely in the darkness, like dark emeralds. Marcus was still holding my chin, and I was vaguely aware of his index finger trailing gently over my jaw. Without thinking, I leaned closer to him.

Sparks filled the air between us, but this time, I didn't flinch from the shock. Marcus exhaled sharply, looking at me. I didn't understand his expression, but then he brought his lips to mine, and the world exploded.

28

I pulled my face away after a minute, startled. "What did you do that for?"

Marcus flexed his hands, as if he wanted to reach for me again. "I'm not sure."

"Well, don't." I glared at him, trying to ignore the churning sensation in my stomach and the way the soles of my feet were tingling from his kiss.

He looked at me for a long moment. "If that's what you want."

I realized my arms were still around his back, so I let go. My body swayed for a minute, like a magnet on a string, but I resisted the pull toward Marcus. I leaned back, trying to sound firm. "Yes."

His eyes hardened, and he stood brusquely. "Are you awake enough to move on?"

Startled by how quickly he dropped it, I looked around at the dark forest. "It's still night!"

"There's no time to waste. Besides, I'm afraid your blubbering may have been heard." His tone was cruel, and I winced.

Seconds ago, he had been trying to comfort my tears. Now he was accusing me of giving away our position to anyone in the woods. My anger rose, canceling the last of the lingering sensations from his kiss. "How dare you? Who died and made you king of the forest?"

His lips parted as if he were about to retort, but I didn't give him the chance.

"We're in this thing together, so stop treating me like I'm something lower than you. Just because I haven't used Red magic as long as you doesn't mean I'm weak."

"Are you finished?"

I screamed in frustration and flopped over, wishing I wasn't acutely aware of his eyes on me. "Yes. And I'm going back to sleep. We'll move in the morning."

He didn't answer and he didn't lie back down. I heard his footsteps shuffle away, and I tried not to care. I shut my eyes, determined to force myself to fall back asleep, but I kept thinking about the kiss. I tried to think of Justin, but just when I had his face in my mind, the image shifted until I was seeing Marcus. What the hell had happened between us? Why had he kissed me? And worse, why had I liked it?

After tossing fitfully for two hours, I stopped pretending to be asleep. I stood up when the first pink wisps tinged the eastern sky and stretched, looking around the campsite warily. For a minute, I panicked, thinking I was alone, but then I saw him.

He was sitting as far away from the lean-to as he could get, and his head rested heavily on his knees. He looked up as I emerged, and his expression was impossible to read.

My stomach flip-flopped, and I looked away. "Let's get moving." I didn't look in his direction again, but I felt him stand and begin taking down camp. We had a system now, and even though we worked in tense silence, it didn't take long to clear away any sign we'd been in the woods.

Soon, we were on the road again. Marcus walked ahead of me, snapping off branches that got in his way. He obviously didn't want to talk, which was fine with me.

As I trudged along in silence, my mind raced down different paths. The idea of nuclear meltdown, my bargain with Loki, Hecate's hatred, and the velvety feel of Marcus's lips on mine cycled through my thoughts, leaving me alternately panicked, angry, and ashamed. I couldn't deal with the kiss right now, so I focused on Marcus's earlier suggestion. A nuclear meltdown was nothing compared to what had happened last night.

He was right: it was probably the safest way to keep my deal with Loki, but the images from my nightmare haunted me. I did not want to be the person responsible for the ultimate destruction of the earth. I only wanted the ability to bind Hecate because I was trying to prevent her from destroying the planet. I'd be a pretty crappy Witch if I ended up doing exactly what I was trying to stop.

My thoughts raced in circles, and I sighed. The idea was risky, but I couldn't come up with any alternatives. If we wanted Loki's help, I needed to make it seem like the world was ending. I wanted to harm as few people as possible, and no other large-scale disasters could be so relatively free from casualty. Despite the logic, something in my gut refused to accept the idea of a massive nuclear meltdown as a solution.

Snow had begun falling while we walked. Thick, misshapen flakes landed in lumps on my arms and hair, and when I looked up at the sky

I was almost blinded by snow. It had an eerie kind of prettiness. When we stopped to eat the last of my granola bars, Marcus looked around nervously.

"We have to move faster."

After so many hours of silence, his curt statement surprised me into speech. "Why?"

"Someone could track us in the snow."

I laughed. I couldn't help it; the statement was so ludicrous. "Marcus, don't you think the people who would want to find us would trace something other than our footprints?"

He looked at me, stunned. "I'm such an idiot. All this time we've been using magic like we're safe. It must have been like sending up a thousand signal flares!" Quickly, he stood up, circling around me in a defensive posture. He looked like a wolf, and I was grateful he wasn't hunting me.

Hesitantly, I placed a hand on his shoulder. We both jerked at the electrical current that snapped between us, but I didn't pull my hand away. "They haven't found us yet. We don't even know if anyone is looking."

He shook his head. "We have to start assuming they are. We need to move on with the plan now, before it's too late."

I paused, trying to find the right words to express my doubts, but he read my expression, and his eyes turned cold.

"You aren't backing out now?"

I put my hands up defensively. "We haven't agreed on anything yet."

He snorted. "Surely you can see that my way would be the best."

I nodded slowly. "Yes, but I've been thinking." I wavered for a moment, but then inspiration struck. "I think we should try to find

Izzy on our own first. The bargain can wait." That was the one thing I could think of that might make him change his mind. Never mind that if we found Izzy on our own, I doubted Marcus would help me keep my bargain with Loki. I'd worry about that later; right now, I just wanted to make him forget the nuclear disaster idea.

His eyes lit up before he frowned at me. "Before, you made it clear that she wasn't our top priority."

"But maybe she can help us!"

Now he glared at me. "Why? Do you want to use her?"

"No! But Marcus, she's smart, and she's Blue. She might see a different solution to the problem. She was trying to help me find a way to bind Hecate when she—"

Before I could finish, he was in front of me, his hand against my throat, sending a painful pulse of energy into my neck. "You dragged her into this? It's because of you that she's gone?" His mood had changed from cranky to lethal, and I squirmed in fear.

"No! She wanted to help me. We were just researching in the library at her school."

"What were you researching?" He didn't let go of my throat, even when I poked him sharply under the ribcage.

"Stories about other gods who've been bound. She didn't know about Loki."

"What had you found?"

"She was reading a book about Egyptian mythology. When I came back to our seats, she was gone but the book was still there."

He released me, and I stepped away from him quickly, breathing hard and rubbing my throat.

"How long has it been since you first met Loki?"

I thought back. "I met him for the first time in a dream on Christmas

Eve. But he didn't try to bargain with me until I was in Scotland."

"And you didn't like his offer, so you dragged my sister into your search for another way to capture Hecate?"

When he put it that way, I sounded careless and cold. "She wanted to help me. When you disappeared … " I paused, remembering the visitation from Persephone, when I had first begun to suspect what Hecate ultimately wanted.

"Well?" Marcus stared at me intently, his face a mask.

"Persephone came to us. She told Izzy we probably couldn't save you. She was the one who told us that Hecate has been trying to set in motion an end to the world."

He sighed. "And my sister wanted to help you." He looked at his hands for a moment, and when he met my eyes again, I was surprised to see tears streaming down his face. "Izzy always puts others before herself. She's the best Witch I've ever met."

"Is that just because she's Blue?"

He shook his head. "No, I've met other Blue Witches. Izzy is special. I guess she was shaped by her patron even more than I was. You know what happened, right?"

"I know your mother promised Izzy to Isis before she was born." I spoke cautiously, not sure if speaking about his family would send Marcus into another rage.

"Mom died giving birth to Izzy. I was six." He swallowed, and I mentally recalculated his age. With a shock, I realized that he was only twenty; he seemed way too hardened and worldly to be so close to my own age.

Marcus went on, ignoring my expression. "That's when Cerridwen took me for training. Isis did the same thing."

I stared at him, open-mouthed. "But how? And where?"

He shrugged. "I don't know a lot of the details. But Isis took her when our mother died, and I didn't see her again until I was fifteen."

My mind whirred furiously. "So Izzy spent the first nine years of her life in the care of a goddess?"

He nodded. "She's never told me exactly what happened, but I think she was raised in the Underworld."

"How would a human child live in the Underworld?"

"From what I understand, the Duat, the Egyptian Underworld, is less like the Greek and more like the Celtic. It's Underworld and Otherworld combined, so the living can pass there with more fluidity."

I processed what he was telling me. "There is no one on earth like your sister."

He nodded. "I've known that for years."

If Izzy had been raised by her patron, then she probably knew as much magic as Marcus did. And from what she'd told me, Blue magic might be able to balance the harm caused by uncontrolled Red magic. "Marcus, we have to find her before we try anything else. We need her," I pleaded.

"Where do you suggest we look?" His tone was icy, and I drew back, startled.

"I don't know, okay? But finding her is the key to everything."

Marcus stalked away from me, his shoulders tense. "Why should I trust you?"

"We both want the same thing," I coaxed, keeping my distance from him.

He whirled around angrily. "No we don't! I don't know what you want, Darlena. One minute, you're talking about binding Hecate, and the next you're back on my sister. Which is it, Witch? What matters to you here?"

"I don't know!" I shouted, feeling helpless. "Stopping Hecate seemed important. I mean, I wouldn't even be here if not for that! But I can't bear the idea of—"

"Nuclear meltdown," Marcus cut me off with a mocking tone. "Because you're not a Red Witch. You want to practice pink magic like a fluffy little Non and stay safe and sound at home." He glared at me. "Well, Witch, that's something you should have thought of before now."

He was standing so close to me that I could feel the heat of his breath, and even though my lips started tingling in anticipation, I drew my hand back and slapped him across the face. *Gods, that hurt.*

Marcus grabbed my wrist as soon as I hit him and started to squeeze. "I'm going to ask you again. What do you want?"

"I don't want to destroy anything. I know that much." I clenched my teeth, trying to pull my hand out of his grasp, but it was like it was set in concrete. My arm tingled, but I couldn't move.

Suddenly, Marcus dropped my arm, and I staggered back. "Too late for that, Red." He gestured around the forest, and I stared in horror.

Flames encircled us, licking up the dry, winter wood. The ground was pitted and cracked, as if an earthquake had happened, and the only thing I could think of was that it all looked like the scene from a bad apocalyptic movie. Black smoke rose into the air, mingling with the snow until it looked like volcanic ash.

I choked back a sob. "What did you do?"

Marcus shook his head. "I'm not the one who can't control my magic."

I wanted to argue with him, but when I looked down at my hands, red sparks were still visible. I dropped to my knees, horrified by what I'd done.

29

Marcus tried to help me clean up the mess, but there wasn't much we could do. Eventually, we gave up and walked away from the smoldering forest. I was a wreck, but he didn't try to comfort me, and I retreated into silence. After an hour, we reached the edge of the woods. I finally spoke.

"I want to find Izzy." My words were quiet, but I could tell Marcus heard me by the way his shoulders tensed and then relaxed. He didn't answer, though, and after a few more moments of silence, I tried again.

"If we want to find Izzy, I think we'll need some help. From a large group," I ventured.

Marcus glared at me. "I don't want their help."

"But they owe it to you. I think the Coven is our best bet."

He grimaced. "Why can't we just figure this out on our own?"

I laughed, gesturing at the woods that surrounded us. "Because we're doing such a great job of that."

He refused to look at me. "I just don't want them involved. They won't act in her best interests."

"How do you know?"

"Have they ever?"

I took a deep breath. "Maybe they feel guilty about it. I think they'll help us. Or, if not all of them," I amended, "I'm pretty sure Dr. Farren can give us some information."

"I thought you said they wouldn't help you before. Why should it be any different now?"

"Because now," I pointed at him, "there are two Reds to be dealt with."

He looked skeptical.

"When it was just me asking for help, they didn't want to do anything. They told me to leave it to them, and they basically ignored me."

A slow smile spread across his face. "But it's impossible to ignore two Red Witches."

"Exactly." I shuddered slightly, thinking of the smoking forest behind us.

The words had barely left my lips before Marcus grabbed my hands. I only had time to register the wild energy pulsing up my arms before everything went black.

When I opened my eyes, we were standing in his messy studio apartment back in Edinburgh. "Gods, why do you have to do that? Can you warn me next time?" My stomach was churning, and I lurched as the ground finished spinning.

Marcus smirked. "I got us here, didn't I?"

"Why didn't you do that sooner?" I grumbled.

He didn't answer, and I swayed unsteadily on my feet as Marcus pulled his phone out of his pocket. Swiftly, he dialed a number.

"Dr. Farren? It's Marcus Welty."

His eyebrows went up in surprise. "No, Izzy didn't find me. Darlena did."

Gradually, the room was slowing down, and I staggered to the sink to get a glass of water. A thin layer of dust coated the faucet, and the water tasted stale. I tuned Marcus out, concentrating instead on getting my ragged breathing back under control. When I turned around, Marcus handed me the phone.

"Here. Why don't you call home? You've been out of touch for a few days, and they might be worried."

His kindness surprised me. I took the phone, but before I dialed I asked, "What about Dr. Farren?"

"She'll pick us up in a half hour. She's calling the Coven now."

I nodded, and then began to dial my parents' number.

My mother answered on the first ring. "Darlena? What's the matter?"

I hadn't realized how much I missed the sound of her voice until now. "Nothing, Mom. I'm okay." I drew a deep breath to keep from crying.

"I would hope so! Did you need something?"

Did I need something? I wanted to laugh; I needed way more help than she could offer. "I didn't want you to be worried."

She laughed. "Lena, you know I never worry about you when you're with Justin."

Time slowed down as her words penetrated my foggy brain. "With—wait, what are you talking about?"

Her voice tightened. "You're not with him? Then who are you

seeing tonight? When you left for a movie, I assumed it was with Justin."

This didn't make any sense. I could only repeat her words in confusion. "A movie?"

Mom's voice rose sharply. "Darlena Agara, you're not doing any drugs or anything like that, are you?"

I stared at the phone, aghast. "Mom! Of course not."

"I should hope not!" Her voice softened. "Enjoy your movie, and make sure Justin has you home by midnight. Not a minute later, young lady!"

Speechless, I hung up the phone. I swayed unsteadily for a moment, replaying our conversation, and then my legs gave out. Marcus quickly grabbed my arms and helped me to the futon in the corner. He sat close to me, not touching, his face concerned.

"Is anything wrong at home?"

Numbly, I shook my head. I leaned against him, seeking comfort, but he didn't put his arm around me.

"Then what is it?"

I opened my mouth, then closed it. Finally, I said, "My mother thinks I just went to a movie with my boyfriend."

His brows furrowed. "She thinks we're dating?"

"No!" I snapped. "She thinks I'm home." The truth of what I'd said sunk in, and I gasped. "How in the world?"

Marcus sat back as if he'd been struck. "What's going on?"

I shook my head. "I don't know. But I need to get home! This isn't right." I started to stand, but he pulled me back onto the sofa. My hand tingled, but he didn't let go.

"Not yet. We have to find Izzy and bind Hecate. You can't leave now." His voice was firm, but I heard the desperate note in his tone.

I wanted to help Marcus, but my family came first. "There's something really weird going on! I have to fix it." My voice broke, and I struggled to maintain my composure.

Marcus squeezed my hand gently. "Think about it, Darlena. For some reason, your mom thinks that you're safe and sound. Maybe this is a blessing."

"What do you mean?"

"Now you can do what you need to do without worrying her. You don't even need to tell her about our plan if you don't want to."

It made sense, but I was still worried. "But why does she think I'm home? This is just weird."

He sat up suddenly. "When you went to the Greek Underworld before, how did you manage it? Weren't your parents freaked out?"

I shook my head, wondering why he brought that up. "No, because Persephone stayed behind and glamoured herself to look like me. They didn't even know I was gone."

He smiled triumphantly. "She's probably done it again. You said you spoke to her at the cairns the day I disappeared, right?"

I nodded skeptically. "But why would she do something like that without telling me?"

"We've been sort of unreachable lately," he remarked dryly.

I thought about what he'd said. It made a certain amount of sense, but I couldn't shake the nagging feeling that something about his scenario didn't fit. "I guess," I agreed slowly, "but I still think we should mention this to Dr. Farren and the Coven. Maybe they know something."

"Agreed. But stop worrying. We've got more immediate concerns."

"Like what?"

He leaned back against the cushion wearily. "Like facing my family again."

"How long has it been since you saw your grandparents?"

His mouth tightened. "Years. I didn't exactly grow up going to Grandma's house on Sundays."

I nodded, feeling awful for him. What must it have been like to grow up the way he did? "But they'll help us. The Coven owes it to you and Izzy." I sounded more confident than I felt, and Marcus stared at me for a minute before answering.

"I'm not so sure. But you're right; I don't know what else we should do."

A buzzer sounded and I jumped. Marcus chuckled and put his arm on my back soothingly. Without conscious thought, I leaned into his hand, feeling safe for a moment.

"That's the bell for the street. Dr. Farren is probably here."

I wished I'd had time to take a shower and get rid of the grunge from our nights in the forest, but it didn't look like that was going to happen. I wobbled a bit as I stood up, and I reached out a hand to Marcus to steady myself. He clasped my hand and gave it a squeeze, and I squeezed back. I'd gotten used to the weird electric current between us, and I almost didn't want to let go.

"Are you ready?" His voice was soft.

Shaking my head, I let go of his hand and walked toward the door. "No. But we're out of ideas, remember?"

He nodded. "Let's hope this isn't a mistake."

30

Dr. Farren didn't say much on the drive, and I shifted uncomfortably in the front seat. From time to time, I caught her glancing at me out of the corner of her eye, but her eyes darted away as soon as they met mine. Marcus snored softly from the back. Somehow, he'd managed to fall asleep as soon as we were in the car; I wondered if he was playing possum so he didn't have to talk to Dr. Farren. When we arrived at the farmhouse in the countryside, the driveway was filled with cars. Nervous, I glanced at Dr. Farren, but she remained expressionless.

Frances opened the door before we had climbed the steps. She rushed forward, crushing Marcus in an embrace. He looked startled for a minute, but then he patted his grandmother on the back, staring down at her white head.

"Mother!" a sharp voice barked from the house, and I looked up to see the bird-like librarian standing there, glaring at Marcus.

"Mother?" I whispered to Marcus. "Does that mean what I think it means?"

Marcus ignored me. "Nice to see you, too, Uncle Sam." Gently, he gently pulled away from Frances.

Samuel's jaw tightened, but he turned on his heel without speaking. Frances stared up at Marcus for an instant longer, her eyes brimming with tears. Then she turned and followed her son into the house.

I glared at Marcus. "You didn't mention that part."

He shrugged. "Doesn't really matter. Just because we're blood doesn't mean there's any love lost between us."

"But still. It makes sense now, how bitchy he was to me before."

Marcus smiled, but it looked more like a snarl. "He's always adored Izzy. Everyone does."

I nodded hopefully. If the entire Coven felt that way about Izzy, maybe they'd be willing to help us.

The hair on the back of my neck stood up as we passed over the threshold, and my skin tingled with magic. We followed Frances and Dr. Farren into the room with the fireplace that I remembered from before, but this time the large space felt small. All nine members of the Coven were gathered in the room. A woman with rich, black hair streaked white at the temples sat on the settee next to Julia. A young woman who looked like a youthful copy of the black-haired beauty stood behind her mother's chair.

There were also two men I hadn't met before. One looked about my father's age, and he was sitting peacefully on the floor, his legs tucked into full lotus position, his eyes closed as if he were oblivious to everything in the room. The second man stood by the window, his back to us as he looked out at the winter sky.

Frederick cleared his throat. "I suppose I should make the

introductions, but I'll be brief about it. Marcus, Darlena, this is Julia, Jewel, Lorna, Matthew, and Roy. You know Dr. Farren, and I heard," he said dryly, "that you've encountered Samuel and Frances already."

Marcus nodded, and I surveyed the Witches with interest, trying to remember their names.

I cleared my throat. "Thank you for helping us."

Julia spoke up, her voice as sharp as her parrot's. "We haven't agreed to anything yet."

Dr. Farren glared at her. "But we haven't turned them away. We agreed to hear them out."

"What I want to know," Samuel began, "is what you bloody well think you're doing waltzing in here after all this time."

I looked at Marcus, confused. "How long were we in the Black Forest?"

He shrugged. "A couple days. Less than a week."

An agitated whisper snaked around the room. Samuel opened his mouth to speak, but Dr. Farren beat him to it. "What are you talking about? Darlena, you vanished over a year ago."

I stared at her, not understanding. "You took me back to Edinburgh before the New Year."

She shook her head impatiently. "That was the last New Year. You were gone for—"

"They were gone for a year and a day." Samuel spoke quietly, but his words caused an explosion from the others.

Confused, I looked at Dr. Farren. "Why is the time frame so significant?"

"It's significant," Frederick began, "because it means we know exactly where you were."

"I never would have thought any Witch would be foolish enough to enter Fairy." Julia brushed her hands across her skirt, smoothing the fabric in agitation.

"It wasn't just Fairy." Marcus spoke quietly, and I could see them straining to listen. "Darlena entered Annwn and found me there. But then we ended up in Hel."

"Two Underworlds! It's a wonder you came back at all!" The younger Witch stared at me with interest.

"That's enough, Lorna. You shouldn't make them any more arrogant than they are." Jewel rapped her daughter's knuckles sharply with her hand.

"What in the world were you thinking? Didn't we tell you not to take action?" Samuel glared at me.

Exasperated, I threw up my hands. "But I had to try to find Izzy! She sent a Seeming to guide me, but I lost her when we shifted to Hel."

"How did you make it out alive?" Julia leaned forward. Her parrot squawked at her shoulder.

I glanced at Marcus and he shook his head slightly. No one else noticed his gesture, but I didn't need to be told twice. I spoke with caution. "There was a volcanic eruption, and we rode the fire out." There was no way I wanted to tell these people about Loki. No one but Marcus needed to know about our deal.

The women gasped and Samuel grimaced. "This is why we do not have dealings with Reds!" He gestured to us. "They are too dangerous to be dealt with safely."

"Samuel! Be kind." Frances spoke urgently, but her son shook his head.

"You all felt it the minute they walked in. Don't pretend you didn't!"

One by one, the other Witches dropped their eyes, refusing to meet my gaze. Samuel crossed his arms in triumph.

"Felt what?" I looked around, searching their faces. It was Dr. Farren who answered.

"The force the two of you give off is almost tangible. I've never experienced anything quite like it before."

Marcus shot me a quick look and I shrugged. I had no idea what they were talking about. I mean, I got zapped whenever we touched, but other than Frances's hug, we hadn't touched any of the Coven. What kind of force could they feel?

Dr. Farren pressed on, trying to steer the topic away from animosity toward us. "Did you learn anything in the Underworlds about Isadora?"

"Well," I began, trying to find the best way to tell them our suspicions, "we think—"

"Set has her," Marcus spoke bluntly and I stared at him open-mouthed. He hadn't acted like he'd known where she was before; what had changed? Lorna gasped, and Frances swayed beside her husband.

Dr. Farren looked from Marcus to me. "He hadn't told you, had he?"

I shook my head. "We'd figured out she might be in another Underworld, but he never mentioned who he thought had her." I glared at him, angry that he hadn't trusted me with his suspicion.

Samuel shook his head in disbelief. "Set would never be so bold. Isadora is—"

"Isis's chosen one. It does make a certain amount of sense." The gentle-looking man who was still sitting on the floor spoke quietly, and everyone turned to look at him.

"Set has always wanted those who are dear to Isis. First it was her husband, Osiris. Then it was her son, Horus. It would make sense that he would take the child she raised as her only daughter."

"Then she's not in the Duat." Jewel spoke softly, fear in her eyes.

"That is not a place of power for the Lord of Chaos."

The title of the god rang warning bells with me. "Wait a minute. Set's another Red god, isn't he?"

Dr. Farren nodded. "One of the fiercest. His powers of destruction and deception are rivaled only by one other god."

I felt my hands go cold. "Who?"

Marcus looked at me in warning as Dr. Farren said, "The Norse god Loki."

Frances made a hissing noise and pushed her hand in front of her, fingers bent in the ancient gesture for averting evil.

"So where would Set have Izzy?" I asked quickly, trying to mask my sense of guilt at hearing Loki's name. Marcus shot me an inscrutable look, but he didn't say anything.

"The Egyptian land of death is under the control of Osiris, his brother and rival." Frederick spoke slowly, thinking. "Set's realm is to make a hell on earth."

Julia snorted. "You don't really believe all that old propaganda, do you?" She turned to me, smiling slightly. "You might like Set, child. True, he is a god of chaos, but the Egyptians understood that chaos was a necessary part of the balance of life."

I ignored her. "But where would he have Izzy? And why?"

The Witches looked around the room at each other helplessly. Finally, a voice I hadn't heard before spoke.

"If Set has had the girl for all this time, then she's lost. It doesn't matter where anymore." He turned from the window and I felt Marcus stiffen beside me. I gasped; the red-headed man might have been a mirror image of Marcus, from his piercing green eyes to his hard jaw. Speechless, I stared at Roy and realized that I was looking at Marcus and Izzy's father.

"Don't say that!" Marcus turned to face his father. "Don't you dare give up on her."

"Son," Roy began, ignoring the way Marcus's shoulders stiffened, "she's been missing for over a year. We have to think logically."

"Do you think she's dead?" Marcus stared accusingly at his father.

Roy paused, then looked back out the window. "Actually, no. But," he went on, "Set has had her this long; whether she's still among the living or not, we may as well consider her to be lost. The Lord of Chaos bears no love for Isis, nor would he care much for her sworn Witch."

Marcus sank onto the sofa, his head in his hands. After a moment, I sat down beside him, close but not touching.

"We'll find her." I spoke softly, but my words seemed to echo through the room, and I felt a prickly sensation that told me the eyes of the other Witches were suddenly on us.

"Does the Coven agree to offer whatever aid is in their power to command?" Samuel's voice rang out suddenly, surprising me.

There was a pause, and then Julia began to nod. Lorna smiled and inclined her head, and one by one the rest of the Coven silently agreed to help us.

"Shall we incorporate them into our circle?" Jewel's voice was breathy with excitement. Samuel turned ashy, and Dr. Farren looked at us for a long minute.

"That's a question for them, isn't it?" She crossed the room until she stood before us. "Marcus, Darlena, we offer you our aid, but there are certain rules that bind us. If you were one of our Coven, we would be more free to help you in your quest." She paused, letting her words sink in. "Would you join with our group willingly and experience the full aid we can give, or will you remain separate and accepting of the least that we can do?"

I looked at Marcus. Finally, he met my eyes. He shook his head imperceptibly, and Samuel let out a quick sigh of relief.

"We understand that you cannot do everything," I said, trying to match Dr. Farren's formal tone. "But we accept what help you can freely offer."

The tension in the room lessened somewhat, but I felt the weight of my words sinking into my skin, binding me to this strange group. I'd never worked magic with another Witch before, other than with Marcus in the woods, and suddenly, the prospect of working with the Coven was overwhelming. Nobody said anything for a minute, but I could feel tension swirling around the room like an invisible current. Excusing myself, I slipped outside to the wraparound porch.

The air was cold, and heavy clouds hung in the sky, threatening some kind of winter storm. I shivered and rubbed my arms. Looking out at the barren landscape, I realized that I was lonelier than I had ever been. I hadn't had contact with Persephone since the day Marcus disappeared, and even though I'd spoken to my mom earlier that morning, it felt like nothing. I thought about calling her again, or calling Justin, but I stopped when I pulled my phone out of my pocket.

I realized that I'd been lucky before, to call when Persephone was out of the house. If I called while I was supposed to be home, I might throw the goddess's careful plans out of whack. Not that I knew what her plans were, but I had to assume she had my best interests at heart. Especially after learning how long Marcus and I had been in the Underworlds, I was grateful that Persephone had taken action to help my parents not worry about me.

Still, I missed them. And I missed Justin. I'd avoided thinking about him ever since Marcus kissed me, but now I let myself remember his warm brown eyes and the way he said my name. I thought about the fragile steps we'd been taking to repair our relationship before I left for Scotland. Most relationships can barely survive mundane concerns, but ours had weathered the storm of my misguided use of Love magic. I knew that what we had was something special, and I closed my eyes, wishing I could feel Justin's arms around me. I tried to surrender to the fantasy, but for some reason, it wasn't Justin's familiar brown eyes that haunted me. I wanted to ignore the thought, but my mind was fixated on a pair of sharp green eyes.

Gradually, I became aware of another presence on the porch, and I stiffened. I didn't know how long Marcus had been watching me, but when I turned around to face him, the expression in his eyes frightened me. He looked as desperate as I felt, but he wasn't gazing off in the distance. He was staring intently at me. I felt my spine begin to tingle and heat crept up my face. Did he have any idea what I'd been imagining?

Quickly, I looked away. Trying to kill whatever I had seen in his eyes, I brought up his family. "Have you met Roy before?"

He clenched his fists, and his eyes hardened. For a moment, I felt a pang of regret that I'd distracted him, but I ignored it. We didn't need to complicate our relationship any further, and there was no way I was going to tell him I had been thinking about the kiss. "Barely. But blood will out, they say. I knew him as soon as he turned around."

"Will he help us?"

Marcus laughed harshly. "He has to, doesn't he? The Coven is bound to us now."

I hesitated. "Did you want to join them?"

"Gods, no. The last thing I need is a sniveling democracy trying to control my magic. I work alone."

"Except for me," I pointed out. He looked at me sharply, and I felt myself blushing again.

"A temporary arrangement, if you remember."

I nodded. "Izzy's been waiting too long. Besides, just because we have some help, would you really let anyone besides you rescue your sister?"

"True. I wouldn't trust anyone else to do it."

"I figured. You just can't wait to go rushing into battle with a Red god, can you?" My words were harsh, but I kept my tone light.

He grinned. "Witch, I fear you have found my fatal flaw."

"Pride? Arrogance?" I teased, trying to make him laugh.

He shook his head, his eyes serious. "No. Love."

I waited for him to say something about Izzy, but he didn't. The air crackled with electricity, but this time, I didn't want to look away from him.

31

Although the Coven had agreed to help us, they couldn't decide which course of action to take. As night fell, Frances insisted we all stay over so we could get back to work in the morning.

I was relieved to find out I'd share a room with Lorna. The other women were all fairly intimidating, but she had a soft smile and seemed nice enough. Marcus volunteered to sleep in the living room on the couch before his father or his uncle could grudgingly offer to share a room with him. No one argued with his decision; of the two Red Witches in the house, they clearly felt that he was the most dangerous.

Lorna picked a room under one of the gables. The slanted roof made the small space feel cozy, like a secret hideaway. There were two old metal bed frames against opposite walls.

"I'll take the one over here," Lorna offered, gesturing to the bed under the low, angled ceiling.

"Are you sure? You might hit your head if you sit up too fast."

She laughed. "Believe me, I'm a sound sleeper, and I never move until I am fully awake. Rushing into things, even daylight, can be dangerous."

I wondered if she was chastising me for chasing the Seeming into the Underworld a year ago, but her face was neutral. Plumping the feather pillow, I flopped onto the bed. I didn't have any pajamas, but I didn't mind sleeping in my clothes for one more night. The springs groaned beneath me.

"So what do you think your Coven has planned? Or is it top secret?"

She smiled and settled herself on her bed without making a sound. "I don't really know. I think we're all waiting for divine inspiration to strike."

I snorted. "Does that happen often around here?"

"No. But we keep wishing it would!"

"Does it ever frustrate you? Being in a group, I mean. Not having the freedom to work alone."

Lorna thought for a moment. "Not really," she finally said. "But then again, I never felt pulled to phenomenal magical workings. I've always been more inclined to use simple charms and arts. The Coven suits me."

"Does anyone in the group go in for a flashier kind of magic?" I asked, thinking of Samuel's fiery temper.

She chuckled. "Of course! We wouldn't be a very strong group if our members weren't balanced. But when we work together, we try to find the middle way between showy and simple."

Other than Izzy, I'd never had the chance to speak so openly with a Witch whose training was so different from my own. "When did you join the group?"

"Mother sort of made me."

Her voice was calm, but I thought I saw a flicker of anger in her eyes. "How did she do that? Was it like what Marcus's mom did?"

"No, nothing so dramatic." She laughed softly. "You see, I had finished up at university, and Mother gave me two choices: join her Coven and receive all the financial and magical support she could offer, or strike out on my own and give up my claim to her."

I stared at her, aghast. "That's awful! She gave you the choice of being disowned or joining her group?"

Lorna shrugged. "It hasn't been a bad decision. Mother is a very powerful Witch; I'm not sure my life would have been as lovely if I'd cut ties with her."

Gods, I'd never realized how lucky I was to have the parents I did. "My mom's a Green. I can't imagine her ever pulling something like that!"

She smiled at me. "White Witches tend to be a little less flexible than Greens. Or anyone else, for that matter."

I wanted to know more about Jewel, but I had the feeling that Lorna wouldn't be comfortable speaking about her mother's patron. "Are you a White, too?"

She smirked. "No. My one rebellion, as Mother calls it. I declared Blue when I turned fourteen."

"That's young. I didn't declare until last year. Who's your patron?"

She stretched her arms overhead and rolled her neck. Instead of answering me, she asked, "What do you already know about Blue magic?"

I thought back to my conversations with Izzy. It seemed like another lifetime when I first met her outside of her school. "Izzy told me that it's elemental. Blue magic is connected to water ... " I paused, searching my memory. "And emotion."

"It's also connected to art. Not the fiery kind of art that made Sylvia Plath kill herself or Van Gogh maim his ear. Blue magic governs a softer kind of art."

"Like what?" I had never thought of magic being linked to art, even though I knew that Shakespeare had been a Green Witch.

"Well, I'm a poet. I write delicate little verses about the natural world. Mostly, I write poems to the moon."

A memory stirred, and I recalled Aphrodite standing in my bedroom, telling me to look at the moon. She had mentioned the duality of the moon as a goddess and the moon as a big rock orbiting the earth, trying to help me see that things could have multiple natures. I shook my head sadly. Sometimes it felt like I still had a long way to go on that lesson.

Lorna misinterpreted my gesture. "It's not crazy," she murmured defensively, "just a mark of my devotion. Like I said, I express my magic in small ways."

"No, it sounds nice! I don't do anything like that." She relaxed her smile, so I asked another question. "What about your goddess?"

She sighed. "It's difficult to tell someone about a patron. Without experiencing her for yourself, you won't be able to understand."

"Still," I pressed, "I'd like to know."

Lorna stared vacantly across the room. Her breathing slowed, and I realized she was putting herself into a light trance. When she finally spoke, her words shocked me. "My goddess is Nepthys, sister to Isis and bride of Set."

I sat up to interrupt her, but she went on. "Nepthys is the last born of her siblings, and the one most ignored by man and god alike." She spoke the words as if they were something she had memorized, the text of some ancient ritual, and I shivered.

"When she was matched with Set, she was not happy and hungered for the husband of her sister. With Osiris, Nepthys bore the god Anubis, and Isis raised her sister's child as her own. Set was furious at his wife's betrayal, and since that time he has done all he can to control the power of his wife." Lorna blinked a few times, her gaze clearing, and looked at me. "That's why I'm not very good at strong magic; my goddess isn't allowed to use her full power, so neither do I." Her voice was back to its normal cadence.

"Why did you swear to her?" The question seemed rude as soon as I said it, but Lorna paused thoughtfully.

"Because I like simple magic. There is so much beauty in the simplest things, and Nepthys helps me to create some of that beauty myself."

I nodded, thinking about what she had said. "That would make sense. But don't you ever wish you weren't limited?"

She shut her eyes and lay back on the pillow. "Has power made your life that much better?"

I couldn't answer her. I sat there thinking in the dark, listening to the old house shift and settle around me. I didn't sleep much that night; my thoughts were too jumbled. Worry for Izzy warred with confusion over the growing pull I was feeling toward Marcus, and the stories of the gods swirled around my mind, making sleep almost impossible. When I did eventually drop off, my dreams were filled with the harsh sound of Loki's laughter. I woke up at dawn disoriented. After taking a few deep breaths, I realized where I was. Lorna's bed was empty, so I padded down the hall to the stairs. I tied my long hair into a messy knot as I walked, not bothering to stop in the bathroom and check the mirror.

When I stepped into the front room downstairs, ten pairs of

eyes turned toward me. Feeling self-conscious, I sat down on a rough wooden chair just inside the door. It was uncomfortable, but I didn't want to draw more attention to my late arrival by moving. I hoped I wouldn't end up with splinters in my ass.

"I say we move now," Samuel resumed the conversation, speaking firmly, but Dr. Farren shook her head.

"There must be more study. We cannot risk harming the child."

Frances twisted her hands. "We may already be too late."

Dr. Farren smiled gently at Frances. "But this must be done with caution." She glanced at me wryly. "Rushing into things has not improved the situation. I say we wait to learn more."

No one spoke, but I saw Julia and Jewel nodding thoughtfully, and even Matthew looked like he was considering Dr. Farren's words.

After a moment, Marcus stood up. "Is that your decision, then?" His jaw was set, and his tone made me want to take a few steps back.

"Understand, boy," Roy stood to face his son, "that we want to save your sister. We simply won't agree to do anything rash." There was a tense silence, but finally Marcus shot me a look that spoke volumes and stomped out onto the porch.

32

"Excuse me," I whispered to the room, not meeting anyone's eyes. Then I followed Marcus outside.

He was sitting on the steps, staring across the empty field. "I told you this was a mistake." He didn't turn around.

"I'm sorry. I thought they could help." Carefully, I sat down beside him. Our knees brushed gently, and I felt a pulse of electricity. I slid closer to him.

Marcus snorted. "They want to study the situation. It's probably too late!"

"You don't really believe that, do you?"

Marcus looked at me, his eyes flashing. "Of course not. But it will be too late if we leave things up to that group." He jerked his thumb toward the farmhouse.

"But what can we do? We don't even know where she is."

"Set has her; he shouldn't be too hard to find, especially for a couple of Reds."

I shook my head, remembering what the Coven had said about Set. "But how will we defeat him, even if we find him?"

Marcus looked at me, and I froze. "There's always plan B." His green eyes bored into me, but I couldn't look away.

"You mean Loki's deal?" I swallowed nervously. "But the Coven says he's just as bad as Set."

"So what? 'The enemy of my enemy is my friend,'" he quoted with a smirk. "If Loki will help us get what we want, why shouldn't we keep our bargain?"

I breathed out sharply through my teeth, looking away. "It's dangerous."

"It might be more dangerous to defy him, now that we made the deal."

My heart clenched. I knew he was right, but memories of the destroyed earth from my dreams rose up in my mind, and I shook my head.

"The world won't really end." Marcus's voice was gentle, and I wanted to believe him.

"But nuclear power is so tricky." I risked looking at him again.

He smiled. "But two Reds together can do amazing things. And," he added, almost as an afterthought, "you'd be able to bind Hecate."

"The problem doesn't seem to just be Hecate anymore," I reminded him.

"Fine! Bind all the damn Red gods. Just help me get my sister back." He stood swiftly, his hands clenched.

I looked up at his tortured face, unable to speak for a moment. Emotion surged in me, and I realized I wanted to do whatever it took to wipe some of the strain from his face. Finally, I croaked, "Is this really what you want?"

He nodded, kneeling in front of me. "I told you," he spoke so low I had to lean forward to hear him, "this is my fatal flaw." The words hung in the air like a spell, and for a moment, neither of us moved.

His lips were inches away from my face. Without considering what it might mean, I leaned the rest of the way in and kissed him. I didn't think about Justin, or Izzy, or the end of the world. For a moment, I just wanted to lose myself in the warmth of Marcus's lips. Electricity tingled through my body, and sparks pulsed back and forth between us. He exhaled sharply, and then he kissed me back, hard.

A year and a day. So much had changed since then, and yet because I hadn't felt the passage of time, I hadn't realized that I was different in any way. But everything had changed. After a moment, Marcus pulled away. I smiled at him, tentatively, and he slammed his fist down on the porch railing. Startled, I jumped.

"Damn it, Darlena, what right did you have to come here? None of this would have happened if I'd never met you." Regret laced his voice, and he wouldn't look at me.

Tears pricked my eyes. He had every right to be angry with me, but gods, did he have to act like such a jerk right after I kissed him? I swallowed, trying to steady my breathing. "I know. But I can't change the past."

"But we can at least save Izzy." His jaw was set, and he strode swiftly down the driveway.

I glanced back at the farmhouse for a heartbeat, but then I turned and hurried after Marcus.

"Shouldn't we say good-bye?" I panted, trying to catch up to him.

He snorted. "They won't care. They're so busy deliberating, it could be weeks before anyone knows we're gone."

I knew he was wrong, but I didn't want to argue with him. I changed the subject. "What did you have in mind?"

"France." He gripped my forearm, and the world spun. Even if Marcus's method for traveling was fast, I would never get used to the way it turned my stomach inside out.

"I wish you'd warn me before you do that again!"

Marcus smirked as I staggered to my feet. The field didn't look that different from the one in the Scottish countryside, but the farmhouse was nowhere to be seen. The air smelled different, too, and I sniffed a couple of times, trying to identify the strange odor.

"Why France?" I was breathless from the trip, and from standing so close to Marcus. He took a quick step back, his eyes hooded.

"Best place I could think of for a nuclear meltdown. In my territory, at least."

"But what about my territory?"

He smirked at me. "I thought you didn't want to mess with things in your corner of the world."

I took a deep breath. "It might be more convincing."

He nodded, smiling sharply. "Have you worked from a distance before?"

"Yes, but only with a map."

"Well, you'll just have to wing this. What's the worst that can happen?"

His words made my skin crawl. "Can't we find me a map or something?"

"There's not time."

"But I don't want—"

"Damn it, Darlena, whose side are you on?"

I stared at the sparks that shot off his hands. "Yours," I ventured after a moment. "I'm on your side."

Marcus took a deep breath. "France relies heavily on nuclear power. They have over a dozen plants scattered around the country."

"So what are you planning to do?"

"It's like we said. If we can trigger a nuclear meltdown, it will look like the world is ending. Once Loki follows through on his part of the bargain, we do damage control. You said you've got control of the U.S., right?"

I nodded.

"Isn't there a nuclear plant somewhere in the desert?"

"I think there are some in the Southwest, but I'm not sure."

He frowned. "Maybe we should just focus on France."

Fighting my relief, I asked, "Are you sure that will be enough?"

Marcus looked grim. "It'll have to be."

We walked as we made our plans, and in a few minutes, we cut into a clearing that was far from empty. Two gray chimneys rose off the landscape, and a tall chain-link fence surrounded the compound. My heart started pounding quickly against my ribs as I realized that we were really about to do this.

"Welcome to Belleville, Darlena. This should suit us; it's almost in the center of France."

I glanced nervously at the smoke billowing out of the chimneys, remembering my horrific dream. "I wish there were another way."

Marcus's jaw tightened. "I can do this without you, but then Loki doesn't owe you anything."

Determined, I shook my head. "I need to stop Hecate, and we both need your sister back. Let's do it."

Marcus knelt down in the field, facing the nuclear plant. "So here's what I'm thinking. If we use this plant as our focal point and project our energy out through the other French plants, we can simultaneously break the cooling mechanisms. Things should overheat fast. Once Loki's free, we can cool them down, fix the machines, and leave without doing any harm."

I nodded. "Can we work from out here?"

"We can, but it would be better if we were inside the plant. The closer we are to the source of the spell, the easier it will be."

I wanted to contradict him; the two times I'd used Red magic on such a massive scale, I had been thousands of miles away. But Marcus had been a Red a lot longer than me, and I had promised to trust him. Hiding my concern, I stood up. "How do we get inside?"

"Easy." He smiled, and his form flickered. "Glamours do more than changing your looks." In a moment, he was gone.

"Marcus!" I kept my voice low as I called his name.

Something pinched my elbow.

"Damn it, Marcus, stop screwing around. Show me how to do that."

He reappeared, smiling. "It's easier than you think."

He was right: it was easy. After only a few moments of practice, I watched my arms and legs fade into nothingness. "Okay. Now we're invisible. How do we get inside?"

"Carefully."

We walked quietly across the dry landscape, and I tried to remind myself that it was just dead because it was winter. We hadn't done anything to destroy the earth, and our plan wouldn't cause the harm that I'd dreamed about.

A car whipped past us on the dirt road, and I heard Marcus's breath quicken. "Speed up. This might be our chance."

The guard at the gate checked the driver of the car, and then waved it through. I started to run. We slipped between the gates just as they swung closed, and I leaned on the fence to catch my breath.

"You're not in very good shape, are you?" Marcus's voice was near my ear, and I could tell he was trying not to laugh.

"I can hold my own. Now," I looked around the compound, "what do we do?"

"Inside would be best."

I glanced at the doors. "Security seems pretty tight."

"They can't see us."

"I'm not sure I can hold on to this glamour for long."

There was a pause. "Yeah," Marcus finally agreed. "I guess we're close enough."

I heard the dead grass rustle, as if he were sitting down. His hand brushed mine, and I yelped.

"Shh," Marcus whispered, "we don't want to give ourselves away." He tugged my hand until I was sitting across from him. It was a strange sensation; sparks crackled where our knees were touching, and he still had a firm grip on my hand, but all I could see in front of me was the power plant.

I flexed my palm, but he didn't let go. Instead, he grabbed my other hand.

"It'll be easier if we're linked. Do you know anything about nuclear power?"

I shook my head before I realized that he couldn't see me. "Not really. Do you?"

"I know enough. Look, we need to raise energy, but I'll direct it. Can you just concentrate on giving me as much Red magic as possible?"

Despite the cold air, my hands were sweaty. "I think so." I hesitated for a moment. "You're sure that we can do this without causing any harm?"

"I promise. I'll stop the meltdown as soon as Loki's free and we have Izzy back."

I drew a deep breath and closed my eyes. "Okay. Then I guess I'm ready."

"Ground yourself first. You know how?"

I nodded again, even though he couldn't see me. "That was one of the first lessons at Trinity."

"Then do it."

I forced myself to take a deep breath, and then another. Carefully, I emptied my mind and just focused on breathing. When I felt intense warmth spreading up my spine and into my arms, I was pretty sure I had managed to root myself to the core of the earth the way I'd been taught. It was a strange feeling: peace flowed through me, but at the same time I felt almost drunk with power. It was as if I were drawing up more magic than I had ever tried to hold before.

I directed the hot energy up through my spine to the top of my head. For a moment, I felt as if I had the worst migraine ever, and then there was a bursting sensation. My eyes opened and I focused on the streams of golden light cascading down my invisible body like I was caught in a rainstorm. As the energy flowed up into me and out my head, the heady sensation dissipated. I hoped we were doing the right thing.

"Okay," I said, my voice sounding far away, "ready when you are."

33

Power coursed through me and swirled around in my chest, but I forced the energy to begin flowing through our clasped hands. It was excruciating. I felt drunk, and the urge to use all that magic myself nearly overwhelmed me. *This isn't about you,* I reminded myself, clenching my teeth. With effort, I sent the power through our linked hands to Marcus. His hands grew hotter and hotter, until it hurt to hold them. I couldn't break his grasp, though, or I risked breaking the spell. With my hands stinging, I drew up even more Red energy and passed it on to Marcus.

I don't know how long we were linked like that; time slowed down, and all I was aware of was the power surging through me and the feel of Marcus's hands in mine. Eventually, the faint wail of a siren came from somewhere inside the compound, but I shut my eyes and focused on directing the energy into Marcus's hands. Another alarm sounded, closer to us, and shouts began to echo around the compound. I shivered, but I didn't let go of Marcus. Whatever was happening, I prayed it would be enough to set Loki free; I didn't think we'd get a second chance.

I could hear the increasing sounds of chaos around us; the sirens wailed, and voices shouted panicked commands in French. With one final surge of heat, Marcus let go of my hands. I opened my eyes and stared at him, completely drained. He was visible again. "Did it work?"

"I think so." He rubbed his arms like he was cold.

I looked around. Smoke was billowing out of the looming chimneys, and the sirens droned on. "Just here?"

He shook his head. "I was directing the energy through the entire nuclear network. We'll have to check the news to know for sure, but that should have caused chaos all over France."

I concentrated on turning invisible again, but I felt like I had the flu. Not even a flicker of magic responded to my attempt. I just felt empty. *Is this what Nons feel like?* I shivered at the thought of a life without magic. "The glamour broke." I gestured to Marcus, and he looked down at himself.

"I know. But I think they've got their hands full. We should be okay." He reached over and helped me to my feet. We were both wobbly, but we managed to stand up, leaning against each other.

I looked back at the building. The smoke billowing out of the chimneys had thickened, and I could see people running frantically on the roof of the power plant. "When do we know if it worked?"

"Oh, it worked all right." The familiar voice spoke from behind me, and I turned slowly to face Loki. He flexed his fingers and bounced on his toes. "Gods, it feels good to be free. Here." He threw something at me, and I reflexively caught it. "You'll be needing that."

Dumfounded, I looked at the chain in my hand. It was slimy and squishy and felt strangely alive. My stomach roiled at the texture. When I pulled on it to test its strength, the links thrummed with an angry sound and I felt like I'd snapped a rubber band against my skin. Loki had kept his promise!

Loki laughed. "Bind whoever you wish with that, but I won't be going back to my prison."

Marcus stood up and clenched his fists. "My sister?"

The god with flaming hair put his hand against his heart as if he'd been struck. "Are you implying, boy, that I would break my word?" Before Marcus had a chance to answer, Loki chuckled. "She's behind you. Use your eyes, Witch!"

Marcus whirled around and I peered over his shoulder. Sure enough, Izzy was lying on the ground, curled up like a sleeping cat.

"Is she okay?" I hurried to her side, but Marcus got there first.

"She's breathing. I think she's just asleep."

I tugged on Marcus's hand. "We can make sure she's fine in a minute. We have to stop what we started. We got what we wanted." He ignored me, leaning over Izzy. The persistent alarms grew louder, and I snapped my fingers in front of his nose. "Marcus! Help me."

With a long glance at Izzy, he grabbed my hands again. "Give me as much as you can."

I tried to summon Red magic, but it was like turning a broken faucet. Nothing happened. Nervously, I looked at Marcus, but his eyes were closed as if he were concentrating deeply. I shut my eyes and reached for Red energy again. Gradually, warmth began to fill me, and I felt it moving sluggishly into Marcus's hands. *Hurry up,* I thought, *hurry up.* The sirens screamed around me, and I struggled to give Marcus as much magic as I could. For a minute, the flow of energy seemed like it was working, but abruptly, I felt the magic rushing back into my body.

Something made a sharp snapping sound, and Marcus's hands clenched mine painfully. My eyes flew open, but I didn't understand what I saw.

Marcus's eyes rolled back into his head, and blood seeped down his chest. He looked like he was about to fall over, and I tugged on his hands, trying to keep him upright. At first, I thought he'd somehow hurt himself by trying to channel too much magic, but then I saw Loki.

He was leaning casually by a guard armed with a frighteningly large gun. They were standing twenty feet away from us, and Loki's hand was on the guard's trigger finger. The guard looked confused, glancing at his gun and then back to the three of us. Suddenly, I understood. Marcus had been shot. For some reason, Loki had betrayed us. I glared at the god, trying to summon the magic I needed to fight him, but Loki just laughed and vanished.

Marcus gripped my hands again, sinking to his knees. "Izzy," he began, blood bubbling up from his lips. I fought back a wave of nausea and terror.

"She's here." I let go of his hands so I could grab Izzy by the shoulders. I shook her a few times, trying to get her to wake up. Glancing back toward the guard, who looked less confused now, I dragged her toward Marcus. That guard was about to realize there were three trespassers in the complex, and I didn't think he'd be too thrilled once his senses returned to him. We didn't have much time.

I shook Marcus's shoulder gently. "Here's Izzy."

She was still asleep, but Marcus smiled. He kissed her forehead, leaving a bloody print like lipstick between her eyebrows. "I love you," he whispered, his voice fading.

"Marcus," I shook his arm, panicked. "Marcus, I need you to help me. We have to stop this meltdown!" His arm was still warm, but it felt stiff, less lifelike. For a moment, everything froze, and then his chest fell as the last of his breath left him. I sucked in air quickly, fighting back tears. How had everything gone so wrong?

"Darlena?" Beside me, Izzy looked up, blinking like a tired kitten. "What's going on?"

Dry grass snapped behind me, and I saw the guard raise his gun. He definitely didn't look confused anymore. Somewhere in the wind, I thought I heard Loki's laughter. What a fool I'd been to fall for this! Loki was free, chaos was rampant, and Marcus was dead. I looked at the guard again and grabbed Izzy's hand, turning her away from the body. "We have to get out of here."

"Okay." She nodded slowly. Her eyes landed on Marcus, and her lips parted in a silent cry.

I gripped her hand tighter. "I'll explain everything, but we have to get away now."

She nodded again, and I pulled her to her feet. With a sudden burst of adrenaline, I started to run, tugging Izzy along with me. She skidded to a stop, still holding my hand, and I jerked backwards.

"There's an easier way." She shut her eyes, and I braced myself for the dizzying experience of Marcus's travel spell. Instead, blue sparks encompassed my body, pricking me, and everything dissolved in a hazy patch of blue light. The last thing I saw before we were whisked into darkness was Marcus's bloody corpse, and then, mercifully, everything went black.

34

Izzy dropped her bag in a plastic chair and sighed. "I need coffee. Want some?"

I nodded, fishing a couple of crumpled bills out of my wallet. I handed them to her without a word, and she headed off. I leaned back, setting my feet gingerly on top of my backpack. Closing my eyes, I let my head hang off the back of the stiff airport chair.

"Leaving so soon?" a cold voice asked.

I kept my eyes closed for a moment, hoping that when I opened them, I would be alone, but unfortunately, I wasn't. Freya sat beside me, her face expressionless.

"I think I've been here long enough, don't you?"

She laughed harshly. "An ocean will not free you from your responsibilities."

I felt my spine stiffen. "What are you talking about?"

"You went against my advice and made a bargain with the Lord of Chaos."

My body felt like I'd fallen into any icy lake. "How do you know that?"

Freya shook her head. "Red magic is connected. As are the Red gods. We all know about your bargain." Her lips curled back, revealing her sharp teeth. "And now that the Lord of Lies is free, we must all band together to stop him."

Her words sank in and I sat bolt upright. "All of you?"

She nodded. "You've made many enemies among us. I should warn you to watch where you step, Darlena."

"Are you threatening me?" I tried to muster up a tone of bravado, but I sounded as terrified as I felt.

The goddess glared at me. "As if I would sink so low. No, girl, I came to offer you a warning. There are not many Red gods left who will side with you, if that is what it comes to. The newest Red Witch is still undeclared, and many are rushing to win patronage of her."

"The newest Red Witch? What do you mean?"

"Marcus is gone. You must have known that his death would open the door for another Red Witch."

Her words chilled me. "But … " I trailed off, stunned. I had never for a moment thought about that, but of course what Freya said made sense. There were always three Red Witches in the world. I shuddered, remembering Marcus's gruesome end. Resolutely, I pushed the image of his bleeding body out of my mind and risked a question. "Will the new Witch help me stop Hecate?"

But the goddess was gone.

When Izzy got back, she took one look at my face and thrust a steaming cup at me. "You look awful."

"Thanks," I said wryly. "I feel pretty awful."

"Still no luck getting things in France under control?" She dropped her voice, glancing around the airport nervously.

I shook my head. "I keep trying, but it's not my territory." Freya's words rolled through my mind; I hadn't really thought about the boundaries of Red magic before now. "And I don't know who the other Red Witch is."

"Should we find out who replaced Marc—my brother, and get her help?" Her voice broke, and I squeezed her shoulder. I couldn't believe that Izzy was still willing to talk to me after everything I'd done.

"That might work, but right now, I need to go home. I've been gone way too long, and if anyone knows what to do, I think my mom might be able to help."

She nodded. "It's not your fault, Darlena. Loki tricked you."

I gritted my teeth and gulped the coffee, scalding my mouth. "Still feels like my fault to me."

Silently, we looked up at the monitor broadcasting the latest news. France had been declared a disaster area by the United Nations, and the world was scrambling in panic. I glanced around the busy Edinburgh airport. It had all been a blur: the nuclear meltdown, Loki's betrayal, and Izzy transporting us back to Scotland. I looked at her. "How'd you manage to get us out of France, anyway?"

Izzy smiled. "Marcus taught me the traveling trick a few summers ago. I figured you'd want to be as far from the accident as possible."

"I wish you could have transported me home."

She shook her head. "What do I look like, the Witch of the North? It was too far for me to control the spell. This is the next best thing."

I nodded, glancing around the Edinburgh airport for the last time. "Did you call your grandmother?"

"Yes." She paused for a minute, her eyes growing dark. "It's a good thing you won't be visiting the Coven anytime soon."

I shivered and tried to force a smile. "Why did you decide to come with me? Don't they want to see you?"

Izzy tilted her head to one side thoughtfully. "I don't know. I just have this feeling that you'll need me." She smiled impishly. "Besides, I've never been to the States!"

I smiled at her, but Marcus filled my mind and I frowned. I had tried to explain everything to Izzy, but I felt like my words kept getting tangled up. She said she understood and that she forgave me, but the guilt I felt threatened to overwhelm my senses. This was so much worse than when Rochelle died. At least then I could try to comfort myself with the knowledge that I'd acted in self-defense. Marcus's death weighed on me, and Loki's betrayal burned. Everything had gone wrong, and it was my fault.

I turned to Izzy, about to make a promise to her that I would avenge Marcus's death somehow, but just then the loudspeaker crackled to life.

"Flight 737 with service to New York is now boarding."

Izzy smiled, picking up her bag and slinging it casually over her shoulder. "That's us. Time for you to go home."

I nodded. I picked up my bag and checked the glamour on it. It wouldn't do me any good if airport security found the athame and the crystal, not to mention the strange chain. Hoisting the bag over my shoulder, I felt a shudder of revulsion: Loki's bonds had that effect on me. I needed to figure out what they were and how to use them, and I hoped that Mom would know more than me. Or even Dad. I was through trying to do this alone, and I missed them.

Izzy and I boarded the flight, and I leaned my head gratefully against the cold window. Izzy turned around, chatting with the family sitting behind us, and the sound of her voice lulled me to sleep.

My dreams were filled with gore and fire. Loki's laughter echoed around me, and Hecate's sharp voice joined in. I forced myself awake and stayed awake for the rest of the flight.

After a long layover, Izzy and I landed in North Carolina early the next afternoon. I gave the taxi driver my address before I collapsed into the back seat. Izzy rode up front, still chattering away. I didn't know how she could be so perky, even considering all the coffee we'd chugged. Jetlag had completely destroyed me.

When the driver pulled up at my house, he turned around.

"Are you sure they're expecting you? It looks pretty vacant."

He was right: the curtains were drawn and there was a sense of abandonment in the air.

"It'll be fine. If they aren't home, I've got my key." I fished it out along with my wallet and paid the fare.

He started to say something, but he shut his lips. After counting the bills I'd handed him, he drove off, not even bothering to wave.

I looked at Izzy, who was swaying on the sidewalk. "Are you okay?"

She nodded. "I think the jetlag is finally catching up to me."

"Don't worry." We headed up the front walk. "We've got a guest room with really thick curtains."

"Wonderful! Maybe I'll sleep for a week."

"First, you have to help me figure out what to do in France!"

Izzy frowned. "I keep forgetting. It's so easy to imagine that everything is normal."

"I know." I sighed. "Except I don't think that anything will ever be normal again."

My key turned easily in the lock, and we stepped into the house. I felt an overwhelming urge to burst into tears. Until that moment, I hadn't realized how homesick I was.

Izzy looked around curiously. "Is that your family?" She pointed to a framed photo, taken the spring my dad turned 50. Mom had thrown a true surprise party, complete with a blindfold and kidnapping, and she'd invited all of his friends. The party had taken up the big private room at the brew pub downtown, and Dad was thrilled. In the picture, he's wearing a paper crown. Mom is sitting on his lap, laughing.

I nodded. "Mom said that's the best photo anyone's taken of them since their wedding."

"I can't wait to meet them."

I dropped my bag and strode into the living room. "Mom? Dad? Are you guys home?"

Izzy flopped down on the sofa. "I could so pass out right now."

I called again, louder. Silence answered me as I headed into the kitchen. My mom always kept a calendar by the phone. I hoped it would tell me where they were.

Xerxes looked up, startled, from his perch on top of the stove. He leaped down quickly and crossed the room to my ankles. Instead of twining around me the way he usually did, he stopped cautiously and sniffed my toes.

I laughed. "I bet I smell like all kinds of weird things, right, buddy?" I knelt down to pet the cat, which seemed to satisfy him. He butted his head against my hand, purring loudly. I scooped him up, happy to see at least one member of my family. "Oh, man, I've missed you." I nuzzled the top of his head, fighting the overwhelming urge to cry.

I headed back to the living room with the cat. "There's nothing on Mom's calendar," I told Izzy, "so they probably just went to run an errand. Do you want to lie down?"

"In a minute. Can I see your room first?"

Her eager tone made me think of something, and I studied her face. "Izzy, have you ever lived in a house?"

She shook her head. "No. Isis raised me, which was amazing, but I went right from the Duat to school." She looked around the room again. "Your house is really pretty."

I laughed, setting the cat down. "Make sure you say that to my mom. She wants to redecorate, but Dad keeps talking her out of it."

We headed up the stairs, Xerxes scampering ahead of us. He rushed past the door to my room and flung himself into the bathroom, hissing. Izzy followed him making soothing noises.

"Crazy cat," I muttered as I pushed open my door. My mirror image stared back at me and I jumped, startled. I'd forgotten all about Persephone.

"I was starting to wonder when you would come home." The voice that spoke had an odd echoey quality. It was like listening to an old home movie. It was sort of creepy to watch another me talk, and I forced a smile.

"Thank you for doing this. I'm glad my family didn't panic."

The other me smiled. "My pleasure. It's been fun. I especially liked hanging out with Justin." She winked.

I grimaced. "I hope I can explain things to him."

"Why would you need to do that?"

I stared at her, confused. "I've been gone a long time. He has a right to know. Plus," I sighed, "things in Scotland didn't go the way I'd hoped. I need Justin's help."

The goddess laughed. It was weird, hearing my own laugh like that. Did I really sound that shrill? "I'll say things didn't go as planned. They went better."

"Better? What are you talking about?"

She just smiled.

I frowned at her, a terrible suspicion sinking into my stomach. Persephone wouldn't stand there and laugh at what I'd done. "How did you get Hades to let you come?" I baited her, hoping she'd reveal whoever she actually was.

She laughed again, and the glamour dissolved. I froze in horror, trying to understand. This was so much worse than I had ever imagined, and for a minute, I couldn't process what I was seeing.

Rochelle smiled at me, her eyes glistening. "No one lets me do anything, Darlena. I do as I please."

I shook my head, stunned. "But you're dead!"

She laughed. "What a shame that such an ignorant fool has so much power."

"Are you a ghost?" I felt a sudden swell of hope. If Rochelle could come back from the dead, then maybe Marcus—

"No, no thanks to you." Her voice was bitter, the voice I thought I'd never hear again. "You did a fair job when you tried to kill me, but I survived."

"How?" I gaped at her in disbelief.

She smirked at me. "Would you believe me if I told you I could fly?"

I stared at her, torn between awe and disbelief. "That's a lost art."

Rochelle shook her head pityingly. "It's not lost to those who listen. And remember, I've had good teachers."

Suddenly, everything came rushing back to me. I reeled. "She taught you how to do that?"

Rochelle laughed. It was a sharp sound, like nails on a chalkboard. "There is much to learn from the gods. Yes, Hecate gave me flight. But she isn't my only tutor."

Her words filled me with fear. "Why would the others help you?"

She clicked her tongue. "Come on, Lena. You aren't that stupid. Did you forget Hecate's promise?"

I thought back, confused. Hecate had promised Rochelle she would become the next Red Witch once I was dead. "But you didn't kill me."

"No. Too bad; she would have really loved me then. But she kept her word, just as soon as there was a need."

My mind couldn't grasp what she was saying. "What do you mean?"

Rochelle's lips curled up in a slow, triumphant smile. "I'm a Red Witch now. You won't defeat me a second time."

Did she mean she'd taken Marcus's place? Panicked, I grabbed enough energy to defend myself. Rochelle raised her arms quickly, but before I could move, a flash of blue light cut through the room and struck Rochelle in the face.

"What—" she hissed, taking an involuntary step backward.

Izzy pushed into the room beside me, her hands raised defensively. I took advantage of Rochelle's confusion to get a grip on my magic, but I didn't strike. I didn't think I could live with myself if I killed Rochelle twice.

"Who are you?" Rochelle's voice held an edge of panic.

Izzy drew her shoulders back and glared at her. "I am Isadora, beloved of Isis." Her hands moved quickly, and another flash of blue shot toward Rochelle. She deflected it, but her expression was changing from triumph to confusion, and finally to fear.

"Why didn't they warn me about you?" she panted, moving backwards into my room, her hands flying frantically as she wove a spell.

Finally, I acted. I singed her hair with a burst of Red magic. She jerked in surprise, and I couldn't resist taunting her.

"What's the matter, Rochelle, didn't your friends teach you how to fight another path?"

Izzy sent another blast of blue forward, driving Rochelle back to the window.

Rochelle glared at me. "This is not over. Remember, Darlena, when I face you alone, I *will* win." She turned quickly, and the window exploded in a flurry of glass. I covered my eyes with my arm instinctively, and when I looked up, Rochelle was gone. Izzy rushed to the window, her eyes wide.

"She's not out there. She really can fly!"

My knees felt shaky, and I suddenly thought I might faint. I leaned against the doorframe. Had that really just happened? I let Izzy lead me down the stairs. She pushed me onto the sofa, and Xerxes immediately hopped up on my lap, purring gently. Izzy left the room, but she returned in a few minutes carrying two steaming mugs of tea. I clutched mine as if it were a lifeline. For a few minutes, we sat in stunned silence. My brain was racing, but I couldn't make sense of anything.

"You know," Izzy finally said, "I think I'm beginning to see the pattern."

"What do you mean?"

She took a careful sip. "Well, think about it. When you didn't defeat that girl the first time, Hecate realized that only another Red Witch had the power to destroy you."

"So?"

"So, think about your trip to Scotland. When they took Marcus, what do you think they wanted to happen?"

I shrugged. I hadn't explained the truth about Marcus's disappearance to Izzy, but it didn't matter now. Let her think he'd been taken against his will; even if he hadn't, he'd still ended up a prisoner. "That I'd try to save him?"

She shook her head. "Sort of. But what if they wanted you to try, but fail?"

Realization slowly dawned on me. "He was held prisoner in the Otherworld. If anything had happened to me there—"

"You would have died instantly. You weren't able to use your magic, remember?"

I nodded, feeling queasy. "But I didn't die."

"No. You didn't." She squeezed my hand. "You saved my brother, and then he started to help you."

I blushed, thinking of our last kiss. Izzy was watching me intently, so I just nodded.

"But then the Red gods really screwed up. They took me."

I looked up at her. She hadn't talked about her captivity yet, and I was intensely curious. Had Set really been her captor, like Marcus believed?

Izzy drew a rough breath and went on. "I'm sure it seemed like a good idea; if you somehow survived, one of you would still have to die to rescue me. And as soon as a Red Witch was gone, Rochelle would be ready to take over."

She was making an awful lot of sense. "Either she'd take over my role, which is what she initially wanted, or she'd become the other Red and finally have the power to destroy me."

Izzy nodded. "But they didn't anticipate us becoming friends."

I paused. "Or that you would come home with me." Her words sank in, and I shuddered. "Thank you. Seriously, I don't know what I would have done if you hadn't been here."

"Rochelle thought she'd get her shot at you here, so she waited for her chance. If you survived, she knew you'd come home eventually."

That thought made my blood run cold. "How long do you think she was here, acting like me?"

Izzy looked down at her hands. "I have no idea. You'll have to find your parents to figure that out."

As if summoned by magic, I heard a car pull into the drive. I gulped, suddenly unsure of myself. "What do I say?"

Izzy smiled at me gently. "Just tell them the truth."

35

They were laughing when they came in the door, and if Mom hadn't been carrying two bags of groceries, I might have flung myself at her immediately. As it was, she looked surprised to see us.

"Darlena? Who's your friend?"

Dad bustled in behind her, carrying another grocery bag and a big bottle of vinegar. He paused, looking at Izzy and me.

"Her name's Izzy. She's a friend from Scotland."

Dad's eyes clouded. "I thought you weren't there long enough to make any friends."

Izzy and I exchanged a worried glance. "How long did you think I was there?"

He chuckled. "You can't pretend we're ever going to forget that our darling daughter woke us up at five o'clock in the morning on New Year's Day!"

Mom had taken the groceries into the kitchen, but she stuck her head back around the corner. "I still can't believe you didn't even stick around to go sightseeing; you weren't even there a week! There are so many cool places in the U.K."

My stomach flipped over, and I took a deep breath. Izzy stood up, and when I nodded at her, she efficiently warded the living room.

Dad looked at her, his eyebrows twitching. "Honey, you better come in here. Something's going on."

He sat down in his recliner, and Mom came and perched on the arm of his chair. They both looked confused.

"Um," I began, looking to Izzy for inspiration. She nodded at me, so I plunged ahead. "Actually, I just got back tonight."

It took a minute for my words to sink in, but Mom got it first. Her face turned fearful, and she gripped my dad's arm.

"What do you mean, exactly?" she asked in a strangled voice.

I took a deep breath, and then I told them about the other magics, and about Dr. Farren and the Coven. It was hard trying to explain it all, especially since I'd screwed up so badly. I told them about Marcus, even though Izzy turned pale when I described how I had tried to save him. They stared at me, open-mouthed, until I ran out of things to say.

"I still don't understand." Dad looked puzzled. "If you haven't been here all this time—"

"It was Rochelle." Izzy's voice was soft, but my parents reeled back as if she'd slapped them.

"You can't be serious!" My dad leaped up and began pacing the room. Anger bubbled off him, and I shivered.

Mom looked at me for a long time. "How can we be sure that you are who you say you are?"

I was stunned. It had never occurred to me that my parents would question my identity. Confused, I looked at Izzy.

She frowned for a moment, thinking. "What about something that only Darlena would know?"

My mom seemed to consider it, but then shook her head. "Darlena and Rochelle were best friends. They told each other everything." She looked helplessly at Dad. "Richard, what do we do?"

Tears welled up in my eyes. Izzy tried to put her arms around my shoulder, but I shrugged her off. "I've gone through hell to get home. Literally, Marcus and I went to Hel to try to save Izzy, but Loki wouldn't help us." I picked up speed, babbling incoherently. "And then the Coven wanted to wait some more, but it had already been a year, so Marcus and I kept Loki's bargain. But Marcus died," I wailed, "and now Rochelle is back and I'm scared and you don't believe me!"

Everyone in the room stared at me in shock. Mom latched on to the important part of the story.

"You made a bargain with Loki?" Her words were slow and measured, but her eyes looked panicked.

Numb, I nodded. "We just had to make it seem like the world was ending."

"Exactly how did you do that?" Dad's voice was tense.

"We forced some nuclear reactors to go haywire." Embarrassed, I lowered my eyes.

"That was you?" my dad exploded, his face turning chalky.

I nodded again.

"I hope you're aware, young lady, that you didn't just make it seem like the world was ending. Those reactors are still spewing waste, and France is terrified. The entire world is terrified." Dad glared at me and I shrank back into the couch.

I hung my head in shame. "I know. I'm sorry."

After an uncomfortable pause, Mom leaned over and squeezed my hand. "We believe you, sweetie."

Startled, I looked up and met her eyes.

"Wait, we do?" Dad raised his eyebrows skeptically at me.

Mom nodded. "Rochelle would never apologize. You said yourself that Lena seemed strange this year, grumpier and quicker to fight." She hugged me, and I almost lost it.

"I'm so sorry."

Mom stroked my hair. "Shh, sweetie, we know. I'm just glad you're safe and sound."

Her words broke me, and I started to sob. Mom held me until I was all cried out, but then Dad cleared his throat.

"Yes," Dad said, "but how are you planning to fix your actions?"

I shrugged helplessly. "I can't. When Marcus died, his territory passed into Rochelle's control."

My parents thought about this for a moment, but Dad seemed to understand. "Do you mean that she's in control of Europe now?"

I nodded. "A Red Witch is bound by her territory. I can't change things there any more than she can change things here."

"So we're safe here for the time being," Izzy added hopefully.

"We may be safe, but thousands of people are going to lose their homes and worse." Mom shook her head. "This is a big problem."

"And if Lena's telling us everything, Loki is loose again." My dad shivered. "Who knows what chaos he'll add to the mix?"

"I think," Izzy began quietly, "that this is no longer a Red problem."

I looked at her, and for a moment, it was like I could read her mind. She nodded, and I leaned forward eagerly. "Do you think they would help?"

"It's worth a try. If they won't, maybe you need to form your own."

I nodded slowly, considering. Izzy might be right; the only way to stop the chaos I'd started would be working with other Witches.

"Form your own what? Who are you girls talking about?" Mom looked at me, her brow furrowed.

"I think what Izzy means is," I took a deep breath, "we need to form some kind of group to face Rochelle and the Red gods. Maybe it's time to think about a Coven."

My parents stared at me, twin looks of horror on their faces, but I ignored them.

Izzy reached out her hand and clasped mine. "I'll help you, whatever you decide to do."

I nodded. "I better decide something fast, or the world really will end."

My parents looked at each other and shook their heads. Dad glanced at me, his face unreadable. "There's something you aren't telling us."

I thought back to what Persephone had said at the cairns, and everything that had happened since. "There's a good chance the Red gods are trying to destroy the world."

ACKNOWLEDGEMENTS

I can't tell you how crazy it is to be sitting down to write the acknowledgements for my sixth book; I'm so incredibly thankful to YOU, dear reader, for supporting my work and falling into Darlena's world!

Thanks and ever more thanks to everyone at Month9Books and GMMG; you're all amazing, and I'm so lucky to be part of such of a wonderful team! As always, thank you to Georgia McBride for pulling this series out of the slush pile all those years ago. It's still so amazing to see it in print! Thank you to Jennifer Million, for helping me hold onto my sanity, and to the wonderful support squad, from editors to cover artists; you've made this book even more magical!

Thanks to Kat for the initial feedback that helped me take this tangled mess of a sequel and figure out what was really going on.

Hugs and gratitude to Kristen Lippert-Martin, Bethany Hagen, and Anne Blankman for reading early drafts of this novel. Thank you for the insight and suggestions, ladies!

Also, love and chocolate to the YA Valentines; 2014 may be over, but I know we've got years of family ahead of us.

It almost feels like it goes without saying (but I'm going to say it anyway) that this story wouldn't be what it is without the loving intervention of my CP extraordinaire, Jaye Robin Brown. I love swapping stories with you, girl!

Sparklers and cupcakes to Ashley Poston for kick ass graphics, amazing ideas, and constant support.

To Laura, Deb, and Amanda for reading this story when it was in its infancy: thank you!

Overwhelming love to the SCBWI Carolinas community; I am so lucky to be part of this wonderful family! Gratitude also to the NCWN; thank you for welcoming me from the beginning.

Glitter and magic to my Witcherific street team; y'all are amazing, and I'm so thankful I get to share this journey with you!

Thank you to my students, past, present, and future, for teaching me more than I ever imagined.

My family has always supported my writing dreams, and I'm forever grateful for the encouragement, cheerleading, and love you continue to send my way.

And to the man who's lived through the all the chaos, thank you; these stories exist because you love me enough to not complain about the way I obsess over fictional characters. As always, Matt, this one's for you.

JEN MCCONNEL

Jen McConnel first began writing poetry as a child. A Michigander by birth, she now lives and writes in the beautiful state of North Carolina. A graduate of Western Michigan University, she also holds a MS in Library Science from Clarion University of Pennsylvania. When she isn't crafting worlds of fiction, she teaches college writing composition and yoga. Once upon a time, she was a middle school teacher, a librarian, and a bookseller, but those are stories for another time. Her fiction titles include YA and NA, and she also writes nonfiction. Visit http://www.jenmcconnel.com to learn more.

Connect With Jen

Twitter: https://twitter.com/Jen_McConnel
Goodreads: https://www.goodreads.com/author/show/ 6451403. Jen_McConnel
Pinterest: http://www.pinterest.com/jenmcconnel/
Facebook: http://www.facebook.com/jenmcconnelauthor
Blog: http://jennifermcconnel.wordpress.com/

OTHER MONTH9BOOKS TITLES YOU MIGHT LIKE

DAUGHTER OF CHAOS

BEAUTIFUL CURSE

NOBODY'S GODDESS

Find more awesome Teen books at Month9Books.com

Connect with Month9Books online:

Facebook: www.Facebook.com/Month9Books

Twitter: https://twitter.com/month9books

You Tube: www.youtube.com/user/Month9Books

Blog: www.month9booksblog.com

Request review copies via publicity@month9books.com

JEN McCONNEL

Nothing is more terrifying than the
witch who wields red magic.

DAUGHTER
OF
CHAOS

JEN McCONNEL

Beautiful
Curse

Nobody's Goddess

Never Veil Series Book One

Amy McNulty